I0585957

# A HARPER'S JOURNEY

## BOOK ONE - ON HORSE AND HARP

## GLENDA UNDERHILL

PIPING SHRIKE PRESS

ULSTER

Cill Ala

CONNACHT

Drogheda

Duleek

LEINSTER

MUNSTER

A Harper's Journey IRELAND

# CONTENTS

# IRISH TO ENGLISH

**Clarsach** - Harp

**Ní thuigim** - I don't understand

**Seanchaí** - Story teller

**Fáilte** - Welcome

**Conas atá tú** - How are you?

**Conas atá mé** - How am I?

**Cailín** - Girl

**Go raibh maith agat** - Thank you

**Slán** - Bye (goodbye)

**Gaeilge** - Irish

# LIST OF CHARACTERS

*Orla Connellan* – peasant farmer – Harper

*Clodagh Moran* – Orla's grandmother – Seer

*Jarleth Moran* – uncle to Orla – Horse breeder

*Seamus Moran* – son of Jarleth – cousin to Orla

*Paeder Connellan* – eldest son of Orla

*Conor Connellan* – second son of Orla

*Kathleen Connellan* – daughter of Orla

*Maura Burke* – harp teacher to Orla and dear friend of Clodagh Moran

*Declan O'Malley* – Boat builder, Trader & blood relative of Maura

*John Earnshaw* – Englishman: as brother to Declan

# PROLOGUE

*M*y name is Orla Connellan, I was born in Duleek, not far from Drogheda, County Meath, Ireland in the year 1610. My life began in a small cottage, and after marrying, my three children were born in that same little house.

Life was hard, but we were happy there; my parents, husband, children and me. We worked long each day on the land cutting turf, clearing for planting of crops of oats and potatoes; some to feed us, most to pay our landlord. Food was often scarce, but love was not. So much love was there in our little cottage.

Often in the evening we'd sit 'round the hearth and Mammy would sing a quiet song, or my father, Da, would tell a story; he was the Seanchaí. My husband, though a man of few words, would betimes tell a tale; that gave the children such a thrill. But things change.

The English were in our land wanting to rule and control us Irish. They'd taken much from us, and this was a time of fighting back. Our land had become so unsettled and dangerous, that my grandmother, living far away from us, had sent for my children, offering them refuge. As a mother, I agreed. As a wife, I must *stay; my husband forbidding me to leave him, and so we were parted, me and my children.*

*I learned to live without them and accept change, we all did. Yet nothing readied us for that day. No one was prepared for the darkness that visited upon Ireland in 1649 in the form of a man, an Englishman... Oliver Cromwell.*

*We knew of his coming. My grandmother had sent my cousin Seamus to give us advanced warning, requesting permission for me to be spared and re-united with my children. Though duty-bound, relieved I was when my husband granted this. His fate, like my parents, was bound up in Duleek; stay they must. But I was not bonded so.*

*My parents were killed. My husband was killed. Our cottage burnt. Our animals slaughtered. Our crops destroyed.*

*My life as daughter, wife and mother would be forever changed on that one morning. Grateful was I that my three growing children were safely away to the western coast, the haven I now rode toward with my cousin Seamus.*

*"Ride faster Orla. Stay up with me. Kick her on."*

*Numbly, I rode. For days I rode. Wet, exhausted and dead inside, I rode. The place I rode to, I knew not. What I rode past, I saw not. Mud, cold and nothingness is all I knew.*

*Finally, we slowed and like a voice in the distance, I heard Seamus say, "We are here. We are arrived."*

*The place we had ridden to was a farmyard with a number of outhouses. Seamus lead me to one of the small buildings standing separate from the main house. I remember a fire burning in the hearth.*

*"Da will be in to settle you."*

*Come did my uncle, settle me, he did not!*

# CHAPTER ONE

# THE HARD RIDE

My head gave a shudder of disbelief! "Play the harp, you're surely fooling, Uncle? I have forty years on me." Looking steadily into my eyes, he said, "I am not Orla. Your grandmother has seen it. I know that with all that's gone on these past few days, this is an odd thing to hear, but it be so... it be so."

"Odd! Can you not see how mad it is, what you're asking?"

"I'm not to be asking, Orla. This is no bidding. As I said, this is how it is to be. It has been seen."

My uncle spoke with such firmness, as if written in stone. I opened my mouth to protest. He raised his hand and said, "You'll not be a great harper, Orla, but you'll be an important one. That should be reward enough for you to know. You've gone through a great deal these past days. You've had much of the suffering upon you. We'll speak of this when you're rested and your mind is less troubled. For now, I'll be leaving you alone with your thoughts."

And think I did. I thought of my parents and my husband; faces I would not see again. I thought of the life I'd ridden away from! The gathering of herbs, and weaving, and cooking, and picking potatoes. Simple things. I thought of the hard riding Seamus and me had done. I thought of the wind, and the cold dark shivering nights spent sleeping on the ground with spirits dampened by far more than rain. I thought of the lives I'd brought into this world, helping other farming women when the time for birthing their weans came, and of those I'd readied for the otherworld, but mostly I thought of my uncle's strange words. A harper... me?

I felt as though I might myself be entering the otherworld! Yes, that must be it! That's why there's the talking of harps. What madness! I shook myself. For if I too was dead, and had gone where the angels dwelt, then surely life would be beautiful. Surely life would be untroubled. In my innards, this was not the peaceful quiet place I believed heaven to be. This was the dirty, tiring war ravaged life that'd been Ireland for all of my years.

I'd suffered much, we all had, so why now was yet another stone being placed in my shoe?

Despite my exhaustion, sleep did not come. I paced and prayed. I could make no sense of this world. One week back, life was ordered, foretold, but now all was wrong side up, all was an unholy mess. Nothing made sense.

Here I was in a cottage, strange to me. There was nothing familiar. Nothing I knew. I did not know truly even where I was. All I knew was my loved ones were dead, and my cousin Seamus and me had ridden from one side of Ireland to the other. Everything was outside of me. My surroundings, my feelings, everything was strange. All I knew was gone.

I felt heavy and hollow at the same time. Bone-weary, but my mind was filled with words and emotions all swirling as if caught up in a fierce wind. Pulling the blanket from the bed which stood in the corner of the room, I wrapped it about me, and sat down at the small table. I did not cry. For the heartbreak and sorrow for my dead was such, if I began, I feared I would never stop. I did nothing, just sat.

I'd ridden away with Seamus with no time to spare. Just as we reached the edge of the woodland, Cromwell's soldiers were on our farm. Trampling our crops, like madmen they killed what little stock we had. My husband ran out and was shot like an animal. Then they were at our cottage door. We stayed long enough to see the cottage set alight, and though we did not witness the death of my dear parents, we knew it to be so. They did not run out. I knew they would not. No sound came from them. I could only think on the horror befallen them, and glad I was to not be among them. I was not ready to die, and they did not wish it for me. Glad they were for Seamus' arrival. I prayed their death be swift, but this was not to be. In my mind's eye, I saw my parents inside the cottage, holding each other, loving each other until the flames took them to heaven. I sent them my blessings. That was the best I could do.

I thought again on my uncle's words. Through the many years we Irish had been downtrodden by the English, I'd heard tell of harps being destroyed, and those who played them being killed. Those, that survived, I felt sure, would have begun their learning as children: I was a woman of middle years. I knew of herb lore and homely things. I knew of farming and caring for people and animals. These were things I could do, not harping. Why me? Why now? My mind was in such a clatter, I wished for the coming of the morning and the return of my uncle.

I heard a cockerel announcing the new day. Slowly the light began to seep in through the window, lighting the motes of dust in the air happily dancing. On another morning I might have enjoyed their fluttering. On this morning, I saw in them no beauty. I said my blessing for the day, silently, as I did every day, more from habit than thinking, and looked around the small room.

It was barely furnished, but clean and tidy. There was a bed and a hearth. I shivered as a coldness ran through me. The horror of the past few days chilled my bones and my heart. I pulled the blanket tighter around me. There was a lamp on the table where I'd sat through the night. I'd not seen it before. Though, it would have been of no service to me, for no source of light could pierce the dark shroud that'd draped itself over me.

I became aware, as is the way in Ireland, that a brief visit from the sun had now been taken over by heavy clouds. The grey matched my gloom. I cannot tell why, but never a once did I look out the window or open the door. Perhaps the belief of closing out the world, lead me falsely to think the past few days were just a visit from the night mare, nothing more, and I would waken, and all the horror and misery would be waved away by the hand of God.

F ootsteps sounded. A light rap on the door announced the arrival of my uncle, followed by cousin Seamus carrying two buckets of water. "For you to wash" he said, and looked to a corner in the small room. I followed his eyes to a wooden tub hiding there in the shadows. He put one bucket down, tipping the other into a large pot that hung over the cold hearth, then quietly left.

"Conas atá tú?" asked my uncle.

Conas atá mé? I had no answer. And he did not wait for one.

"I've brought turf," said Jarlath Moran moving towards the small hearth.

I watched as he deftly set the fire and gave it life. He was a strong looking man, not overly tall, with grey hair and kind eyes. He must be nearing seventy, as he is, or was, my mother's elder brother by twelve years. I'd met him ten years earlier when my grandmother had sent him and Seamus across our green land to take my three children. She'd seen life in Duleek becoming harder and more dangerous with the rise of English soldiers; a place of little hope for children.

"My children, are they well?" Without turning away from his task, he said, "They are".

Small curls of smoke wafted out of the hearth's open mouth. The burning turf smelled sweet, earthy and comforting, and made me to think of church. Perhaps I'd once smelled it there. "Uncle, I know we are many miles from Duleek, but what is the name of this place?" This time he turned to look at me. "We're in County Mayo."

Seamus returned carrying a basket and a bundle. "Granny sent you a linen towel and some clothes. There's food in the basket."

Like before, he made his delivery and left. Strange the way he'd said Granny. Familiar like. As if I should know her by that name, but, I'd never met my mother's mother. I'd heard plenty of her, for sure, but never met her.

"What's she like... Granny?" I asked.

My uncle thought for a moment. "She's a queer woman. She has the second sight, and a rare wisdom. You'll meet her in the morning, but for now, she says you needs be alone. She says you need some time to ready yourself before the greeting of kin."

She was right.

"Have the day to yourself. Rest up, get some sleep if you can bid it. I'll come for you in the morning. And this time, keep the fire going. It'll do none of us any good for you to have another cold night." He smiled kindly and looked at the lamp. "You can light it from the fire, if you've a mind to."

I was glad to be alone. And when the water was hot, gladder still was I to make use of the tub. The warmth of the water gave comfort. Sitting in the tub, I leaned forward to put my head into the wet warmth. Then sitting up again, trickled the sodden bathing cloth over my body. I stayed doing this a long time, soothing myself. When done, I put on the nightdress and wrapped the knitted shawl around my shoulders that were among the clothes given me by my yet unknown grandmother. I sat by the hearth and ate the bread and cheese that I'd found folded in a linen cloth in the basket. I hadn't much mind for food, but my rumbling belly demanded an offering.

I thought on my grandmother. How did she know or understand that I was needing to be alone? Often was I a one for the wanting of my own company, how did she know?. Was she a fiercesome woman, like some warrior? Or just quietly head-strong? I knew her to be the head of our family, yet I did not know her, or how she worked. I had many questions, but they would have to keep. Finally, an all-embracing weariness came upon me, and sleep called.

Next morning I followed my uncle Jarlath across the muddy yard, glad to own a pair of shabby boots when many did not. We walked toward a farmhouse, bigger than any known to me. He opened a door. It lead into the kitchen. A large table stood in the middle of the room. There was a cooking chamber over which hung two pots. A woman, a little older than myself, was attending them. Everything about her was round. Her face, her fingers, even her friendly smiling mouth had a roundness to it.

"This be Seamus's wife Mary, so it is."

I smiled weakly, as she bid me to sit at the table. I could see in her eye a tenderness for my pain, though she'd never known my husband or parents.

"I've cooked porridge. I expect you'll be needing some nourishment after what you've been through. Did you sleep?"

I welcomed the mothering Mary offered in the warm room that smelled of wholesomeness.

"I did."

Mary set down in front of me a bowl containing a small helping of porridge swimming in warm milk.

"There's seconds if you'll be wanting."

Grateful was I that Mary did not give me enough to feed three grown men as was the custom in Ireland when food was plentiful. Though, that was a rare thing where I'd come from. Nothing here was like where I'd come from. It was like I'd gone to another land. A land where everything was good. Everyone was kind.

"Eat up Orla. Else it'll go cold."

Eating! The oddness of all this came over me. How could I be sitting here eating porridge in this warm kitchen, with this kind motherly woman, when just days ago...?

"Where are my children?"

"Seamus and the young folk have gone into the market town. They should be back before midday. So surprised you'll be Orla when you see them. They aren't children anymore. The boys are now grown men. Paeder has twenty years, Conor eighteen, and Kathleen, is quite the young woman. They'll be so pleased to see you. They've been asking and asking to see you, but Granny thought it best to leave you alone for a bit."

Almost ten years had passed since I saw my children last, that awful day when Jarlath and Seamus had taken them from Duleek. Crying our goodbyes, peeling them from my skirt. I had no want for them to go, but knowing in my breaking heart, it too dangerous for them to stay. If they were to have the best chance in life, then go they must and stay must I.

So badly was my want to go with them. A mother should be with her children. We argued about this, my husband and me. A wife's place, he said, was with her husband. My parents, though knowing the grief this caused to me, agreed it was a wife's duty to do as her husband bid, so stay I did.

Mary was getting on with her tasks; my mind wandering. How little choice we've had in this life, robbed of all we hold dear, yet how resilient we Irish are, with death and destruction so much a part of all our lives. Through my own mother's words, I knew of the English attack that had killed her father and most of her brothers and sisters. The attack that had forced my grandmother, Jarlath and his pregnant wife, Niamh to flee Duleek. The attack that forced my newly married mother into hiding with her husband, when he refused to leave that piece of Ireland. That farm in Duleek he loved more than life. The land that in the end took his life, and hers.

I don't remember all the details, but my mother told me the journey was long and hard for Jarlath, his wife and his mother. They travelled far across Ireland in the hope of a better life, to where I now find myself. My grandmother's family had been well-off until their land had been taken, but wisely her parents had hidden from the English, an amount of coins, buried in the Irish earth, and on their death it became my grandmother's. It was with this, she'd purchased the farm here in what I now know to be County Mayo. She'd seen this farm in her mind's eye, in a vision. Yet, she'd not told of all she saw. Jarlath wanted to stay and fight, but had left with his mother because of the coming child that Niamh carried. What his mother didn't tell was that the birth of their wean, Seamus, would take Niamh's life.

Jarlath's mother, my grandmother, tended the wee child while Jarlath's heart mended. Then together, my mother told me, they'd built this farm, raising horses, fine horses. Not like the shaggy donkeys that the few fortunate in Duleek owned. The decision to breed fine horses gave credence to the older woman's wisdom, for horses were in great demand and valuable. Being able to breed these fine mounts, and care not who they were sold to, afforded them a protected and thriving life here in Mayo. Only twice in my life had I seen tall sleek creatures such as these. First time, was when they'd carried my children away, and then when Seamus came for me, it was one of their fine horses that carried me across our green land to here.

As if waking from a dream, I saw that Jarlath was no longer in the room.

"Where's my uncle?"

Mary softly humming turned to me, "He is with Granny. He'll come and take you to her soon, I'm sure."

Granny... I could not make a picture of this woman in my mind. She's a wise one, of that there's no doubt. Was she one sheathed in a cold hard shell as might be suggested by her not telling Jarleth of Niamh's going to die? Or did she not tell him out of kindness? She did care for Seamus as a wean, and he was grown into a good man, as was his father, my uncle Jarlath. And my own dear mother was a kind, gentle and loving woman who'd always spoken with fondness of her mother. Everything I knew of my grandmother was from my mother's lips.

I knew she'd loved my grandfather, and he her, from the moment they met at a gathering in Duleek. My grandmother had come from a neighbouring village. It was a rare thing for anyone to travel further than a mile or two from their village, and rarer still to marry out of your own village. But my mother had told me, my grandmother was not as others. Like Jarlath, my mother spoke of her mother having the second sight; the ability to see things that others could not. To know what was to come before it happened. It was because of this that my children still lived. Because of this, that I lived. What else had she seen for me?

"Come Orla, it's time for you to meet your granny," Jarlath said.

I stood and followed him down a long hallway. Halfway down there was hung thick dark curtains tied back on each side. Passed the curtains we walked. There were doors leading off to each side. This building was big. So unlike our two-roomed cottage in Duleek, or the single room where I'd spent the past two nights. It felt like being in some great hall, perhaps where a royal person might live; where I might be taken to meet The Queen!

"In here," Jarlath said, and lead me into a room on the left.

Though I did not know the woman I was to meet, I thought she must be grand; a witch, or warrior like. Yet she was not. She was strikingly ordinary.

"Fáilte! Fáilte Orla!" said the older woman, extending her hands to me and moving with the grace of a woman half her age.

I was stunned by her plainness. There was nothing remarkable about her. She was a similar height to myself which was neither tall nor short, her grey hair she wore in a long plait. Her clothes were the same as the borrowed ones I wore myself, a woollen skirt, linen shirt and a wrapped shawl. These must be surely hers.

"I am pleased that you have arrived to us safely. I know you've had a dreadful time. We all have the sadness upon us. Let me look on you, child."

Child! Hardly can I remember being a child, it being so long back. So much had passed since those days. Now I was a grown woman of middle years. No, I was not a child. It struck me in that moment, bringing a sudden sense of aloneness, with the death of both my parents, I was no longer anyone's child. I was an orphan!

She stood back and eyed me. We eyed each other. It seemed I was just the way she'd seen me in her vision, and Clodagh Moran was nothing as I believed her to be. My mind was all a swirl. I'd followed Jarlath down the hall expecting to meet some magical being, or some fierce warrior woman; expecting something to mark her, as my uncle said, rare. In the eyes of God, I swear truthfully, I was more than a little afeared of the greatness that I had wrapped around my grandmother. Yet here she stood, plain and ordinary, and I found myself though never having met her before, feeling a closeness, and an ease I'd not bargained for.

"Your hair is dark as mine was at your age. And you have my green eyes. I think you are a lot like me, though your beauty is far greater."

Was I like her? From what I'd heard tell of my grandmother, she was able, strong-willed and decisive. She could make harsh choices when needs be. She had a good head on her. I did not think myself to be very much like her. Then as if she had a knowing of my mind she said.

"You do not know what you can do Orla until you are tested. Only then do you find out. In time you will come to understand this, but you are yet young."

In that moment, I did not feel young. I felt old and tired, and sad, and bewildered. And in truth, I was not young, still, to a woman of her years, I may seem so. I had many questions. Of this woman, Clodagh Moran, I knew very little, and dearly wanted to know more. And what of the learning to play the harp that my uncle had spoken of when I'd first arrived. What did she have to say of this? All of this was going through my head when footsteps and excited voices began to fill the air.

"Your children are here. This is a special day Orla... treasure it!"

"Mammy," said Paeder.

# CHAPTER TWO

# KIN AND BLOODSTOCK

Embracing me was a very tall young man with dark hair. Conor, my second born, quickly followed Paedar's lead. He too, was tall and dark. It was sadly striking how much in height, and looks to their father these boys were, though they had my dark hair. Kathleen was different. She was small, more like me, yet she had father's fair hair. It was plain to see she felt uneasy, and why would it be otherwise? She was so young when our lives had parted. "Mother," she said awkwardly.

I felt like I was trying to charm a small bird that was unsure of me. I so wanted the little bird to trust me, but knew I needed to be quiet and not make any bold moves. So many emotions flooded through me as we carefully and briefly enfolded each other. Surprise, joy, sadness that their father was not here to see them, and the knowing they'd never look upon his face again, but most of all, I was filled with love, and the wanting to weave the fabric of our lives together once more.

Mary's voice sounded. "Come to the table."

Paeder took my arm. "I remember when we'd all eat together when I was a boy, you, Daddy, Pa, Maga and the three of us. Never have I forgotten how loved was I there was in our cottage. I hated leaving." I was glad he'd been able to hold these memories, even Maga, the children's pet name for my mother, for I'd often feared we'd be nothing more than a dream.

Then Conor spoke. "I don't remember much, but Granny has often talked of you, our family, and life in Duleek, saying we must always remember from where we came."

I cast a brief glance at my grandmother.

"Orla, why don't you call me Clodagh."

My grandmother was such a mystery to me. It was as if she felt my feelings; knew my thoughts.

We bustled in and sat at the table that Mary had got ready. Once more, I was struck by how agreeable life seemed here. Everyone so at ease. There was no place set for fear at this table. Its absence was strange to me.

For all of my living days, even in the happiest of times, a cloud of worry hung over us. We knew our lot as farmers, but we never knew what'd be visited upon us by others, those who, through cruelty and conflict, ruled over us. Here there was food aplenty and laughter, and a strong, undeniable love shared between all who took their seat. Blessed I was to be here with my loved ones, though it would take time for me to fully feel at ease. How much? I could not say.

"Mary told me you'd all gone to the market town with Seamus. Is it a long walk?" Everyone began the laughing. Clodagh, seeing my puzzlement, said, "They went on horseback. The young folk each have their own horse."

How could this be? Back in Duleek, very few had a donkey and cart. No one had a horse. All of the back breaking work, and much there was of it, was done by the efforts of men, women and children. How is it that here, my own children enjoyed the wealth of not a shared horse, but one for each?

"Horses are our living, cailín," said Jarlath. "They were in Mammy's vision, and they be what keeps us safe and provides us with a good living."

Mammy's vision! Like the horses, Jarlath had told to me my playing of the harp was one of her visions. When would she speak to me of this strange and wild vision?

"O rla must have her own horse," said Clodagh.

My own horse! I'd only ever been upon the back of one. The one I rode away from all I knew in Duleek, and of that ride I recalled little.

"How did you find the black mare that carried you here?" asked Jarlath.

Was the horse I had ridden black? Was it a mare? "She did not deliver me to meet the ground in our journey here, though I do not know but how given that I've never ridden before, so I think her a kind animal."

"She is yours. You must name her and care for her. The young folk, Jarlath and Seamus, will show you how," said Clodagh.

All nodded in agreement, and so it was decided that after our meal I should be taken to meet properly, my unasked for gift. All were excited. I tried to share their feeling, but my stomach knotted with uncertainty.

I spoke little during the meal, but heard and saw much. It was clear my children were closely bonded to Mary. She and Seamus had not been blessed with weans of their own, and it was plain to see that mine filled their hearts. As painful as it was to have been parted from them, I never thought their lives to be one as blessed as they had here. They'd been in my heart every day, and the best I hoped for them, was that they'd have enough to eat, and a warm bed to lay in each night, but this! I must soon waken from this heavenly life. Peace, love, food, and now horses. This surely cannot be true!

"Come Mammy, let's go to your mare," said Paeder, taking my hand.

We all, except Mary and Clodagh, walked out into the fresh sharp air to a long building. Inside the building was a row of faces looking out at us. Faces with large velvet eyes, and soft nickering voices that seemed to say, we are pleased to see you. The smell of hay filled the air.

"These are our horses, Orla. These ones are not for the selling. Your mare is down there, why don't you go to her on your own." said Jarlath.

I walked forward as if drawn to the glossy black horse; my heart thumping. She was big! In the madness of the ride, escaping death, I hadn't seen her so. And though I felt fear as we galloped away, it was not for this horse. She made a soft nickering sound that spoke to something inside me. I reached out my hand to her whiskered muzzle. It was soft like I thought velvet cloth might feel, though I'd never seen or touched such cloth. She nuzzled me as if asking for something.

Jarlath came to my side. "Here, give her this, but mind how you hold your hand. It must be flat like this." He held out his hand, palm side up, flat with fingers outstretched. On it was a piece of carrot. "Now you do it."

I took the carrot and placed it as shown. I reached out my shaking hand toward the mare. I felt her lips nibbling on my palm as she gently took the carrot. It gave to me such a thrill!

"There, said Jarlath. You have much to learn, but now it has begun."

"I'll call her Raven."

As we walked back to the farmhouse, I was filled with joy. Once more to be with my children and kin of my own, and now to have a horse. Expecting change to sneak up on you, my mother always said, was a good way to live. A way, she said, that was useful for dealing with the good and the bad of life. I thought these wise words, and like her, had taken on this way of thinking. It'd helped me rise with the good, and deal with the sinking of disappointment. In Duleek these last years, there were many low times. The change that came to us was mostly not for our betterment.

Glad I was, that my children had not the need to share the disquiet that was often my companion. I gave a silent blessing that I still lived, and for the bringing of me to this moment in time. As my grandmother told me this very day, this was a special day, and one to be treasured. And always would I.

As we neared the main house, the men parted from us, having work to do. A weariness was seeping through my body. I thought to excuse myself at the earliest chance to return to the quiet of the small cottage that had given me shelter these past nights. Another had a different notion.

We entered the house through the kitchen, and I followed my sons and daughter down the hall and into the gathering room on the left once more, where their great-grandmother sat by the small fire chamber. She smiled as we made our noisy entrance.

"Which room will be Mammy's?" asked Paeder.

Clodagh looked to me with a knowingness. "I think your mother might prefer to remain in the cottage for now."

"She cannot live in the tack room," protested Paeder. I turned my questioning face to him.

He scowled. "Well, it was a tack room until a few weeks past. Granny had Uncle Jarlath and Seamus clear it and put in the fire chamber, but it is still a tack room. Surely now you will want to move up here." I looked to my grandmother for I knew she understood.

"Why don't you and Conor walk your mother back to the cottage and light the fire for her. Kathleen, you go to Mary and ask her to make up a small food basket. You can take it to your mother when it is ready."

Paeder readied himself to continue his protest, but Clodagh raised her hand and looked at him in a way he knew. It was clear this exchange was at an end.

"Rest well Orla. You are safe here."

My sons walked with me as told, back to the cottage. They quickly had the fire crackling, and though Paeder plainly unhappy with me sleeping away from the main house, bid me goodnight, each kissing me on the brow. How strikingly different were their lives to mine.

This room, the one I'd slept in since my coming here, was half as big as the cottage where I'd lived all of my life. The cottage, that before their leaving, had been home to my three children, my parents, myself and their father, my husband. I was comfortable here and welcomed the quietness. I was thinking on this when came a soft knock on the door. It was Kathleen carrying a small basket.

"Some food for you, Mother." Her eyes were cast down. "We're glad you are here."

"I am glad to be here." I reached out and touched her cheek. Startled by my hand, she looked up. Just for an instant, our eyes met. "How beautiful you are. I wish I could have been with you all these years." Her face took on some colour, and her bottom lip trembled. Quickly, she turned away.

When her feet had put between us a few safe steps, over her shoulder she softly said, "Goodnight, Mother."

The next morning I dressed, gave my blessing for the new day, and walked to the stables. It was early, but work with the horses had already begun. Uncle Jarlath was doing something with one of them, lifting up its feet. Seamus was in the now empty stall raking the straw. I could see Paeder and Kathleen approaching carrying buckets of water, and Conor was cutting the strings of a bale of hay. Down the end of the row was the black mare, my mare, her ears forward, watching me and softly nickering.

"She knows you already," said Uncle Jarlath.

I carried in my hand a small piece of bread that I'd saved from last evening. I held it out flat on my hand as shown the day before, and once again she took it from me. "You are a lovely thing." I stroked her soft muzzle. Suddenly the air was filled with a loud clanging sound.

"Come. It's breakfast time," said my uncle.

As we sat round the table eating porridge, I was reminded that this ideal life in County Mayo, like all farms, was built on hard work, and everyone shared in it. The talk at the table was about horses, planning of meals, the tending of the vegetable garden, and the selling of, or slaughtering of sheep. I saw by the way my grandmother Clodagh kept a close eye on the oatcakes being cooked, getting up to turn them, placing them to cool along the bench, that this was a task she was charged with. And Mary busying herself with the large pots in the fire chamber seemed to do most of the cooking. These were everyday tasks that I was used to doing and had done none of since my arrival.

"Where can I be of the best help?" I asked.

"This morning and perhaps many more, Jarlath will teach you the care of your horse, and this afternoon you can help in the garden. This untamed land is not easily willed into providing food for those who tread upon it," said my grandmother.

T hat morning, I did learn much about the caring for a horse. It began with the cleaning of hooves. I watched my Uncle Jarleth face toward the back of my mare, and run his strong hand down Raven's leg. She lifted it. He cupped the hoof in his hand and checked it. He said I should be sure to see that the hoof was clean, and most importantly, that there were no stones lodged there.

"Your horse is not just for pleasure, as you'll find out in time, and a horse cannot work for you if it is lame."

I learned about leading a horse, what to feed it and specially what not to feed it; how to brush it and clean its stall. Then he showed me how to put the bridle and the saddle on, something Seamus had done on our ride from Duleek to Mayo.

T hat afternoon we all, except for Jarlath and Conor, who were killing a sheep for house meat, worked in the large vegetable garden. This was work I knew and enjoyed. I knew a lot about the growing of plants and how to use them for both food and for healing. My mother had taught me well.

I had seen this morning in the stables that Kathleen did not wear a skirt, but a pair of long frieze breeches akin to the men, and still in the garden she was dressed this way.

"Kathleen, why is it you do not wear a skirt?"

Kathleen looked to me, but before she could answer, Seamus said, "It's best for others to think her a lad... she's safer that way."

I understood. Well, I understood. I pushed down the vile memory that was wanting to rise and turned my mind back to my work. That night when I was alone, the memory, uninvited, visited me, curdling my blood, filling me again with the powerlessness, disgust, anger... hatred!

I t had been a summer evening in Duleek. We'd just begun supper, my parents, my husband and me, when without warning the English soldiers burst through the door. We'd heard nothing. Like wasps, a swarm of them grabbed my father and husband. Another four having cast everything from the table onto the floor roughly threw me face down over one end of the table, and my mother the other. We'd had no warning of them coming. It all happened so fast. We had no chance to defend ourselves.

Lifting our skirts they pumped our bodies, making our struggling menfolk watch. Our men were strong, but not strong enough to free themselves. Though they struggled with all their might which only earned them the fist of their captors. They were well outnumbered, each being held by three soldiers. The best they could do was turn their faces away. All the while, the soldiers laughed. The smell of liquor strong on them. Their rough hands wrenching at us. My mother's words whispered to me; I hear still. "Do not struggle... do not cry. Deny them that." I did struggle. Though it be in vain, I kicked and bit, I did struggle!

When they had each, in turn, abused us, laughing, they were gone as quick as they arrived. In the distance we could hear the pounding of horses' feet, and the fading laughter. The four of us stood silent, numb and broken. We never spoke of this. Not ever, but the shame and anger, I know, stayed with us all. Even now with years gone, the red of their coats, the smell of them, the disgust and my mother's words stay with me. Do not struggle, do not cry!

I spent the next few weeks learning not only how to care for Raven, but how to ride in a proper way. Not just sitting, holding on as I had on my ride from Duleek. To make the riding more easy, Mary made me some breeches like Kathleen's. I took quickly to the riding. It gave me such pleasure, and a sense of freedom that never had I felt. Being new to riding, and not knowing the land, beyond the farmyard, for the few days, my kin each took a turn in riding out with me. It was grand. It gave me a chance to get to know a bit about them.

Jarlath, as was his way, spoke little as we rode. Mostly it was to offer something about riding or to point out something of the land. Conor was quiet like Jarlath, he spoke little, but was reassuring to be with. As we rode, he asked me to tell him of his father. I spoke of his father's kindness, told him he was a man who held to his values and beliefs steadfastly, and of his love for the land. I thought Conor to look most like his father. As I spoke, he listened in his own quiet way. It was clear this young man was a thinker.

It was less clear to me if Paeder shared this quality. He's a one for the speaking of his mind, leaving no doubt of his meaning. I like that. There's no guessing with him. And, as already shown himself to be, of a protective nature. Perhaps that comes from being the eldest, or from being told to look out for his younger brother and sister when they had left my care ten years earlier. I know not which. Kathleen, she has the deep thinking as does Conor, and though she does not say a great deal, when it's needed, will speak her mind and stand her ground. Of the three, I think her most like me in nature. These are good young folk. They be raised well. There was no doubt they were well-loved, and encouraged to be independent and capable... and they lived! For this, I could never repay the debt.

Though riding alongside me took each away from their work, I was sure they enjoyed it as much as me. We all shared a love of the land. This was a wild and beautiful land, where one could feel totally alone, yet always belonging. It held the farm nestled in a valley, surrounded by hills, and further away mountains. All cloaked in its rich greenness. Jarlath told me Clodagh had seen this farm in one of her visions, believing it to be chosen because it was hidden and hard to get to. Below, the hills were almost, encircled by bogs. I remember his smile and the glint in his eye as he repeated... almost!

After a few days, I rode alone. I had such a love of this! Just to be with Raven, the wind, the rain, the bushes and trees. How I loved the greenness. I mostly rode on the paths that I'd been shown, and on this day I rode my favourite. The path lead up to the top of the largest hill. You could see far into the distance. When Seamus had ridden with me, he pointed from here to where the town lay. As I was wondering about what the town may be like, a movement caught my eye.

Riders! No one had come to the farm since I'd been here. I knew only my kin. All others were strangers. Unease flooded me, my heart thumped and kicked Raven's sides. She lurched with a startle but responded and galloping carried me swiftly to the farm. I pulled up by the stable doors. Calling riders are coming.

Jarlath grabbed my reins and barked, "Kathleen." Suddenly, she was there. "Take your mother and go into the house."

"Come Mammy" said Kathleen, snatching my hand and pulling me toward the back of the stables.

I thought, why are we not running for the door, but we were. Kathleen pushed open a small door in the rear wall of the stable, a door I'd not seen before. It opened to the back of some outbuildings. Kathleen, still grasping my hand firmly, hurried me to the farmhouse.

"Riders," she said as we entered the kitchen. Mary quietly moved to bolt the door.

Seeing my eyes on Mary, Clodagh said, "We are safe, but let us not invite unnecessary trouble." She stood watching at the window as the two riders passed the farmhouse to the stables. I saw her whole body settle. She gave Mary a nod. "All's well."

My mind was whirling with Jarlath's urgent barking, the running, the door being bolted, but what was ringing loudest in my head were the words, *come Mammy*. I'd struggled to get close to Kathleen. Hearing these words meant so much to me.

Knowing the riders, my grandmother now untroubled, said, "Orla, come with me. I have some things I need talk with you about."

I followed Clodagh to her room. "Kathleen called me Mammy," I said with a lightness in my heart.

"I know that is important to you, and I am truly pleased for you, Orla, but that is not why we are here." There was a firmness about the way she spoke these words. "When you arrived, Jarlath spoke to you of playing the harp. That time has come."

That time has come. Dear Christ, what does she mean? I had let Jarlath's words about me playing the harp to fade from my mind, hoping too, that others would think no more on it. In this moment I knew I was wrong. I'd faced much hardship in my life, always meeting it head on, but playing the harp? This was a thing I knew nothing of. Glad was I for my mother's advice of expecting change to sneak up on you. This one had surely caught me cold.

# CHAPTER THREE

# THE TELLING

"**G**randmother, you cannot mean this! I know you know much of me, and I am not a one to shy away from the hard or painful, but you cannot surely be willing to place my life in such peril for the sake of music; I am your own flesh and blood. You of all must know what you are asking of me. There must be someone else!"

"Would you have it that one of your own children stand in your stead?"

"No. For sure, I would not, but why this? Am I not useful enough on the farm? Am I not doing my share?

"Of course you are! Orla, what is being asked of you is a privilege not a punishment. In these days, yes, there is danger for a harper, but those who live in our land need you to do this. There is much sundering. Hearts and spirits are broken. You with the harp can bring about the mending, the bringing together, the crossing of the unseen bridges. The harp has been with our people for a long time. It holds within its strings a magic that no other instrument holds. And you ask why you? I have seen this. In a vision, I have seen this. You are the one. You know what it is to suffer as many in our land have suffered. This duty can only be accepted by one who truly knows. One who has the spirit for it. I know you to be that one. I have seen it. I beg you do not resist."

Do not struggle... do not cry! My shoulders dropped. Torn I was. I wanted to please my grand-mother. I wanted to do what I could for my land and our people, but I did not want to give my life. Not now. Fate works in strange and sometimes cruel ways. If I say yes, what will that mean? Am I to be cleaved once more from my children?

"I have forty years upon me." I could hear my voice say, sounding as from a far distant place.

"That is so, but you have the quickness of mind to learn easily, and in learning you take joy. I know this to be true. You have the sensitivity, a love for the natural world, and through all that you have lived, your spirit has never deserted you. You are brave. You are the one."

"It would appear that you see much, Grandmoth-er. When you saw me playing the harp, in your vision, when was that, how long have you known of this?" This time, though I meant it not, my voice was a sharp-edged sword; accusing! Like someone a secret is not shared with, though the secret it is about them.

"I see much and feel much Orla, but not all things. Most of what comes to me flows through a connection of blood, but this is not without exception, and in answer to your question, I was given this vision some three or so years back."

"Then why wait until now?"

"I have held off, but could no longer. It had to be now or you would be dead. The Englishman Cromwell decided this was the time."

We sat there for an eternity, neither speaking, sitting with our own thoughts. Clodagh Moran possibly, probably, knowing mine, me knowing nothing of hers. I thought on the heart-breaking history of Ireland, the invasions, the dispossessions, the burnings of our buildings, the trampling of our beliefs; this had been our reality for many lifetimes, including mine. I thought on what she had spoken of regarding my liking for the learning. This was true. I did have an eagerness to learn. I thought on herb-lore, and spinning and weaving, on farming and cooking, on mothering and love, and most recently horses. I was a one for the learning.

Again as if knowing my thinking, my grandmother said, "See you know you are good at learning."

"Are there even any harps left in Ireland?"

"Do not worry yourself, Orla, that part is for me, yours is to take up the mantle. Ah, I hear the voices of men, our visitors have gone. Let us leave this now and find out what our visitors wanted."

"They were looking to buy another horse," said Jarlath. "The man fancied a certain black mare."

I gasped and looked hard at him. "Tis a shame that when I brought her out of the stall, she had a lameness in her front leg. He was disappointed, but without too much talk, he decided on the other black, the one in the field."

"Lame! Did I ride her too hard in my hurry to get back?"

"As luck would have it, she'd only a stone in her hoof." He winked at me. A canny man my uncle.

Everything settled back into the rhythm of the ordinary. The speed and calm actions carried out on the arrival of the horse buyers, the escape through the rear stable door, the bolting of the kitchen door, told me this had been done before. This was a known plan, and reminded me that in these uncertain times, nowhere are we safe. Danger can be found without looking for it, even in this beautiful wild remote place.

After taking supper and bidding all a good night, I walked back to my cottage. I set a fire in the hearth. I cannot say if the cottage was cold, or it was me, that was cold. Picking up the tinderbox, taking out the flint, striker and a piece of char cloth, without thinking, I made a nest of dry grass. Placing the char cloth on the flint, it only took a few strikes to produce the small glow needed. Wrapping the grass around it, I blew softly. As the flame burst, I placed the bundle in the hearth, feeding it with small sticks. Dancing flames quickly grew, taking my mind into them. As I stared, I thought on the speaking with my grandmother. Her words were spoken with honesty. She did not deny that the life of a harper would be a dangerous one, but her reason for wanting me to become one was powerful. Could the music that I might play be mending music?

I'd heard little music other than the music of nature; birdcall, windsong, soughing of the trees, water over stone, this was the music I knew best... and loved. I did once hear a Scottish travelling man in Duleek play the bagpipes. They were loud and rang out across the land. My heart was moved by the sadness in the music he played.

What does a harp sound like? Are they heavy? And what sort of wood are they made from? And the strings? I was a one for always asking the questions, and hunting for the answers, that was part of the learning for me. What would it feel like to hold? How does one hold a harp?

I felt a thrilling as I thought on these things, though blunting, was the danger that ran alongside of such an undertaking. I'm not ready to die. If I was, I'd have stayed in Duleek and died with my husband. I took comfort in that my grandmother saw me playing the harp in her vision, so at least for a time it seemed the hand of death would not fall upon me.

D ays passed in the way that most did, tending the horses, working in the garden, clearing rocks from the fields, preparing char cloth, sharing meals, then one morning after breakfast Jarlath and Seamus rode into the market town, for what reason, I knew not, nor was it my business. Their going afforded me time to spend alone working with my children. In this I found much pleasure. Such pride I felt, though I could take little credit. They were not afraid of hard work. They were quick to help one another, never a once did I hear them grumble, and their lively spirits shone through it all. I would be lying if I were to say that my heart was not swelled. All three were a joy to be in the company of. I told them some of my life in Duleek, and they, in turn, told me of their happy lives growing up here on the farm, lives that had they stayed in Duleek, would have been very different.

Sitting at the breakfast table, a day or two after their going to town, Jarlath said, "Kathleen, you and Conor catch up the chestnut in the field, the one with the white socks, he's off to market next week. You'll be needing to work him each day, to get him quiet. Conor, you be sure to give a hand now. Take a bucket with you. It'll be easy to get him to come to you if he thinks there's a feed in it."

I knew from listening that most of the horses going for sale were kept in two fields close to the house. Fields enclosed by dry-stone walls built up over the years by my family, and those that were here before them. Built from the limestone that dotted the land here; a blight and a blessing.

The farmhouse and outbuildings, the shelters for the horses, the fencing and small yards, were all made with this stone. So much of it there is. This was no land for the ploughing. This was good pasture land with rich grass, ideal for horses, sheep, and cows. The milk from the house milker was rich and thick with cream, and when churned made the grandest golden butter. Mary and Clodagh shared the milking of the cow, a chore I'd willingly take on if asked. Me thinking for the most part, cows lovely animals. We had one for a time in Duleek but she had to be sold to pay the landlord.

K athleen and Conor worked with the chestnut. Kathleen doing most of the riding. She was a good rider, and it was plain she loved the work. For the first few days, the chestnut was nervous and flighty. Kathleen didn't seem to mind. She worked him in one of the yards with Conor close by keeping an eye on her. After a few days when the horse was settled, they took him out. Conor riding alongside the chestnut on his horse.

"He's a grand ride," said Kathleen to Jarlath at supper one evening.

"Good, we'll take him to town the day after tomorrow. Orla will come as well. Seamus'll stay ahint. Be sure now, you cailíns, wear your breeches and tie up your hair under a cap, and when in town, Orla, say nothing. Do you hear me? Say nothing. This is a good town, friendly like, but there are not many womenfolk, so let's not be offering any temptation for trouble."

How exciting! Going to the town. Ever since my arrival a month or two back, I'd not left the farm. I had no real mind for it. In Duleek, I never left the farm much, but now the prospect of seeing the market town, and me being curious and all, I looked forward to it. What it would look like? Would there be many people? Would it be a large town? What would the buildings be like?

What's the town called? I asked.

"It's a port town. It is Cill Ala," said Jarlath.

# Chapter Four

# THE KEY

T he next day passed slowly. I went about my chores quietly as usual, but inside of me were feelings of excitement and curiosity... and unease. Eager as I was to see Cill Ala, Jarlath's words of warning and my own memories were with me. Would there be soldiers, English soldiers? I thought that was the truth of what Jarlath was saying. This vexed me and I slept little.

The day of the ride dawned clear and fresh. I'd done as was told and plaited my hair, pinned it up with a strong wooden comb given me by Clodagh, and topped it with a cap from Conor. At breakfast, Kathleen and me, were given a keen look over. Strange it was, us riding away from the farm that morning as lads, but liberating too; throwing off the fetters of being a woman, if only for a while.

The ride took about two hours with most of it being through wild and unfriendly land. Bogs and marshland stretched as far as the eye could see. I now understood what Jarlath had meant when he said the farm was almost unreachable. A person needed skill and good knowledge of the land, especially on horseback, to make their way without stepping into the bog.

Mostly, we rode at a walk, in single file with Jarlath leading. Kathleen rode the chestnut without a saddle, due to its being sold bare. She said she liked to ride this way as she could truly feel the horse. I was glad of the walking pace. I could look around at the land, these parts being new to me. I loved this land, it living in my every breath, living in the breath of us all. I prayed to live long, and never have my love for this land leave me.

After picking our way carefully through the bog we came to a road. Here the ground was firmer. Running away from the road the grasses were studded with buttercups and bluebells. We were now able to ride in pairs.

"Not far to go," said Jarlath, kicking his horse into an easy canter. We all did the same. It felt good to have a change of pace. As we rode, I could see in the distance a tall upright structure. Jarlath followed my eye.

"Ah, that be the round tower of Cill Ala. Very old, it is. Built out of limestone like the stones on our farm. No-one knows exactly what its for. Some thinks on it as a bell tower, some say it was built for religious worship or for keeping treasures, others say it's military, and that people would lock 'emselves away in it from the attacks of Vikings. There's other towers the likes of it across Mayo, but this one's the tallest, so they say. Given their age, and all who would know being long dead, we'll probably never know, but it's a welcoming sight after a decent ride.

R iding toward the town we passed a crumbling stone ruin standing on the bank of a river. Though in ruins it was clear this had been an important building. "Uncle, what was that building?"

"Rathfran Abbey. It was destroyed, not long before Mammy, Niamh and myself arrived to the farm. Burned by a man named Richard Bingham, acting for the English queen, Elizabeth."

"And the river?"

"The Avonmore."

"Uncle, are you religious? Do you have a faith?"

"I have a faith alright. It's called staying alive. That's my religion and much devoted to it I am. You'd do well to take it up Orla. It's the faith your grandmother raised me in. It's the faith Seamus has been raised in, and it's the faith we've raised your children in. It's done us well so far. Praying to one god or many, works for some, but I believes godliness lives within each of us, just as does the devilment. We has a choice which way we goes."

I love my uncle Jarlath. We're kin. But too, as a man, I have of him a fondness and high regard. True it is, I've spent little of my forty years in his company, yet I've found in him a kind, patient and wise man, one that if it were not already so, I'd be pleased to be bound to by blood. He's a one that can be trusted, and though he claims his faith to be staying alive, he's a one for doing right by his family, and I think he'd die to protect us. That's what I believe of my uncle, Jarlath Moran.

W e were now on the edge of Cill Ala. As we got closer, the round tower stood high. A feat of wonder, unlike anything I'd ever seen. The town itself was bigger than any I'd ever been to; people everywhere! Stalls and shops lined the street as we rode. Bustling, rushing, things and people moving everywhere. I had no mind for this! No longer was I wanting to know. My shoulders stiffened, my stomach tumbled, my heart banged in my chest. This was not a place for me!

"Peadar," said Jarlath, "give Kathleen your horse. You and Conor take the chestnut to the yeoman. Mind he pays you what we agreed. Then go to the grain store and put in our order. Tell 'em we'll be back in a week to collect it. We'll meet you by the abbey. Kathleen and Orla, you come with me. And remember, say nothing!" Kathleen swung down from the chestnut. Peadar got off his horse. The exchange was made. My sons continued down the street with Paedar now upon the back of the chestnut.

Following Jarlath, Kathleen and me went back the way we'd come. Though I hadn't seen much of the town, I'd seen enough. As we neared the ruins of the abbey, we went up a lane running beside it. I hadn't seen this on our recent passing. At the top of the lane was a house.

"We're calling here," said Jarlath. "This is where your journey as a harper begins."

What! Ní thuigim! My eyes widened, but from my gaping mouth, no sound came. What did he mean?

Before I could ask, Kathleen said, "Oh, Mammy, we're so proud that you would do this for all who love our land. For our land itself. For us!"

Such a pride was there in her voice, and me being keen to bridge the years lost to us, closed my mouth. I could hear my mother's voice as though she stood by my side. Expect change to sneak up on you. Change, surely wore the softest of shoes!

"These are good people. You'll be well cared for, and we'll be back for you in a week," said Jarlath.

"So, I'm to be staying here? Is that what you're saying? For a week? Why didn't you tell me of this? What of Raven?"

Nodding, he said, "Kathleen'll ride her home, she'll be well seen to. And when we come back, we'll bring her for you to ride home. She'll be alright. We said nothing of this to you because we thought you'd refuse to come with us. I'm sorry. You'll be alright. It'll work out. You'll see."

Reaching the house we got down from our horses. I would do anything for my children, and if that meant spending a week with people I didn't know, then that I would do. I'd agreed to take on the duty of a harper, and Uncle Jarlath would not see me wrong. He trusted these people, and I trusted him. Though, if the truth be known, before Kathleen had spoken, I'd be lying to say the thought of turning Raven's head and galloping for the farm had not passed through my mind. It was her words, and the giving of mine, stopped me.

W e tied our horses to the lower branches of a tree that stood near the house. Jarlath knocked on the door. A woman opened it. She was an older woman, though not so much as my grandmother.

"Céad Míle Fáilte," she said.

"Go raibh maith agat, Maura," replied Jarlath.

She bustled us in saying "Fáilte, fáilte," as we passed. I nodded and thanked her for the welcoming.

Looking to me, Jarlath said, "This is Maura Bourke, she knows much about the harp. Kathleen you know, and this is my niece, Orla. It's Orla you'll be teaching."

"Your grandmother has told me much of you, Orla! Now, Jarlath, you and Kathleen will be taking some food with us before you leave."

She took down four bowls, laying them on the table, Maura Bourke filled them with a stew of meat and barley. We ate, then Kathleen and Jarlath left us, left me! There was no bluster. A quick embrace, Kathleen atop Raven, they were gone. Though left behind with a stranger, odd it was, I was in no way troubled. Maura had a way that put me straight away at ease. To my mind, like Uncle Jarlath's words, if I was to be taking up the harper's journey, I had to make a beginning of it... and this was it!

"Come Orla, let's be settling you in. We have much work to do, and little time. Jarlath tells me you're a quick learner, and a strong and brave woman, these are good qualities, and ones that'll serve you well in your life as a harper."

My life as a harper!

That afternoon and evening, sitting by the hearth, broken only by supper, Maura told of many things about the harp and its music. That harps can be made of different woods, and like people, have different voices. She told me some harpers play with the harp on their left shoulder, nearer their heart she said, and some play with it on their right. She told me that most surviving harps have strings made of wire, players of these use their fingernails. Some older harps, have strings made from the hair of horses, or from the innards of some animals. These were called gut strings. She spoke of harps being different sizes and some having many strings, and others having less.

My first lesson in the harping tradition went on for hours. Maura had much to teach me, and the patience of a saint, with my constant interrupting questions, finally she said, "It's time for us to rest, we'll talk more on this tomorrow." As she headed to her bed, she turned. "Ah, there's one more thing you need to know, a very important thing, a precious thing, every harp has a key."

As I lay down that night, in another place strange to me, I thought on the day's unfolding. Someone has a plan for my life, and it's not me, perhaps this is the same for all. Is this the work of the Lord as I'd been told in the teaching of the church in Duleek? I recall someone saying, the Lord works in mysterious ways. Now that be the truth of it! I'd lived when many others had not... why? I fell asleep thinking on Maura's words, every harp has a key. What did it unlock?

"Make yourself ready Orla, there's much for you to see. Tie up your hair, and put on your cap. Cill Ala's a friendly place, and I'm well known here, but I think it best, for now, if you keep in the way of a lad."

There was a spark in Maura's voice as though we were setting out on a grand adventure. I felt swept along by her eagerness. What would this day bring? Something had shifted in me overnight, this I knew to be true. I was accepting and even a little thrilled by the unknown journey I was taking. A giving in to the one who has the plan, though uncertain of who that was or my part.

"Where are we going?" I asked as we walked down the lane.

"I'm not sure, but I'll know when we arrive. That is the way of life."

We stopped by the ruins of the abbey. What a grand building it must have been before the burning. Such wilful useless destruction. To undo the labours of the hands of many, and for what? To make those who think differently come to heel. To stand over those with less might. The wielding of power in such an evil way, makes me to boil! Looking at this forlorn building that once stood in a glorious celebration of its people, filled me with sorrow and anger.

"No," said Maura. "I'll take you into the abbey on our way back. Come."

Spending only a few hours with this woman, Maura was such a riddle. One moment serious and learned, the next spirited as a hare. She was slightly built, quite tall, and like most her age, wore her long grey hair in a plait. Her hands, well her fingernails, were striking, like none I'd seen before. They were long and shaped to a point. But the point was not in the middle, it was to one side. From her talking last evening, I got the notion that Maura was the player of a wire strung harp. My curious nature had me to wonder what life had delivered Maura? Why was it that we'd been brought together in this place? At this time?

As we walked, Maura said, "We'll go to the port. There's someone you needs be meeting."

We arrived at a large wooden building, its doors opened onto the street. As we entered, I could see that the back of the building had no wall, it was open to the water. In the middle of the building stood a partly built boat, it was big, on which many men were working. In one corner away from the others, was a man shaping a piece of wood with a sharp tool. Maura lead me toward him. We stopped a ways back watching as he fashioned a rounded edge on a large piece of wood. Now and then he'd stop and run his hand along the edge, though I'd not seen a man work like this before, it was clear he knew his trade well.

Feeling our eyes on him, he looked up and said quietly, "Ah, Maura, so this is Orla?"

"Yes. Orla, this is Declan O'Malley. He's the builder of boats, and a very fine craftsman he is."

"Hello", I said quietly not wanting anyone to be hearing my voice and reveal me a woman.

In such a short time my life had become a maze of questions and puzzles. Why did Maura bring me to a boatyard to meet this man? Who was this man? And how is it that my name is already known to him?

We three walked outside, not talking. The day was fair, a lovely, soft Irish day. We walked by the water. So much water! It seemed to me to be endless. I was thinking on this when, although almost whispering, Maura startled me by saying, "Declan's a stringmaker."

"But, I thought he was a boat builder?"

"He is that," said Maura. "He is many things. A trader, a smuggler, the getter of the unusual... things like perhaps a harp. And... he is a stringmaker."

The way she said stringmaker made it sound magical. As though it was some mystical rare craft, known only to the chosen ones. While Maura spoke,

Declan O'Malley did not interrupt. The corners of his mouth ever so slightly turned upwards. A fondness for Maura showing in his eyes. He was a tall man, perhaps in his late forties, with dark hair flecked with pewter, worn long to his shoulders. The front of his hair tied back. I thought to be out of the way of his work. He was a handsome man, not bold, yet there was a confidence about him, and determination shone in his green eyes.

"You must be careful Orla," said Declan. His voice deep and warm. "You are embarking on a beautiful, but dark and dangerous journey. One that will find your life forever changed."

As he spoke those words, if his face and tone were not so serious, I might have laughed. Forever changed! Of late, in almost every moment my life was changing. Nowhere in it was a sureness. Nowhere in my life was there a knowing. I did not laugh, instead I said, "I have not the knowing where this journey will take me, but if it is one that will do good for the people of this land I love, then it is one I'm willing to take." This I said with a true heart.

"We'll help you, best we can. Come now, follow along."

W e walked around the harbour and along the shoreline for a way to where the water became edged with rocks, big dark rocks, not like the limestones we picked in the fields, these were strong, jutting, jagged rocks. These rocks were solid, unyielding rocks, these were bold rocks!

"Now we climb," said Declan.

Climb! How does one clamber up the face of these foreboding rocks?

"This is one of the doorways to our sanctuary," said Maura.

Her words caused my mind to spin and swirl once more. The reverence in the way that Maura spoke of these rocks was as though we were entering a holy place. I knew from the sureness of their steps I was being lead to a place well known to both my companion and the one who guided us.

At first, I did not see the steps cut into the rocks, but following Declan was easy, it was more as walking than climbing, yet we were getting higher. Up an invisible walkway of rock. After many steps we rounded a large jut, and ahint, obscured by this jutting monster was an opening. This was like no other place I'd ever seen. Since leaving Duleek, so much was new to me. Declan reached down into the darkness and took up a tinderbox and a lantern. Setting alight some stranded jute, he lit the lamp, and put back the tinderbox.

We made our way along a dark rock-lined tunnel, which after a time opened out into a chamber-like room. It was filled with barrels and chests.

"These chambers hold many secrets," said De-clan.

Perhaps the spoils of a smuggler I thought, but said nothing. On we went in this rocky burrow, opening out every now and then into a chamber, some stacked like the first, some empty. I'd never known anything like this place. Some of the lintel rocks above the openings into the chambers were carved, some with faces, some with crucifixes; thinking on it being under the ground filled me with wonder.

"Not far now," said Declan. Maura smiled knowingly.

As the lamp filled the next chamber we came to, in the soft light, there stood two harps. The wonder of the sight stopping my breath!

# CHAPTER FIVE

# HARP AND CRANE

The shape of each harp was a little different from the other. One with the wood being light, the other made from darker wood. Having never seen one before, I could only stare... frozen to the ground by their beauty. Declan's words broke the spell!

"So, Orla, this is your place of learning, a little different from most, I'll grant you, but you'll be safe here. No-one but those who need to know, will know your secret. I'll leave you now and let you two to get about your work, and I mine."

With that, he took up a lamp from within the chamber, and with a small twig, transferred the flame from the lamp that had been our guide, to the unlit one, and left us.

"**C** ome," said Maura, "This one is yours."

She was standing next to the harp made of the darker wood. A thrilling, mixed with fear rippled through me. What if I couldn't do this? What if I was not such a good learner as my grandmother believed me to be? What if I was not brave enough? Not knowing my thinking, with her hand, Maura beckoned me to sit on one of the stools standing by each harp.

"I don't know how to hold it! I don't know how to sit at it! I don't know what to do with it!" The hurry of my words giving away my fear.

"Of course you don't Orla, that's why I'm here. I will teach you. Don't be afraid. Come! These harps look alike, but they are not. They are very different. Mine is strung with wire. Yours is strung with gut strings made by Declan. Because of this their sound is different. Mine has a louder bell-like voice, and I play with my fingernails. Yours is much softer, a more soothing sound and you will play with the fleshy part of your finger tips. Your grandmother, Clodagh, thought the more gentle sound would suit you well."

With that, she ran her thumb nail down the wire strings on her harp from the shorter strings to the longer ones. The chamber filled with a sound like no other I'd ever heard. It was both sweet and shrill, and as Maura said, it rang out like a bell.

Holding up her hand with her thumb raised, she said. "Now you do the same Orla, but use the fleshy part on your thumb."

I did as instructed. Oh, the sound was heavenly. It rang out into the air softly, and into me, touching my very soul.

"It causes me dismay Orla that what should be done over years and with joy, needs to be done with haste, being that you're here but for one week. Yet, it is the ways it is. My hope is that joy will not be completely absent. But now we must eat."

She took from the small bag carried over her shoulder, a flask, some bread and two boiled eggs. While we ate, Maura told me what she knew of the tunnels and chambers, which was very little. She said their reason for being, like the round tower, was uncertain, but because of the positioning of entrances and exits, and some of the stone carvings, she believed they were somehow connected to the holy buildings of Cill Ala. Not many knew of the tunnels, as they were rarely spoken of by the local people, and those that did know of them were becoming fewer as old age and death overtook them.

As we finished eating Maura reached into her bag. This time from it she took out a small wooden handled metal tool. "This Orla, is a harp key. This is a tool of great importance. It is with this key you will tune your harp. With this key you can change the voice of your harp. You must keep it forever safe. In times past a key could be replaced if lost, but now with the coming of the English this is not so easily done."

She handed me the key. The wood of it was smooth in my hand. Its colour, a little darker than the harp. As I looked upon it, running my hand over the grain and I thought on those who before me, had held this key. Who were they? Was it the touch of their hands that darkened its wood? Where were they? Had they been killed for their music?

"Mine is a little different," said Maura, holding another key for me to see.

It was plain that each was meant for the same purpose, but the handle shape was different. The wood of the key Maura held was lighter, though they had the same metal bit. Maura slid the metal bit over one of the pieces of metal that stuck out at the top of her harp near a string, it fitted perfectly. She then handed it to me and told me to do the same. This I could not do for the key did not fit. Then she asked me to try with my key. It fitted as perfectly as hers had done on her harp.

"You see they look alike, but are not. Harps and their keys are like people. We may have two eyes, but what we see and how we look are to ourselves alone.

"Let me have your key, Orla. Today we will not be tuning, and as you have no bag to keep it safe in, until you do, it's best it stays with me."

We next spent time with Maura showing me how to sit on the stool holding the harp. She said for me to tip the harp back on to my shoulder. She did not say to me which shoulder. I pulled it back onto my right shoulder.

"Ah, that is the side for you. That is your natural side. That is the way you will play."

The wood was hard against my body, and though I felt clumsy and awkward, it felt right to pull it to that shoulder. Then Maura had me tip the harp forward to stand by itself again, and for me to get up, walk about, sit, and take up the harp again. This I did over and over, becoming more at ease each time.

Maura brought her stool up next to mine, lifting the harp away from me, we now sat one beside the other. "I want you to follow what I do with my hands."

She held out her hands in front of her and softly opened and closed them in a way, that though not the same, brought the milking of a cow to my mind, crinkling my face.

"Ah, tis good to see that you're already enjoying the being of a harper."

I told her the reason for smiling. She could see it too. We laughed. It felt odd and grand to laugh.

"There's one more thing for you to do. Then we must make our way home. I want you to pick up your harp and place it back by the stool."

I stiffened. Pick it up, this precious thing! What if I am to drop it? It was one thing to tip it back and forth... but to pick it up!

"If you're to be a harper, you'll be needing to carry your harp now and again. You may as well learn how from the beginning. You will come to love your harp, but you must not be afraid of it, Orla. It is more hardy than you might believe."

Maura patiently showed me each movement. Where to hold. How to lift. How to balance. The harp was heavier than I expected, and though I cannot say I moved it with confidence, I did as asked. A small task, perhaps, but done.

M aura took up the lamp and began going deeper into the tunnel.

"Maura, are you not going the wrong way? I'm sure Declan brought us this way. Stretching my arm in the direction we'd come." Now it was her turn to smile.

"Follow and you'll see why we go this way."

I followed. Deeper we went. Down here was cool. Not cold. Not warm. No breeze. Still as a fine Summer's evening. A rare thing in Ireland, yet it was a rareness, etched it into the mind. Down here was as that. Fixed, without change in either chamber or tunnel, and the smell of old. I was glad to have Maura leading the way, for on my own, I would surely be lost. By her confidence it was clear she knew her way through this underworld hidden beneath the green land above.

As we went along, I saw other tunnels leading off. I asked Maura where they lead. All she said was I would come to know, as needed. It was odd to me, in this dark place of mystery, enwrapped by these huge rocks, that I'd feel so at ease. Lost, but more safe than I ever could recall. These beautifully built tunnels running this way and that, were so high that even a tall man like Declan had no need to crouch when walking them; the rocks lining the walls and the roof, shaped flat and smooth, and the carvings, though few, hewn with care.

After we'd been walking for a time, I thought the ground beneath my feet to be running gently uphill. I asked Maura about this. She told me what I was feeling was true and needed. The rising would allow our issue from this otherworld and the rejoining of the world we'd left earlier on this day. She was telling this to me when I saw that the tunnel was being lighted by a source other than the lamp.

"We're near a doorway back into the every day, though I fear the evening is closing in," Maura said, blowing out the lamp and placing it down by the opening, where another lamp and tinderbox sat waiting for the next visitor. I wasn't surprised by the light we stepped out into, that dull light that comes before nightfall, but my eyes widened in disbelief at the place we came out! The years of abandonment had allowed the growing of brambles and trees, useful for the hiding of a secret world whose doorway stood among the ruins of the abbey, inside the buildings walls.

"Ah, I see we are in a place you did not foresee," said Maura with the delight of a small child eluding the seeker one might hide from.

"I'd no idea this would be where we would come out."

Being inside the ruins showed to me just how big the abbey was, a knowing one could not tell as a passerby. There was something else. The remaining walls held within them a sorrow, this I felt within my very soul.

"We'd best be hurrying along now," said Maura. "Good fortune has it we've not far to walk, but it is late. The fire will need to be kindled, there's supper to make ready, and we need to prepare for tonight's learnings."

I was glad her words drew me away from my thoughts, less pleased was I at the notion of more study. I'd taken in much today, and more learning presented a burden I was unsure I could bear. Tiredness and uncertainty wore itself plainly on my face.

"Do not worry Orla, what I teach you tonight, one hopes you'll not find too troublesome. You might even enjoy it."

While we worked together preparing supper, then eating, Maura asked. "Are you skilled with the needle and thread?" Puzzled, I nodded. "Good when supper is done, we shall sit by the fire and ply our needles."

What could sewing have to do with learning the harp? My mind could make no sense of the two. But then I knew little about the playing of the harp, and Maura knew much. She'd already reminded me earlier in the day that if I knew all there was of harping, then I'd be having no need for her. Beginning the harping tradition in my fortieth year, I was not so foolish, nor my pride so grand as to deny my need, or my want, for Maura's wisdom.

A s we settled ourselves by the fire, Maura asked, "Would you be wanting a skirt to put on? The cap and breeches are useful when we're about; an old woman and a lad attract little attention, but back here, you can return to a woman if that be your liking."

Having hung up my cap on coming into the cottage, I was at ease in my clothes. The truth be known, I enjoyed the wearing of breeches. "I am comfortable as I am, and being as I am, an unexpected visitor, you've been kind and provided me with much. I already sleep in your nightdress and comb my hair with your comb, to wear your skirt is a liberty I'd rather not be taking."

She did not ask again, but looked at me. Not a glance. A deep long look. A look I felt.

"You're not an unexpected visitor Orla. Quite the opposite. We've been waiting for you to come. We've known of your coming for a long time now."

Who is the we? How long had they been waiting? Before I could ask, Maura asked a question of me.

"Have you heard of Manannán mac Lir?" I shook my head.

"There is an old tale among our people, that his wife was turned into a crane by one of his enemies. When she died, so the legend goes, he made a bag from the skin of her. In this bag, he placed treasures important and precious to him. It is also said that

Druids made use of such a bag, though theirs, I do not think, to be made of the skin of a crane.

The Druids, it is told, used this bag to carry and hold their spell-making and healing tools. Our tools may not be wands and potions, but as harpers we are indeed spell-makers and healers, and in need of such a bag. I believe if the bag is made by the hand of the one that will make most use of it, it will carry the essence of the maker, and all things carried in the bag will be charged with that essence. Tonight, Orla, is the night for you to begin the making of your Crane Bag."

M aura stood and began collecting things and laying them on the table. Drawing me to her side, she said we first needed to settle on the size of the bag by knowing what was to be carried in it. She laid out the harp key, a coil of harp strings, being sure to tell me that Declan had made them, a flask, some pieces of bread and cheese, a kerchief and a pair of gloves. Once she'd gathered these, Maura went to a cupboard near her bed. From there, she brought out a large piece of fine brown cloth. Linen! The finest I'd ever seen. Each strand close and perfect. The skill of the weaver plain to see. Maura agreed.

"You can thank Clodagh for the linen. She had Declan get it on one of his trading voyages. It's the best linen I've seen in my long life."

"My grandmother?"

Maura smiled at the surprise on my face.

"All of this may seem like a sudden, unforeseen turn in the journey of life Orla, but your grandmother has known of this for a long time. Declan and I have known of your coming for more than two years now. We've had many visits to the farm, and much has been set in place for your significant campaign."

That turn of phrase, that choice of word, campaign, was I setting out to war?

"Enough talk, this is not getting the task done."

And so we began.

It was decided, to give it strength, the bag would best be made using two layers of the linen. And did I want to hang it over my shoulder or wear it on a belt? Maura, suggested a strap would be her choice, as she said she always had a shoulder, but not always a belt. I agreed with her wisdom. She was easy to be with, even though we were new to each other. It was as we'd always be known to the other.

With the fabric folded and the contents laid down, Maura handed me a large pair of shears. My hands shook. "You cut it Maura."

"This is your bag. I'll not be cutting it. You can do this Orla."

My body stiffened, my heart thudded in my chest. The fabric was so fine, what if I get it wrong? What if I ruin this?

"Go on Orla, make your cut. Trust yourself. I trust you."

I made my first cut. The sharpness of the shears made it a clean one. The world did not end! On this night, my Crane Bag began its life.

Our time together began the same each day. We rose, took breakfast, and with me dressed as a lad made our way to the abbey, lit the lamp and descended into the otherworldly place, the chamber where our harps lived. And in the evening, under Maura's watchful eye, my Crane Bag took shape.

I thought often, mostly as I lay waiting for sleep to come, of my children, and Raven. How I longed for Raven! Since coming to County Mayo, when I felt scared and daunted by the task of becoming a harper, and many a time there had been, it was Raven who comforted me, who nudged me with her soft muzzle. The times when I could not be strong and heed my mother's words, do not struggle, do not cry, it was into Raven's mane I shed my tears. She did not judge me. She loved me, and I her.

The days passed quickly, with much learning and a few words of urgency uttered by Maura. "There are two things that need attending to before you take your leave. The first is the tuning of your harp and the second is the changing of a string. These are important and often bring about a foreboding when one is starting out as a harper."

This I could easily understand, as I had felt discomforted when Maura talked of these things, but she was patient and her instructions clear. For three days we spent time tuning, but mostly changing strings on my harp. Maura would take off one or two, never more, then I'd put them back. The first time was awful. I was afeared. The shaking hands came, the thumping heart banged. How would I ever be brave enough to play when I could hardly change a string?

Maura said, "You are a mother, think on one of your weans learning to walk. They fall down. You urge them to try again. Up they go. They fall again. Sometimes they cry, but after a time of trying they get better, and so will you!"

And I did. With each try, I got better, more sure of what I needed to do, more sure of how to tie the knots, wind the string, and use the harp key.

"Ah, you're doing grand Orla," said Maura, as we made our way home.

"Yes, but in two days my family will come for me. By the time I come back to you, and who knows when that will be, I will have forgotten all you've taught me."

"That will not be so Orla, your harp will be making the journey to the farm. It will not travel with you, but it will be waiting when you arrive."

"I don't understand."

"You will. We will talk more on this tonight while you finish your Crane Bag."

With my Crane Bag being near to finished, needing only the fastenings, Maura impressed upon me to give this part careful attention, saying many times, that if the closures were not made well, then all could be lost. I felt she spoke of more than the Crane bag!

"We must also proof your bag against the damp."

While I worked on the fastenings, Maura hung a small cooking pot high up on a hook in the fire chamber. I was surprised to see her putting in beeswax candles. I knew these to be valuable and hard come by. Then she poured in some golden liquid, this Maura told me was oil from the flax plant, the same plant the linen for my bag had come. It seems the getting of this oil too, had been another of my grandmother's requests to Declan.

Every so often Maura would stir the pot, telling me the melding of the two ingredients, must be done slowly and thoroughly. I was glad this was a slow process, as the smell given off was pleasant to the nose. Maura took great care in the making of this simple brew, treating it as the holy anointing concoction that it was.

"It is ready. Are you?" she asked, placing a stoneware jar on the table. Flapping her hand for me to bring my bag close.

With the same care given the brewing of the mixture, Maura poured it into the jar. I brought my bag to the table. I was pleased with my work. Under the watchful eye of Maura, from the beauty of the fabric, and my skill with the needle, a fine Crane Bag had been made. A sturdy, handsome bag that would serve me well for many a year to come.

"We must wait for the mixture to cool a little. Not too much. It needs to be still as water, but so as not to burn. When it's ready, dip your fingers into the jar and rub the wax well into the weave of your bag. The better you do this, the more your bag will withstand the dampness, and protect its contents from the rain which well blesses always our travels.

I worked quickly covering the whole bag while the mixture was still, as Maura put it, like water, then I spent time working it into the fabric, inch by inch, working it carefully into the seams, for this is surely where the rain would take the opportunity to seep in, if allowed. The warmth of my hands keeping the wax pliable. This was a most enjoyable thing to do. I worked up and down the strap, around the fastenings. I worked both the inside and outside equally.

The wax changed the appearance of the bag completely. The sheen of the fabric was now dulled, and what began as a fine well-made bag for carrying, now took on a different look. This was a serious bag. One that offered strength and protection to its precious treasures - a true Crane Bag!

While I worked to finish the bag, Maura had been clearing, cleaning and packing away. I looked at her, questioning whether I'd done enough, whether my work was complete? She took the bag from me and inspected it thoroughly. She smiled.

"It is done Orla. Tomorrow you will carry your own harp key. The hour is late, we must be off to bed."

"We cannot go yet, you were going to tell me about taking my harp to the farm."

"Sure, that will have to wait. I will tell you, but not now. I'm too tired."

CHAPTER SIX

# BACK TO THE FARM

While we made ready to go to the tunnels, Maura said, "Tomorrow your family will come for you. There is much to do today, hurry yourself along now."

I quickly plaited my hair, tucked it under my cap and we set out for the abbey. This time, me with my Crane Bag slung over my shoulder, carrying my own belongings, including my harp key. Into the ruins we went, ahint the brambles. Taking up, and lighting the lamp, we made our way to the chamber where our harps sat waiting. Silence in the tunnels and chambers was not like silence above ground, it was a thick, dense nothingness, eagerly awaiting a visitor of sound. Maura touched her hand to a string on her harp. This was what the chamber waited for. With just one note, the chamber filled with sound. It rang out clear like a bell.

"Find that sound on your harp Orla."

We hadn't done this before! We'd spent time tuning, changing strings, running thumbs and fingers up and down the harp, and how to pluck a string. But not this. I was not ready for this!

"How can you expect me to do this when your strings do not sound like mine?"

Maura gave me a stern look. "Do not shy away, when you have not tried. You know how to pluck a string. We have not much time, now pluck a string!"

"What if I pluck the wrong string?"

"How will you know it's the wrong string?"

"It won't sound as yours."

"Ah, there you have it! If it's wrong and you know it's wrong, then we will be making good progress. Now pluck a string." Once more she played the note.

I plucked a string as quietly as I might. It did not match the sound! Maura played the note again, asking if my note was higher or lower than hers.

"It's lower."

"Move up one string at a time, slowly, let each string ring. Give it its full voice. Really listen. Open your ears Orla and let your soul search for the sound. Don't be trying too hard now."

I plucked three strings, listening with care. None matched her note. I plucked the fourth string. There it was! I knew this was the one. Maura's face told me I was right. This was how we spent most of that day in the chamber. Maura played a string, I matched it. Betimes instantly, Betimes taking much longer.

"Trust yourself. Listen with your ears and your heart."

After going through the tuning again, making sure my harp's voice was sweet and true from the low strings to the high ones, our day in the chamber ended. We left our harps to rest again in the dark silence.

That night after supper when there was no more work to be done, the bag was finished, I asked Maura about taking the harp back to the farm. I knew that Jarlath and the others were coming for the grain order... and for me. I knew they'd bring Raven, but how would the harp, my harp, make its way to the farm? Would it go in the cart with the grain? Would I, or one of the others carry it on our horse? Was it wise to shift the harp? Many questions I had.

"Do not vex yourself Orla. All is in hand. You and your harp will travel safely back to the farm, let that be enough for you to know. There is wisdom in knowing and accepting that betimes you do not need to know all the details of a thing. Not knowing, in the future, may at times even save your neck, now let me tell you something you do need to know."

"In our land, great store is held in poetry, song, myth and legend. The seanchaí is much revered, as is the harper among our own. These arts hold much power! They bring people together, stir our hearts, and fill some, particularly the new English with fear that we will rise up. We will of course. When the time is right. My words wander.

"The tale I wish to tell is that of Dagda. He was a king of the fairy people known as the Tuatha Dé Danann. It is told Dagda had a magic harp that travelled with him wherever he went. In this enchanted harp there were three noble strains of music, that when played, would affect the person hearing it in different ways. The first is the Goltrai, the strain that would cause the weeping. The second, the Geantrai, the joyful strain, causing people to laugh and be merry, and the third the Suantrai, the sleeping strain.

It is said that the Fomorians, enemy of the Tuatha Dé Danann, stole the harp of Dagda, making of it an ornament to be hung upon a wall. Dagda and his son Aengus Og, searched for the harp. On finding it, Dagda called it to him with a spell. Legend has it, that the harp flew to him killing some of the enemy, and stunning the rest. Dagda then used the three noble strains to subdue the Fomorians allowing him and his son to make their escape with the beloved harp."

Maura's eyes sparkled as she told this story, but I knew, even knowing her this short time, there'd be a reason for me to hear it.

"Tell back to me, the noble strains."

"Goltrai, for the weeping. Geantrai, for the merriment, and Suantrai, for the sleeping."

"Good. Good! Now Orla, when you play the strings of your harp think on the noble strains. Choose one and go deep into it. Feel it. Embody it. Become it. Do you think you can do that?"

"I... I think so."

"Which do you think would give you the most trouble?"

"Not the sorrowful strain, the Goltrai. Though not through the strings of the harp, sorrow has touched me many times, and the gentle Suantrai, I have known through the lullaby from my own mother. This I passed to my own children before our parting. The Geantrai, I think the most troublesome. Of course, I have known joy and merriment in my forty years, but cannot with ease bring it to mind, or know how this sounds on the harp, I cannot know."

"Then this is the strain you must work with. Call to the Old Ones, they will come. Think on this as you wait for sleep."

I thought on Maura's words as I lay in my bed. I thought much on Maura. Though only being with her one week, I felt a closeness to her. The times when we laughed, or she put her arm around my shoulder, her patient teachings, her offerings of encouragement, even her scolding of me, all of this I would miss. Sleep, after a time faded my sadness.

"I'm frightened, Maura."

She reached across the table and took my hand, I could see in her eyes my sadness for leaving mirrored there.

"You'll be grand Orla, and you'll come back again, many times. Look forward. Now is only a moment. This is a time for you to get to know your harp, and she, you. Do not be afeared. You are strong Orla. You do not need me to hold your hand."

That she was holding mine, made us both to laugh.

The sound of horses saved us from the weeping bidding itself out from behind our laughter. I rose and dashed to open the door. There stood Raven, black, shining... beautiful! On seeing me, she nickered. Running to her, I wrapped my arms around her neck. She nuzzled me.

"Never be minding a hello for your dear old uncle," said my uncle with his usual twinkling eyes.

"Oh Uncle, I am pleased to see you. Thank you for keeping your word and bringing Raven."

"You're alright lass, but you best get back inside and hide away those beautiful long locks of yours. You need always be alert, Orla. Never be letting your guard down, never!"

I knew him to be right. I'd been in such a rush to see Raven I'd taken no care. I drew back into the cottage while Uncle Jarlath tied the horses.

"You'll be after having a cup of tea with me before you go?" said Maura.

I checked my bag once more, making sure I'd not forgotten anything. Sitting at the table Maura and Jarlath talked in Irish. It was grand to hear, though my ears or my thinking was not in truth, in the room.

"Well Orla, it's time we took our leave," said Jarlath standing.

Wearing my newly fashioned Crane Bag over my shoulder we mounted our horses.

Waving our goodbyes, "Slán leat," said Maura.

"Slán agat," said Jarlath.

"Slán Maura. Go raibh maith agat."

When we were partway down the lane, I turned. Maura waved. I blinked away the threatening wet in my eyes.

The ride back to the farm was slow and quiet. The cart filled with grain, and surely my harp, though it was not showing itself, taking up all the road. The soft bog running close to its wheels gave rise to little talk between Conor and Paeder. Jarlath and I rode ahead of the cart, mostly not saying much which was often the way we spent our time together. It was grand to be atop of Raven's strong back. Every so often, as was his way, Uncle Jarlath would say something, mostly about the land or sky, or offer me a learning.

"Always pay attention Orla to the ground you're covering, you can learn much from this. Look down, tell me what you see?"

I could see the tracks made by the cart running over hoof prints. They were going the other way, I reckoned them my kin's tracks heading into town, but I saw something else!

"I see fresh hoof prints. Going the way we travel."

"How many horses?" asked Jarlath.

I looked at the ground. "I see only one set."

With his twinkling eyes, he said, "You see well my girl, that'll be the bearer of your harp."

I knew he would tell me no more.

As we neared the farm, a wash of knowingness came over me. I knew where I was in the land. If I'd lived in this place for a longer time I might have named it as homecoming. It was almost that. Smoke wafted from the farmhouse chimney, and passing my tack room cottage, our arrival being late in the day, it heartened me to see smoke rising from my own hearth. How I looked forward to being alone in that small place. Going into the stables; the smells, the sounds, these I knew. I did not know the face though, of the black with the white blaze that watched our arrival with bright eager eyes.

"Whose horse is that?"

"Declan's," was the reply.

We unsaddled our horses, put away our gear. I gave Raven a light brush down; so happy was I to be near her again. As I brushed, she nudged and nibbled at my arm, my clothes, my hair, swelling my heart. Looking into her warm dark eye, "I've missed you." I kissed her face. She nudged me again.

The boys and Jarlath unloaded the cart. I fed the horses. When finished, we made our way to the farmhouse. Mary was there in the kitchen brewing up supper. The smell was grand. She was gifted in her way to make wondrous food from almost nothing. I was greatly pleased to see her and receive her warm greeting.

"The others are with Granny, they'll be well pleased to see you home safe. Welcome back Orla," she said with a touch to my arm.

Like a noisy gaggle of geese we filed along the hallway. There was Clodagh, holding court! Attended by her loyal subjects, Kathleen, Seamus, and there too, being suitably attentive, was Declan O'Malley. With great affection, I'd come to think of my grandmother as *Our Queen*. She was surely a one to get things done, or make them happen, that was plain! Her orders seemed to me, to be obeyed by all, such was the regard for her quiet grandness.

There was much excited chatter on our entering Grandmother's room, her room; the very air within, held the essence of the woman that spent much time here. I thought this a place of business, of planning and deal-making, a place of visions. My mind went back to the day my grandmother and me had sat in a long silence. The day that Kathleen called me Mammy. The day my grandmother first spoke of the harp.

On that day in the silence, as I looked into the flames of her hearth, I wondered after her. What pain, what destruction and death visited her in her visions? I thought it a terrible burden to witness such events; it placing such a weight on the seer and sent a blessing to God that I was not so graced.

"Mammy. Mammy, we're going for supper now." I felt a shaking on my arm. As if back from a dream, Conor's voice fell upon my ear.

A s we took supper, it was plain that Declan O'Malley was well known to all at the table. There was an ease among them I did not share. I did not know this man. And my past saw me slow to trust. Maura had spoken well of him. Talking a little of him being the one to get the harp that was now called mine. I knew nothing of how this had come about. Him being among other things, a smuggler and a trader. As Maura had counselled me, maybe it was best for me not to know everything. Eager to know though I was!

"Did Maura tell you she and Declan share blood?" asked Clodagh, looking to me. My face told her clearly she had not.

"It goes a ways back now, but the thread remains," said Declan. It was not in the words he spoke, but the way they were said, that told me kin meant much to him. Maura had told me very little of this man, save him getting the harp.

"Declan and Maura, betimes visit with us, not often enough I am afraid. They are honoured guests in our house. We are much in their gratitude," said Clodagh, touching her hand to Declan's. He gave her a small nod. A look of a shared regard passed between the two.

"Raven has missed you Mammy," said Kathleen.

"And I, her."

"What of us then? Did you miss us?" Asked Paedar.

If the truth be told, during my time in Cill Ala, I'd rarely thought on anything but Maura's learnings, the harp, and Raven. Though there'd be nothing to gain in saying this. "Of course I've missed you, all of you. I am glad to be back."

Paeder pulled himself up tall in his chair. "Glad to be back. Don't you mean glad to be home? This is your home now."

"Thank you, for thinking so on this, Paeder. Much has happened in the past few months and I'm not yet used to thinking of this place as my home. It will take time. But know, I'm much pleased to be here." I touched my hand to my heart.

"I will take my leave now. It's been a long day and I slept little last night with the joy of seeing you all again," I said in the hope that my grandmother was not knowing my mind.

It was not sleep I was after, it was the being alone I wanted. Having little need or the craving for the company of others, even my own loved ones, I walked swiftly across to the cottage. Opening the door, I placed my bag on the table. Thankful for the gentle light given off by the still glowing embers. There standing in the dimness was a form. It was the shape of a harp, but solid.

I stirred the coals and put more turf in the hearth. Poking and blowing, trying to urge a flame. Finally a flickering. This was what I was wanting. Taking the lamp from the table I put a twig to its wick. Bringing the lamp closer to the harp shaped object. I could now see my harp was wearing an oilskin coat, beautifully shapen, following well the lines of the harp. Crafted with great care.

Pleased was I, to not have the eyes of others upon me as I fumbled and struggled to release the harp from its protective skin. Twisting and wrenching both my face and my body, grappling with fastenings, trying to remove the cover and at the same time stop the harp from falling. In my mind's eye, I thought how foolish was this, how foolish was I! Among the many harp lessons given me by Maura, never a once did she learn me how to wrest an oilskin coat from the instrument.

Struggling and falling about set me to laughing. A sound I hoped would not meet the ear of another. At last, I finally parted the cover from the harp. Thinking to fold the oilskin, a hard thing stopped me. Feeling about the cover, I found a pocket sewn into it. In the pocket was a thing made of wood. I thought it something to be carried, for it had a handle. Having enough trying to work out how to take the oilskin off, I was not about to start another trial. This wooden mystery could wait till morning!

I plucked a string, how loud it seemed in the quiet of night. As it rang, so did my doubt. Who was I to be doing this? Who was I to be thinking I could be a harper? Then so clearly did I hear Maura's voice it made me to look around the room. *Trust yourself Orla!* I was alone.

I'd done many things in my life of forty years. I'd learned much, I'd seen much, but to play the harp was more daunting than anything I'd ever done. It was not so much the playing that troubled me. I knew in time, this I could do. It was the weight of the burden accompanying the undertaking. Could I as a chosen harper, someday bring a healing to people through my music? Of this I was less sure.

# CHAPTER SEVEN

# GEANTRAÍ

I slowly opened my eyes, making of them a squint, wanting to hold the pleasure of my harp greeting my sight. Never would I have thought it'd be here with me, in my cottage! Giving my blessing for the day, still in my nightdress, I ran my hands up and down the strings. A few did not sound as they should. I took the harp key from my bag, plucking with my left hand, I placed the key on the shaft of the string that did not sound true. Slowly turning it a little this way and that, tightening and loosening, listening deeply to the sound. Plucking the nearby strings to check the evenness of sound. It took little time to get it to sing sweetly once more. The journey from Cill Ala to the farm had done it no harm.

"Did you work out the stool?" Declan asked across the breakfast table.

"So that is what it is. No, I didn't."

He smiled. "I'll show you before I leave."

I did not want him in my cottage, my sacred haven. "When will you be taking your leave?" Just at that moment Seamus came bustling in unaware of our talking.

"Declan, Granny, Da and me would like to sort out the arrangements for your next trading voyage, we want to send three horses. Can we do this after you've had your breakfast?"

I quietly released my breath. I had no reason to fear this man who had only treated me with kindness. A man who Maura and my family thought highly of, but to think of him, or any other, coming to my cottage, entering my small piece of the world, unsettled me greatly. It was a place I wanted no others in.

The morning chores of tending the horses and other farm animals, and working in the garden took longer than usual without Jarlath and Seamus, though I enjoyed these rare times spent alone with my children. Kathleen was now much warmer toward me than when I first arrived, yet, I knew in my heart that Mary would always be the one she'd turn to, the one she thought of as her mother. I could not deny or begrudge Mary her closeness with my children, her having no issue of her own, and being the one to care for them. My regret was founded in the cruel circumstance that had forced their leaving from me. My body stiffened when I thought on the cost the superior English had levied upon my life; my people!

Before going to the farmhouse for the midday meal, I went by the cottage and collected the wooden thing that confounded me the evening before. Carrying it by the part I thought a handle, I gave no time attempting to understand how it worked, this I would leave for Mr. O'Malley to tell to me. I twitched with annoyance. It was unfair of me to refer to him, if only in my mind, in such a way, he'd done nothing to warrant such disrespect. I leaned the thing he said was a stool, though I could not see it so, against the farmhouse wall and went into the kitchen. Meal times were sacred times. This had always been the way in our family. Sitting, I thought on my dead parents and husband far ahint in Duleek. The four of us sitting together, sharing the little we had. Cherished times. Now they lay cold in the ground, and me away to a new life.

"This soup is grand Mary, thank you. I think it betimes easy for us not to notice the good things that life presents, your cooking is one of those fine things," I said.

"Oh, away with you," replied Mary, "Stop it now or you'll be having me red as a beet."

We all laughed as Mary's face reddened, her eyes growing moist with love. Too many times, praise, kind words or love, I'd not shown or spoke. The death of my loved ones, had opened my eyes to this, and brought much regret upon me. I vowed, when I thought well on something in my life, I'd tell of it. I wanted that my children, growing up in such a safe and favoured house, thank the Lord, would value their lives and the way they lived, knowing that this was not the way for many Irish-born of our time. This they would hear when needs be from my lips, me being one of those who suffered.

"You'll be away shortly then Declan?" Asked Jarlath.

Dropping his shoulders and sighing, "Yes."

He seemed in no hurry to leave the farm, and it was plain my kin enjoyed his company, especially my grandmother. There was a bond between her and Declan O'Malley that I didn't understand, but then why would I? I'd only arrived here a heartbeat ago, they had shared years. Indeed, when Clodagh and Jarlath had come to this place, Declan would have been, by his looks, a boy.

"Well, I can put this off no longer. Though there is one thing I must do though before I go. I must show Orla how to set up the harp stool I made her."

He'd made the stool! Why should that be news to me, he was a worker of wood after all.

"I brought it over. It's stood outside the door."

**I**t's a travelling stool, that's why it folds up, but I have made it the same height as the stool you used in the chamber. I thought that best for you."

As he picked up the stool, although to me it did not look as a stool, I saw how beautifully crafted and finished it was. There'd been much thought and care taken, even the choice of wood matched the wood of my harp.

"This bit, which you've already worked out, is the handle by which you can carry the stool when folded. Now these cross ways sections on each side, if you lift them, and push them together they close up over the handle; there is your stool. To pack it down, lift again the two sides and push them down and there's the handle. Now you have a go."

The ease that it could be set up and folded again was grand, and clever.

"There you are Orla. Now I must ready my horse."

I took the stool back to the cottage, and for practice set it up beside my harp, it was perfect! As I was admiring how well paired they were, I suddenly thought how rude of me. I'd not once uttered a word of thanks, not for the stool or for the bringing of my harp to the farm. Here I was telling my kin to be grateful for what they have, what we have, and I'd shown little regard to a man who had done much for me, this I needed to remedy.

I quickly made my way to the stables. On seeing me, Raven whinnied. I gave her ear a scratch, as I walked by. Declan had taken his horse out of the stall and was pulling up the girth strap, securing the saddle.

"Thank you Declan for all that you have done for me, bringing the harp and the making of the stool, it's grand, it truly is, and I am muchly grateful. I want you to know that."

My words caused the horse to turn his white blazed face to me. A strong horse, taller than Raven with four long white stockings. I stroked his nose.

"You're alright Orla. I enjoy a challenge, though I think I will have to give some more thought to carrying your harp on a horse. That was not an easy thing to do, not even for me, being a man." I felt slighted by his last words, being a man.

"He looks a fine mount," I said.

"Oh, he is that," said Declan getting on with his readying.

Stinging from his words, that I took him to be thinking a woman lesser than a man, I said with a slight sharp edge, "I recall Jarlath once saying, that a horse with white stockings is best avoided."

With that Declan stopped what he was doing. With a steady deep look, and raising his hand to his chin, he said, "Sometimes we love, or are so drawn to something that we are willing to accept or overlook the flaws; my black is such a thing."

With that, me feeling a fool, he mounted, nodded at me and rode away from the farm.

I met Clodagh as I was heading back to the vegetable garden. She'd been after bidding Declan farewell.

"I think it best if you spend less time in the garden now that your harp has come. The horses I know you enjoy working with, so that you should continue to do, but now the harp is where you need to spend your time."

I opened my mouth to protest.

"There'll be no arguing with me on this Orla. As head of this household it is my responsibility to ensure that each of us do what is best for all. And what is best for all, is for you to grow your skill calling forth the music from the harp... the music that will bring healing to this land. This will take time, and this you must give. Do you understand?"

I nodded.

"The bell will call when it is time for supper."

With that she turned and continued on her way to the garden. I watched her for a few moments, this woman of many years, who moved with grace, purpose and determination.

Of course I understood, and if the truth be known my want to protest was borne out of habit, not out of resistance. I knew I had to give my time to the harp, in this I was more than willing. I closed the door of the cottage and stood for a long while looking at my harp with its neatly paired stool. It was a plain harp, well made and free of decoration. Maura's had carvings on it, Celtic knotwork.

I liked that mine did not. Its lines were clean and plain. We were well matched. I thought on who had played it before me. Whose hands had called music from it. A man? A woman? Which of the noble strains had they played? All of them perhaps. I moved closer running my hand down the back of the sound-box, feeling its smoothness, feeling the curve of it.

I sat on the stool. The stool made by Declan O'Malley's hands, and as I did, tears found their way down my face. Not being a one for the tears, I felt overcome, as though my heart would burst! Since the leaving of Duleek, so many had done so much to bring me to this moment. Now it was for me to give the only thing I could, the only thing I had... myself!

I ran my hand over the strings as taught to me by Maura, up and down, listening to each with care, there were some needing to be put right. I stirred the fire and put more turf on it, got my harp key and began the tuning. It was important Maura said to give time to the tuning to teach the ear and do right by the harp. Listening and turning the key, slowly I worked my way across the strings. When I was done, I checked as Maura had shown me, plucking strings with others to see they sounded well together. Now with the tuning done, what was I to do with the harp? Call forth the music? How?

I sat, having tipped the harp back on my shoulder, waiting. For what I know not. The music to come? In the silence, I liked how the harp felt against me, its smell, that special smell of wood! I thought on the three noble strains, and Maura's counselling that Geantrai, the joyful strain, may be for me the most difficult, and so the most useful strain with which to begin.

I set my mind to a wandering. Seeking out the things in life that brought to me, joy. My children, Raven, making love, my mother's arms, blue skies, falling rain, Raven, Jarlath's twinkling eyes, the sound of the harp, flames dancing, Raven. Again, and again Raven returned. Her soft dark moist eyes, the smell of her, her nuzzling, the sound of her nicker, her warm sleek neck, her muscles. To me Raven was pure joy. Raven was Geantrai!

I closed my eyes and lifted my hands to the harp, thinking on Raven. I let my hands follow my spirit. At first my notes echoed my own lack of belief, but Maura in our short time together had taught me well. *Trust yourself Orla*. I sank deeper into the feeling and listened less to the sound, as I surrendered to the feeling, other things that brought me joy began to seep in. The call of the thrush, the bright yellow of buttercups, fine craftsmanship, the smell of fresh herbs; drifting, I let my hands play what I felt. I let the notes come from within, from my heart. I was lost to the world. Nothing else existed, just me, my feelings and the voice of the harp singing my soul.

A s if far off in the distance the sounding of a bell joined my notes drawing me back from my dream world, slowly returning me to the cottage. I thanked my harp for sharing with me her sweet voice, and walking to the farmhouse muttering about talking to my harp, I knew, like it was with Raven, the beginning of a bond was happening. A love was growing.

After the spending of time with my harp, joining my kin, listening to their talk of the ordinary, was as watching the soaring of an eagle, then being in a chicken coup among a flock of scratching chickens. I scolded myself. How unkind of me to think on them such. What was happening to me? Not long back I celebrated the ordinary. I must not, will not, forget my place. These past months had been beyond the ordinary, but I was not.

I am Orla, a displaced farming woman from Duleek, a widow who cannot read or write, who is not much travelled, who is used to being poor and hungry, one who has struggled to exist, that is who I am. I must remember that, and guard against the power held within the harp to encourage me to think otherwise!

E very day on the farm had its own rhythm. The horses, midday meal, harp and riding, supper and back to my cottage, betimes spending more time playing my harp, betimes sitting watching the turf burn, lost in my own thoughts, thoughts of sound. In my mind I heard the wind soughing through trees, the beating of horse's hooves, the clear ring of the house bell, droplets of water at the end of rain, the crackle of fire. As I sat alone in the quiet, these sounds played in my mind. It was as though the sounds from my harp were a key. A key that opened my ears to sounds that were ever-present, but now I heard them truly. I heard them as the sounds of wonder they truly are.

I was constant in my work on the harp, tuning and recalling the way for changing a string. I'd had no need for this skill as yet, but I knew from Maura's teaching that a string could break any time. *Strings get tired and suddenly snap.* How like people harp strings are! I kept my focus on Geantrai, and each day it took less effort to bring to mind the joys of my life.

I struggled betimes though. Knowing that while I played my harp there were many chores needing to be done, and me not helping weighed on me. I liked hard work. It was all I'd known, and though my family did not mean it so, denying me, made me feel less valued. This troubled me most during the day when there were things going on. In the quiet of night it bothered me not at all.

Some evenings I would sit at my harp, close my eyes and pluck one string. I would float away on the sound as it faded, and the silence returned, then I would pluck another. I never tired of this. Like the waves in the harbour at Cill Ala, rolling out and back in, only to roll away once more. When I did this, nothing else existed, only sound. Everything was slow, even the beating of my heart slowed. A feeling of peace flowed through me, washed over me, became me, I became one with the harp. I knew this feeling. It was the one I had when I rode alone on Raven. The joining of horse, rider and land. A feeling ever so rare in Duleek, but on coming to County Mayo, a feeling that was with me more than it was not. A feeling to be cherished until my last breath.

# CHAPTER EIGHT

# THE FIRST TUNE

I'd been back at the farm with my harp for nearly a month, when one morning at breakfast Clodagh asked me to come and see her when my work was done. Just before midday, I made my way along the hallway to her room. There was a desk by the window at which Clodagh now sat, writing with a quill.

"You can write?" No one I knew could write.

"Yes. I can read as well. It is most useful for doing business. It took time to learn, but I had two very good teachers. Now, I find it quite pleasing. You would do well to learn yourself Orla, though I think you have enough learning to be doing for now."

"That's the truth of it. What was it you wanted to talk to me about Grandmother?" I always found myself calling her that when I was unsure of happenings. I knew it. She knew it.

"In two days Maura and Declan will visit us. They will stay overnight, and you will return with them to Cill Ala. It is time for you to do more study."

My body thrilled with the exciting thought of spending time with Maura. Such a pleasure she was to be with.

"That will be grand. I've a good deal of learning to be doing. Thank you Clodagh for all you've done for me. I hope I'm able to become what you're expecting. If there's nothing else, I'll be away now to do some thinking on what I'll be taking to Cill Ala. To get myself ready." Unlike last time. I did not say it, though she knew.

"I know you have been troubled at times Orla, not knowing what direction you are going, but this has only been done to protect you."

I stiffened, I'd heard these words before. "It's very unsettling to have things thrust upon me with no warning."

My grandmother looked warmly at me and said, "I know."

Being my way of it, the words "Do you?" tumbled from my mouth before I could gather them back.

Of course, she knew. Her leaving from all she'd known had not been much different from mine, though I'd been carried away from death on the back of my beloved Raven. Clodagh, Jarlath and Ni-amh had made their escape on foot with nothing but the clothes they wore. Not a cloak to wrap about them, no food to fill their bellies; such were the trappings Clodagh made certain I had when Seamus came to take me from my home.

"I'm sorry Clodagh, that was unkind of me. I know you've known the suffering. Mammy told me." My grandmother came to me, wrapping her arms about me in the warmest of embraces, an embrace I'd only known from my mother. I sobbed with the pain of missing her. Clodagh said nothing; holding me until I became quieted.

"Thank you, Grandmother."

I carried the kiss she placed on my cheek back to my cottage.

It was late afternoon when our visitors came. I was working with my harp. Maura came directly to my cottage, keen to know she was, of how I was getting on. She made no sound, but stood outside the door, listening. I was lost in my work. Without knocking, quietly she opened the door. Though I didn't hear her, I could feel her in the room, but her spirit was gentle and did not bring me back from my otherworld state. I don't know for how long she stood, as time had no meaning when my mind was away on the strings.

"You've done well Orla," said the voice in my dream world. "You've done much work on both your harp and your heart. There's been much healing. I can hear it in your playing." She placed her hand on my shoulder. I was back!

I stood and greeted her. How glad was I to see this woman I felt truly at ease with. The one I trusted. The one I could be my true self without fear or judgment. My teacher, my fellow woman, my friend.

"We best be getting along to the farmhouse. They'll be thinking us lost, or worse, ill-mannered. That would not be doing then, would it? Though, I think they'll well understand today our tarrying," she said.

A s we walked across the yard, we could hear voices and laughter coming from inside. Opening the door it was as though we'd arrived at a fair. Everyone was in the kitchen chattering away. All talking at the same time. Us arriving and the greeting of Maura adding to the noise of it. The voices, the smiling faces, the pleasure surrounding these two visitors showed how much looked forward to, and welcome they were.

"Granny, why don't you get Maura settled in with you, and Paeder, you and Conor take Declan to your room. That will give me a bit of a chance to get supper organised. I'll ring the bell when it's ready," Mary said.

As they left the room it grew less noisy, but the joy on the faces of Mary, Seamus, Jarlath and Kathleen remained. It was clear not only were Maura and Declan welcome, my kin well loved them.

After getting their bags stowed, the house became more quiet. The menfolk went outside, Maura stayed on with Clodagh, and Kathleen and me helped Mary in the kitchen. It was rare they'd kill a sheep, this being only the second time since my arrival, but the cooking of it set my mouth to watering. Mary fussed, and ordered Kathleen and me about in her affectionate way. We in turn dutifully obeyed, peeling vegetables and beating eggs. It was grand to see the usually quiet Mary working her magic in the kitchen.

When all was made ready, Mary had Kathleen ring the bell. It only had to be rung once to bring everyone scurrying in. Ah, the life that filled the room as we ate was as lively as a crackling fire, and as warming. During the eating it was told to me we'd be leaving after breakfast the following morning, so after a time, I bid all a goodnight and made my way to the cottage, wanting to be fully ready.

K nowing I was going this time, and I'd be staying in Cill Ala for two weeks, meant I could pack the few things that had become mine. In truth, I had very little. I packed my comb, a skirt, and nightdress. The thing I wanted to do most was the packing of the harp. I wanted no eyes on me as I returned it to its oilskin cover.

On our last meeting we two had fought a great battle! Me wanting to free the harp from its confines, and the cover not wanting to be separated from the one it protected. The cover had proven itself a worthy opponent. This time, though, it would not be so. There'd be no battle. I'd thought much on this. I had a plan.

I took care to lay the cover on my bed, straightening out the folds, I eased the harp in. Slowly. Inching it. Easing it little by little until it was fully inside the cover. Doing up the fastenings, I thought on how perfect was the fit! Next, I folded the stool and placed it in its special pouch. I did not think I'd be needing it in Cill Ala, but as it took up no extra room, I thought it good practice to take it. Once packed, I carefully lifted the harp down and stood it in its canvas finery near the table with my packed belongings and Crane Bag. I was ready!

Maura and Declan had travelled to the farm in a small cart pulled by a large heavy horse. After breakfast with the cart hitched to the horse, it was drawn up close to my cottage. Placing the long strap over my shoulder, I stood lifting the harp off the floor, its weight causing it to follow. I carried it out to the cart, bent down slipping the strap from my shoulder, standing the harp on the ground.

"Oh, Declan what a fine cover!" Maura said. It being plain this was the first time she'd seen it.

"Yes, my sailmaker can work wonders with a piece of canvas, a needle and some thread."

With trust not coming to me with ease, I asked, "Is it wise for your sailmaker to know of my harp?"

"My men are true to me. I would not betray them, nor they me. Such is our bond."

Having spent time with my kin and Raven, my harp loaded into the cart, goodbyes made, wearing breeches, my hair braided and tucked under my cap, we took our leave. Maura and Declan up front on the seat of the cart, and me in the back with my harp. They spoke to each other mostly in Irish as we made our way to Cill Ala. I watched the land pass by, and in my silence, wondered about Declan O'Malley.

I'd watched him load my harp, done with great care, such was his regard for the instrument. He appeared a man loyal to those he was pledged, and from his own words was repaid in kind. Did his loyalty extend to me? Or did he do for me because of his loyalty to Clodagh and Maura?

Though we travelled mostly at a walk, I being lost in my thinking, I was surprised when the round tower came into view signalling our journey to be almost done. Passing the ruins of Rathfran abbey my heart quickened with a keenness of knowing soon we'd go down the tunnels to our secret world.

"Will you take supper with us Declan?"

"Thank you, Maura. No, I have much to do."

Climbing down from the cart I began to pull my harp toward me.

"You best be leaving that Orla. I'll make certain it is waiting for you in the chamber by morning. I'll keep safe the cover and stool until they are needed again. If that is to your wanting?"

My wanting! Declan was asking if it be my wanting. Being such a rare thing, the asking, I was slow to answer.

"Orla, is that to your wanting?" he asked.

"Yes. Yes, Declan that is well to my liking, and thank you for all that you have done for me. Go raibh maith agat!"

He cast me a brief smile. As Maura stepped down from the cart, he kissed her brow, climbed on the cart and started back down the lane leaving Maura and me at her cottage door.

The air inside the small house was as chilled as the early winter air we'd just travelled through, but having set it in readiness for our return, in no time at all Maura had the fire away. It taking the edge off the cold. Watching Maura made me to give thanks for the ease we all had at striking the flint. For without fire, in this beautiful, yet cold and damp land, we'd be after eating cold supper and sleeping in a cold bed. Glad I was on this night to be doing neither.

R eturning to the tunnels thrilled me greatly. It made me to think on the evening Maura had told me, how, though nothing was written down due to them having only a spoken lore, the Druids found sacred spaces among the trees. Places where they gathered and gave worship to the gods and goddesses, where they chanted and danced, where they passed on their knowledge. Down here in the darkness, in this seemingly nothingness, this was our sacred grove. It had not the trees or the night sky as its roof, but the rocks held secrets, many blessings, and like the groves, this was a place where knowledge was passed from one to another. This was a truly sacred place. This was our grove.

With Maura leading the lantern lit way, we soon came to the chamber where her harp stood. And true to his word, Declan had returned mine to its place beside it. They looked so grand, and at the same time, humble. As was their way, they waited patiently in silence for the hand to give them voice, for without the hand they were destined to remain mute.

Taking my key from my bag, knowing that from the journey, some strings would surely need to be put right, I ran my fingers across the strings, surprised and delighted that only a few had lost their tuning. Using the key, I returned the strings to their proper place, then Maura did the same. With our harps both tuned our work began.

"Today Orla, you will begin the learning of a tune. It's a tune in the noble strain of Geantrai, the strain of joy and merriment. The one while on the farm, you have spent your time on. First, you must understand, that as the harper, just as you have been practicing, play with intention. Geantrai does not mean you have to play quickly. It means when you send out your music it is done with a heart that holds joy within. And the ear of those your notes fall on, will feel the joy from your heart and take it into their own.

This is true of all the noble strains, it matters not which of them you play. What you hold in your heart and desire to share, of this you must be sure. Of this there should be no doubt."

She said this again to me. The graveness with which Maura spoke these words, told me of their importance. I sat, taking in the lesson. Maura asked me to think on her words, she did not hurry me, quietly waiting. Until now, I had in truth, thought Geantrai was to be played quickly, now though, thinking more deeply on the ways that joy and merriment are felt, how joy is for me, how this may be for another, I understood Maura's words. If one has the clear intention, filling their heart with this, then the music can be the messenger.

Once satisfied that I understood the first part of the lesson, Maura continued. "The melody is queen, the drone is the ground she walks upon. I will play the tune through a few times. I want that you listen deeply. Listening is the most useful skill a harper can have. Now listen."

She began playing. This was the first time Maura had played for me a tune. It was beautiful and her hands moved like butterflies, I could not take my eyes from them.

Then Maura stopped and asked, wearing her stern face, "Are you watching' or listening?"

I thought for a moment. "Both."

Seriously she looked at me. "What is it I asked you to do?"

"Listen."

"Then close your eyes and do as I ask!"

With my eyes closed, Maura began once more to play. It was true. Now I heard the music more clearly. Now I could follow the path of the sound as it wandered, lead by Maura's fingers, this way and that, across the harp. I heard the slowing as the tune neared its end and began again. The second time through, I heard that the first part was played twice. This was so for the next part, and the following one, returning then to the beginning.

Maura continued in this way several more times. I was beginning to feel where the music would go, be-times higher, other times lower. After a time, Maura stopped playing. The sound drifted away down the tunnels. I sat with my eyes closed until I could no longer hear any trace of it.

We two, sat there in the chamber, neither wanting to speak, neither wanting to break the spell. Our bodies filled with sound. Each time I sensed the music leaving my soul, I would close my eyes and bring it back. I felt so light, so peaceful, and at once so alive; this was surely magic! After a long time Maura spoke in a voice so quiet,

"This is your work Orla. You will bring to others what you have experienced here, this is the magic of our music. What I played for you, I did with inten-tion, for you have suffered much, and this I do not forget."

These words, the way they were spoken, and the music... my tears began to flow. Never had I spilled so many tears since coming to Mayo. Never had my heart been so soft!

"Weep freely Orla for that is the release. Let the pain wash your lovely face. As a harper, your music will often bring the tears. Betimes these will be your own, betimes they will be the tears of others, you must not be afraid or discomforted by the weeping. In time you will learn that sorrowing aids the healing of the heart and spirit. This is the touching of the soul. This is your work!"

We sat once more in silence.

"**F**ollow me. Not my hand. Follow with your ears. Follow the sound," said Maura playing the notes I recalled as the beginning of the tune.

"Find the first string. Find its sound! This is as your lesson from your last visit. It is no more than that." She plucked the string.

"Now you can work from this place to the next sound."

I found the sound. Maura plucked a second string. This too I found. Then a third. We did this until I had a small piece of the tune. Then we returned to the first note. This we did over and over. At first, my notes were awkward and separate, but as I came to know their order, Maura asked me to listen again. Now Maura gave to them feeling. Now I could hear the change from sounds to music.

"You try Orla. Make the music."

We worked this way for a good many hours, pausing only to share some food. When my notes began to muddle, Maura said it was time to stop. As I stood, my back ached, as did my shoulders. Yet, pleased was I to have the first two parts of the tune under my hands. Though Maura warned, *that as I slept,*

*what I had learned on this day, may not be with me on*
*waking. As often in her elusive way, the queen may slip*
*away to play among the stars and the moon.* I prayed
this would not be the case.

Returning our harp keys and flasks to our bags,
bidding our harps good night we made our way
along the passages. As we did, Maura lilted the tune.
It was beautiful. I listened with care, thinking my
fingers on the strings.

"Join me Orla, sing with me. There is no better way
to learn a tune than by singing it."

Dread flooded my body. Stiffening, I thought I
cannot. What if I open my mouth and am to sound
like the honking of a goose? I cannot! "I've never
sung Maura, I think it best I listen to your sweet
voice."

She stopped walking. Turning to her stern face.

"The music is not about you. You are just the messenger. Do you think yourself so important the gods
care what your voice sounds like?"

She returned to the walking and her singing. Shyly, whispering, I joined her. She made no sign, she
just kept to walking and singing.

That night in Maura's cottage, after supper as we
sat by the fire, she said, "You have done much today
Orla. You learn well. Tomorrow it may be that we'll
be able to give the queen some ground to walk on. If
she does not take her leave in the night. Let us sing
once more to her."

Sitting in the warm by the hearth we payed homage to the queen with our voices, singing the tune.

Before sleep visited upon me, laying in my bed I sang again through the tune though my mind wandered to Maura's words. *Do you think the gods care?*

Never have I heard her speak of God, nor are there any holy signs, not about her neck, or about her cottage. This was also true of my kinfolk's home. Yet, they did not speak of God or the gods in the curious way Maura did.

## CHAPTER NINE

# WHO DO YOU SERVE?

The day that followed began as the day before. I made my blessing to the day; we took our morning meal, and with me as a boy, made our way to the abbey. Maura took up the tinderbox, set the lamp alight, and along the tunnel we went.

"Does the tune stay with you Orla?"

I did not reply at once, trying the tune in my mind. "I have most of it still." I knew she would ask me to sing it. I began softly. I had the first part, yet when I came to the second, there was a bit missing. I recalled the notes that came before, and those that came after, but the notes that fell between, I could not bring to mind. Maura urged me to keep trying, assuring me that the missing notes would come. And they did.

On reaching our harps, tuning done, we contin-ued with the tune. Maura played through, and I listened, again with my eyes closed. How different our harps sounded from each other. Becoming aware that my mind had wandered, with such ease does that happen, I returned to my task. Maura played three times through the tune, then the work of my learning the third part began. The task seemed less difficult on this day, why I cannot say. Perhaps, it was that the sounds were nearer each other, or my mind and hand better prepared. I thought little on the reason, taking delight as my hand shaped the sounds into music.

"It's time now to lay the ground for our queen to walk upon. The melody you hold in one hand, in the other will be the drone. Hold your hand like this."

Maura held up her drone hand, her thumb pointing toward the roof of the chamber and her fingers together showing the way down the tunnel.

"Your thumb will play one string, and your longest finger, or the one on which you wear your wedding ring, will play the same sound, but lower. You will find the sound seven strings from the first."

She then plucked the two sounds at the same time. They rang together in the chamber, one lower, one higher, like the ringing of bells.

"You try now Orla."

Maura had made this look an easy task. For me, it was not so. I could pluck each string as told, but they did not sound as one. Though the melody had asked my hand to play many notes, each string was played with one finger. Now to make a hand shape, one not known to me, and sound the notes together, this I found more difficult. My dismay showed.

"This is long work Orla, do not be in a rush. Think of the abbey or the stones that line these walls. Those who laid the stones did so with a true heart, they believed in their work, they knew why they lay down each stone. Yet, they did not know at first, when boys, how to shape and place the stones, little by little they learned their craft, and so it is for you."

P atiently, Maura learned me, showing the action, then encouraging me to try. When finally I made the one sound, I yelled with the pleasure of it. Though Maura laughed, she said, "Do not be too pleased with yourself, once does not make you a harper."

Of course, she spoke the truth. The next pluck sounded as two strings, but after a time, the sound came more often as one. We spent some time plucking this pair of strings, and other pairs of strings, always one and the string seven from it. When I could do this most times, Maura said it was time to bring both together; it was time for the queen to walk upon the ground.

"Play slowly the beginning of the tune, where do you hear the place for the drone?"

I did as asked. I felt it should fall with the third note of the melody.

"Have a try of it."

Yes, that was the place for it. Maura agreed, but asked, "Who is the queen?"

Looking to her, I said, "The melody."

She need say no more. I understood why she'd asked, for my drone was so loud that the queen's voice was heard as faint.

"Try again, now that you are aware."

The next time was much better, though not easier. Playing both hands together, each doing a different thing, one playing louder than the other was hard, so was it for finding the drone that married well to the melody.

"This is the beginning, like the boy, you are learn-ing to choose the best stone. Not all stones are a good fit, but in time you will come to know."

We worked a little at a time. I played, listening for where to put in the drone, and finding the drone that sounded best with melody. Betimes, there were more than one pair of drone notes that sounded well, when this was so, Maura encouraged me to choose the one that I found most fitting. To do this, would make the tune my own, she told me. By the end of the day, I had worked through the first part, playing both the tune and the drone. It mostly sounded well, though my drone was at times unruly and muddied the queen. This would come with time and practice, Maura told to me.

That night, I welcomed sleep. My mind and my body had worked long and hard. Not hard in the way of carrying bales of hay, or picking up stones from the field, in the way of sitting in one place with my arms held in a certain way, paying attention for many hours. Hours, that as they passed I did not notice. Hours spent lost in learning. Grandmother's words came to my mind, she was right. I did have a love for the learning. It was only when I rose to make the journey home that the tiredness made itself known, only then; sitting at the harp... only pleasure!

"We'll not be needing to pack any food today, we'll come home before midday as Declan is coming to take supper with us. I want to prepare."

This surprised me, as during the time I'd stayed with Maura, Declan had never eaten with us. Having many unforeseen things come upon me these past months made me wary, and made me to ask the purpose of his visit.

"Is there a particular reason that brings him tonight?"

Maura replied with little regard for my question, as though she was thinking her mind aloud, "He comes often to take a meal with me, us both without a spouse and being related."

I had not thought much on the life of Declan O'Malley. Yet, I thought a man of his years, and a handsome one, to be wed and father to children. That he lived alone seemed to me, odd. Was he a hard man? In the few times I'd met with him, I'd not found him so. I found him to be a confident man. One who did not waste words, yet when needed, was more than able to speak his mind in a clever way. Betimes in a way that caused my face to blush with shame at the use of my own words. Thinking on this dulled my awareness, and in a trice our harps stood before us. I hadn't noticed Maura light the lamp, or seen the rocks that walled the tunnels we walked through, so lost was I in my thinking.

The morning passed quickly, though I cannot say I was a good pupil. I tuned my harp nicely, and recalled the tune and the drones, but my playing was aimless. I could not keep my attention, my mind kept wandering to the evening. Thinking on sharing the table with Declan O'Malley unsettled me, why I did not know. I only knew that when he was around, I felt this way. I promised myself I'd keep a close watch on my tongue tonight, he was after all Maura's relative, most welcome in her home, and he'd done much to see that my learning progressed well.

So distracted was I, Maura threw her arms in the air. "It's plain you do not have a head for this. It is time to leave our harps." So, back to her small house, we made our way.

When we got there Maura asked me to begin the preparations while she went to one of the fish-mongers in the village. The fare she planned was a simple one, there was not the need to impress this visitor. As kin he would be pleased with a bowl of gruel, Maura told me. Yet, she was given to make an effort when Declan came, she said as she set off cheerfully. It was plain that a great fondness was held between these two. I peeled the vegetables, gathered the eggs dutifully laid by Maura's three chickens, and as I was setting the table Maura returned.

"It's odd to set for three."

Maura looked at me thoughtfully. "Yes we can become used to doing, or behaving always in the same
way. When Declan shares our table this evening, do
not sit across from him as a boy. Sit as you are, a
woman."

I had not thought of myself as a woman of late,
but now, wearing a skirt, with a shawl around my
shoulders and my hair let down, I did feel a woman,
though shyly so. I scolded myself for my foolishness.
Me, a woman of forty years, recently widowed, had
no right or reason to feel as I did.

"Oh Orla, you are pleasing to the eye. Wearing
your hair down suits you well."

As Maura's words fell on my ears, I tugged at my
skirt, my face growing warm.

"Do not wear your loveliness with shyness Orla.
You are beautiful! The gods have blessed you well,
do not dishonour them by keeping your beauty in
the shadows."

Just then a knock sounded on the door. A motherly love showed in her face as Maura hurried to open
it.

"Come in Declan," she said bustling about him. He
placed a stoneware bottle on the table, telling us the
contents held within was mead, come his way on a
trading voyage. As he said this, he winked at Maura.
This was the first time I noted a hint of mischief
about him.

The corners of Maura's mouth curled. "We are indeed fortunate that your trading voyages yield such delights, and that you have the wanting to share them with us."

The look that passed between them, told me there was much about this pair I did not know. I asked no question, as I recalled the wisdom shared to me, that betimes it was better not to know.

Maura took down three glasses, and poured the deep rich, golden coloured liquid, into each. The smell was grand, honey and spices... and the taste was wonderful! I was careful to take a small sip, not being used to liquor, and wanting for it to last long; this was not so for Maura and Declan.

"Is it not to your liking Orla?" asked  Declan.

"Oh, yes! Indeed it is. I do not think I've ever tasted anything more delicious."

"Then come now, drink up. The gods have been kind enough to bless us with this fine brew, it is surely our duty to enjoy it," he said filling up my glass again.

As we sat by the fire waiting to have dinner, and it being many hours since our light midday meal, I felt my mind less clear than I was used to. I'd no want for the liquor to cloud my thinking, or to make me speak out of turn, or forthrightly, like I'd seen others do when taking in too much. I sipped slowly and was careful to keep my glass from the attention of both host and guest.

"This is a fine meal Maura. Thank you," said Declan.

Sitting across from me at the table, he then turned his interest in my direction. Looking steadily into mine, with his own green eyes, he spoke.

"Maura tells me that the gods have gifted you generously, and your harp playing progresses well. Does it please you to play?"

When did Maura tell him this? I was forever at her side. Was it when she went to the fishmongers?

"Yes, it's grand. It pleases me a great deal." Then without time to rein back my words, I said, "You and Maura speak of the gods and goddesses, who are these? For surely there is only one God. That is the teaching of the church?"

He poured himself another glass, and quietly said, "Now that depends to which church you go."

Perhaps I was emboldened by the liquor. "Which church is it that you attend?"

This amused Maura. "Yes Declan, tell Orla about your church."

He sat thoughtfully, looking unwaveringly into my eyes, gathering his words. Such a steady man. As was usual, I felt unsettled by his gaze. It was as though he looked through my eyes into my very soul. I moved uncomfortably in my chair.

He began. "Church means much to some, and little to others. For some, attending church requires of them to go to a building. Beautiful as most of these places are, they are not where I go to worship. I find my church in nature. My church is nature! The roof of my church is the sky, and the earth, the floor. Birds, trees, flowers, lakes, and oceans decorate it. I have no need to enter a building to be filled with wonder, I am surrounded by it!"

"But who is your priest? Who teaches you right from wrong? Who shows you the way to live a good and proper life?" I felt as a small child asking questions of an elder, though he did not mock me.

"Ah now. What you speak of is religion. This is a different matter. You ask who teaches me? Nature teaches me. My family teach me. My own mind and heart teach me. I learn from my own ordeals, and when I have questions that are not readily answered, I ask the Old Ones. They know."

"Who are the old ones?" I asked, finding all this talk strange. Finding this man strange... and yet I had a wanting to know him. His words, the way he spoke, was not the way of most men. Indeed, in the short time of meeting him, never would I have thought to hear Declan O'Malley speak the way he did that night. So worldly, so open and wise. Is this what he and Maura speak with my grandmother about? Did she share these beliefs? Did she know the Old Ones?

He continued. "The Old Ones are those who have gone before us. Whether or not we know, we remain connected to them. The air we breathe, is the same they have taken in through their nose and mouth. The thoughts and thrills that filled their minds and bodies, linger still in the air surrounding us. It is through the Old Ones, that Maura and I, and those that choose to hear, remain connected to the gods and goddesses. The beliefs and practices carried in the blood of our forebears, the way they lived, how and who they worshipped, the remnants of their lives flow through our blood. It lives on in us!" Then lowering his voice to almost a whisper, he said, "They live on in you, Orla."

"I think you're mistaken Declan. These Old Ones, and the gods and goddesses you speak of are unknown to me," I said firmly.

"Are they not?" Asked Maura. I looked at her puzzled. "Every morning what is the first thing you attend to?"

I thought briefly on this, for that was all the time needed. "I give my blessing for the day."

Maura smiled, "And where do you think this blessing comes from? Did you learn this in your church? Did a priest teach you this?"

Where did I learn this? We sat silently while I thought on this. "I think I must have learned it from my mother, but in truth, I cannot say."

Maura then asked, "And she, from where?" This I did not know, so could not tell.

She went on. "The Old Ones revered nature, think on this tomorrow when you give your blessing. Now, let us take some more of Declan's fine mead with our pudding."

"Does it trouble you to be away from your family Orla?" Declan asked, in a way that I knew he was truly interested.

"A little, though I'm long used to being parted from them. If I am to be honest, it is my horse Raven, I miss more." As I spoke these words, I found myself having to blink back the tears threatening to fall from my eyes. I did not want this man to see me weak, though recalling the way he'd spoken of his own horse, I thought him one to understand, but I was not ready to reveal any more of myself than was needed.

"Next time when you come, you could bring her. She could be stabled with my horse. No one would question that," said Declan with more confidence than I thought wise.

"Would not the English?"

"The English give me no bother, I service them well," he said indifferently.

I gasped as a wave of emotion washed over me, a mix of contempt and panic! Had I just supped with, and shared a table with a supporter of the English? No, that could not be so! Maura, I knew, did not trust them, and loathed much of what they represented.

"You serve the English?" I asked rather too loudly. My disdain in plain view.

"As a harper you must learn to listen well. That is not what I said."

Declan O'Malley had a knack for making me regret my tongue, and on this night, I feared once more, this may be the case. "If I misunderstand your words, then perhaps it is that you have not chosen them wisely, or delivered them with a meaning that is unclear." I said curtly.

"I like you Orla. You have spirit! Most women wear demure as a coat, all the while plotting and planning in ways to further their own station; you say what you think, I like that. It is late now, and I must away; we will talk of my relationship with the English another time. Do give some thought to bringing your mare. I can safely stable her, and I'm sure that between Maura and I, we can find a way for you to visit her... shielded from the eye of the English." He grinned, casting me a mischievous glance.

# CHAPTER TEN

# THE WEEPING

The time spent with Maura passed quickly. It was filled with practice, playing and learning another tune. I now had tunes from two of the noble strains to take back to the farm. I had a want to learn more tunes, but Maura spoke to me of the value in learning a little, deeply, rather than much, that would live only briefly in the shallows of the mind. Maura, I thought to be a wise woman. I learned much from her, not only about the harp and harp playing. She was unguarded with me, and with suspicion and doubt being my long-time companions, this I regarded highly. One evening, I wondered aloud, why it was she lived alone. Without any thinking or holding back, she told to me this story.

In her twenty-third year she'd met and fallen in love with a man, his name was Liam. He was fourteen years older than she; a man of the sea. He built boats, sailed trading voyages, and on occasion undertook dangerous voyages, aiding enemies of the English. He also gave counsel to Declan's father. They were fast friends. A request was made of Liam and Declan's father to take a number of Irishmen being hunted by the English across to France.

Two galleys were needed. Liam and Declan's father would captain one each.

Liam and Maura had planned to wed on his return, but return he never did, nor did Declan's father. No one knows exactly what happened, whether it was a storm, a whale, or an enemy; lost were a great number of men and both galleys. Maura and Declan's mother were heartbroken. Maura told me she made a vow. Never would wed another as her heart was given wholly to Liam. Declan's mother's spark of life died as the darkness of their death took hold, such was her broken heart. Declan was just a boy, and he and Maura being related, she took him in. Herself with the helping of his only other living relative, his grandfather, raised him to a man. Now I understood the closeness between them.

Though devoting herself to raising Declan, teaching him the values of his kinfolk, encouraging him to be strong and of a good nature, benumbed the pain felt in her heart, it was clear that the loss of Liam still wounded Maura deeply. As we two sat by the fire, her the teller of the story, and me the listener, tears flowed from our eyes. A heaviness took over my body.

Loss and suffering was not known to only a few of my kinsman and countrymen, but to many. Most had felt pain in some way. Yet, we obstinately, those who lived, resisted death in every way possible; holding firm our grip on life, doing whatever was needed to ensure the opening of one's eyes each morning.

"I 'll not be making the journey back to the farm with you today. I have much to do here, and too I'm sure you've had enough of my company, for the time being anyways." Maura said at breakfast.

I did not think I would ever tire of this woman's company, and told her so! I'd quickly grown so fond of this woman that I thought on her as my kinswoman. In truth, just as caring for Declan had offered Maura a distraction in her time of loss, Maura, along with Raven and my harp, afforded me comfort, easing my own misery of loss.

"Grandmother will miss the opportunity to spend time with you. She enjoys your company greatly."

"And I hers," said Maura.

And I thought, I will miss having you by my side, for my own reasons. The slow journey back to the farm would take almost two hours, what would I speak of to Declan? It was more than kind of him to collect and return me to the farm, though I was sure he had tasks he would otherwise have chosen to attend to.

And, that the journey was by cart, a means by which neither of us was fond, would only add to the discomfort, us each rathering to be atop a horse not following its tail. I took comfort in my finding pleasure in silence, and enjoyment in looking across and around at our beautiful green land.

We did not go ahint the brambles down the tunnels to our harps that morning. There was no need, as Maura assured me that Declan would have already packed my harp. As I readied myself for the journey, I wondered if cloaking my harp with its firm fitting cover, would offer him the struggle, it did me.

This thought amused me, as I saw in my mind's eye, his tall handsome figure being thwarted by the formidable oilskin bag. No, that would not be Declan O'Malley's way. He would surely, quietly and with ease, persuade the bag to the shielding of the harp. Declan O'Malley, I was certain, was a man who would maintain presence of mind, no matter the situation, and not one to be coerced into battle with a harp cover.

D eclan arrived shortly before midday, took a meal with Maura and me, then we set off. He, holding the reins, and me sat next to him dressed as a boy. Most times I was comfortable wearing breeches enjoying the ease in which I could move about unencumbered by a skirt. Yet, on this day sitting upon the wooden seat of the cart next to this man, I did not.

I felt discomfited by my dress. Out of place. As though I was pretending to be a person I was not. I knew well why it was necessary for me to dress as a boy, but on this day I felt dishonest. Knowing the value that Declan O'Malley placed on one's word being their bond, it was for an unknown reason, important that he knew me to be a person worthy of his trust.

We travelled quietly along in delightful silence for a time, then out of my mouth tumbled, "Maura says you live alone, why is that?"

It was as if I was taken over by some madness of curiosity. What business was it of mine to ask such a question! I cast my eyes out to the surrounding countryside, not wanting to meet his, as my face blushed with my brashness.

Not turning, he said evenly, "Did she now. What else did she tell you of me?"

I told him what I knew of his parents, and his growing up with Maura.

"Did she tell you about my Pa?"

"A little."

He went on to tell me, though most of his time was spent with Maura he also spent time with his grandfather. He was his father's father. An old man, but a man who taught him much. Like how to be a man, and how to shoot an arrow from a bow. He was a string maker.

"Maura has spoken of you being a string maker. What is a string maker?"

He laughed. "A person who makes strings."

The way that Maura had spoken of it, made it sound both ancient and mysterious. When I asked Declan why this was so, he told me it was ancient, though not mysterious to him. Like many of the old ways, it was a mostly lost art, no longer needed since guns had replaced the bow in the killing of men, and perhaps that is where the mystery was to be found.

"How do you make a string?"

Once more he laughed, and said with kindness and amusement, "Orla, you do ask a lot of questions. When next I am making strings, if you are in Cill Ala I will be sure to collect you so you can see for yourself."

I did ask a lot of questions. This I knew. I had a greedy hunger for the learning. I wanted to know. It mattered little to me the subject. I do not know why or where this curiosity in me comes from.

"I'm sorry I ask much."

He looked at me, there was a warmth in his face. "Don't be sorry, and don't stop asking. Now it is my turn. When we supped together the other evening, Maura spoke of your morning blessing, tell me of it. What is it you say?"

Most often, if another made a request of me such as this, I would refuse or feel awkward, yet, the way it was asked I offered my reply without battle.

*I give my thanks for this day,*
*May wisdom and learning come my way,*
*Under sun and moon; in the trees, I say*
*An honour to this land, I pray.*

"Ah, now I see why Maura challenged your knowledge of the Old Ones. From what has been passed down to me, my understanding is they spent little time in prayer. Yet I think, a prayer such as yours, would have been the kind they'd have made. It would be enough; an offering! The Old Ones did not have churches crafted by the hand of man. They did not drop to their knees and pray to one holy God. Theirs was not a fixed way of worship.

The time of the Old Ones is a long way back so none knows for certain their ways, but I know they had special places of gathering. These I've seen, mostly marked by stone here in Ireland and other places I've travelled. These places might not look as churches of today, yet, they are surely just as holy! And I know too, they raised altars. On these, they made offerings to the gods or goddesses of the elements. The offering you make each day may be made with words, but the echo of nature is there. One more thing I cannot leave unsaid."

He looked to me wearing a face of mischief.

"The Old Ones had a lust for learning. Never could it be satisfied. It too is in your blessing. I think you may be afflicted so! What do you say to that?"

I smiled broadly. "You may be right. You've told to me much, and plenty curious I am! You've not told to me why a man such as yourself lives alone?"

His expression changed, and a seriousness came upon him.

"There are many who do not hesitate to kill us, these we call our enemies, and are known to us as such. But sometimes, it is the thing we love most that causes us pain, or brings our life to an end. We have a love for this land and are loyal to it, rightly so, for it has much beauty, and we have a need for it. Yet, it cares little for us. It has no need for us. We are of little importance to it. Nature is the one with all the power!

The marshes would fill your mouth with mud and choke you to your death. The winds would sweep your body like a feather from the cliff top. The oceans would gladly feed you to the fishes, as was the fate of my own dear father. And in turn, brought death to my well-loved mother from a broken heart. Like my father, I have a love for the seas and the sailing of oceans. I have no want for a woman that may love me to die like my mother from a broken heart, so I do not take a wife. That is why I remain unwed."

As he said these words, our journey ended. We now stood at the door of my cottage. He gave to me a warm, wistful look. I nodded my thanks though I felt numb with sadness that a man of such quality as Declan O'Malley plainly was, would never know the sharing of love known between the heart of a man and a woman!

I stepped down from the cart and went to the rear where Declan was now hauling out my harp. I saw his saddle in the back. I did not ask. As my harp cleared the cart I reached for it still having no desire for anyone to enter my haven without good reason. Delivering my harp was not that reason. I slung the strap over my shoulder, thanked Declan and walked the few steps to my cottage door.

This seemed an odd way to part from my travelling companion after the talking we'd done, yet, I could think of no other. Setting my harp on the floor I made my way to the stables. I knew I should be greeting my children and kinfolk, but did not have the heart for it. It was Raven I was needing to be near.

On seeing me she issued her soft welcome. Hearing her I was flooded with love. What I felt for Raven was, to my mind, the way I thought it to be, to have a true, dear friend. One to tell your secrets to, knowing they'd be kept safe. In all my years, I had never had such a friend. There was not the time. Life was filled with work, family and staying alive.

As I stroked her nose, I looked into her eye. How different from the eye of a man or woman is that of a horse. So dark and large that as one looks upon it, the image of the one looking into the eye, and the surroundings, can be seen as if gazing into a looking glass. There was I, my hair tucked under my cap still. I wondered who was I now? My mood was strange. I had no want for people. I had no want for talk, though I knew I must go to the farmhouse and greet my loved ones. Yet, in this moment, if free to choose, Raven was the only one I wanted to be near.

Out of duty I returned to my cottage. Removing my cap I let down my hair and combed it through. I hoisted my harp on to the bed taking off its oilskin bag while there was still the light of day. I stood it back on the floor. I would not play tonight, that I knew, for my heart was not for it. While I did these tasks I tried to remedy my dark mood. I did as Maura had instructed me in my harp work on Geantrai, I thought on what brought me joy. Yet, Declan's words, and the weight of them, kept finding their way back into my mind like a creeping murky shadow. Gathering myself, it was time. No longer could the greeting be delayed.

"**M**ammy," Paeder rushed to me, embracing me. He was always first to my side; Conor and Kathleen following. I returned their embraces with a love for them that was true, though the years apart had seen our need for each other weaken. This unbinding known to them as surely to me. Still, I would give my life for each and all if called to.

It pleased me greatly seeing my kinfolk. Having them all greet me warmly. This time though, on my return I did not feel the pull of home coming that I'd had on my last journey back from Cill Ala. My mind greatly unsettled from the journey!

"Orla!" My grandmother came to me, casting a knowing eye over me. "Do tell me how your harp playing is coming along." Always, did I feel vexed in her presence when my mood was such as tonight. Though, she had told me the visions did not always come upon her, still, did I feel her to know my thoughts. It was as another, uninvited, was privy to one's secrets.

"Tomorrow Clodagh. I'll tell you all about my time with Maura, tomorrow. She sends her fond regards to you. Tonight, let us dine together on Mary's fine fare, and enjoy the being together again."

I tried to lighten my words with a smile, yet, the firmness borne in my voice made it clear that speaking of my harp playing would not be had at this time.

"Have you been working up any new horses Kathleen?" I asked in a bid to shift away the attention from myself. I heard the beginning of her reply, but my own thoughts took her words over. I thought on my dead husband, and my own heart. Was, that it did not break on his death, to mean I did not love him enough?

What horror it must be to be caught on the ocean, with the fury of the water tossing your galley about with no more regard than the tide washing up on the shore. How must it feel to drown? Was it the way many had told, that your last moments are filled with your whole life? Or worse still, to die the slow painful death of a broken heart.

The evening passed, yet my distraction did not lessen. I recall little of the meal, and less of the words spoken. Knowing that it'd be dark when I made my way back across the yard to my cottage, I'd brought my lamp with me. Asking Conor to light it for me, I bid everyone goodnight. Welcoming the silence of my cottage, I deeply breathed in my aloneness.

S itting at the table in the lamplight, I thought much on my own self. My grandmother's words returned to me. *I think you are a lot like me.* When she spoke those words to me I thought them untrue, yet, now alone I was not so sure. She, a woman that has kept a firm hold on life, betimes at the greatest cost to herself and others.

And me, a woman unwilling to die at the side of my husband. Leaving him. Forsaking him, knowing his death was guaranteed and I'd never look upon his face again. Even the knowing of this was not enough to make me stay. It may after all be true. That my

grandmother, Clodagh Moran, and me, Orla Connellan, were, each in our own way, much alike!

Thinking on this, a moonbeam appeared suddenly at the very edge of the window. It cast its golden
ray upon my standing harp. How it pleased my eye.
The moonlight showing the curves of its body, making the strings to appear as the threads of a spider's
web. What a precious gift to be the custodian of!
Overcome by the emotions this day had delivered
I began to weep gentle tears of sorrow and regret.
I wept for the parting with Maura, and her pain
on losing Liam. I wept for Declan's unwillingness to
be loved, and the death of his parents. I wept for
my own dear dead ones. I wept for the time spent
parted from my children.

Yet, as my tears fell, I felt a shift within. A washing
away. A lifting up. A comfort began to move into my
being, relieving the sadness. What was happening
to me? I felt half mad. How could a mind filled with
grief in the one moment think on joy in the next? It
was as if all the reasons I had to be grateful came
forward from the shadows, lifting me from a dark
place. Holding my soul to the golden moonlight,
affording me a mending of spirit!

I woke as the light of day replaced the moonlight
through the small window, glad of the mildness of
the evening, as I was still sat at the table. I splashed
water on my face from the basin on the bench,
combed my hair, felt in my pocket for the piece of
bread I'd placed there during last night's meal, and
went to the stables. Jarlath was there, getting about
his chores. He was always first up.

Giving the treat and a quick pat to Raven, I joined my uncle; mixing up feeds, cleaning stalls, and carting buckets of water. Seamus and the boys, arrived, then Kathleen. With ease taking up their share of the work. I enjoyed the work with the horses, its heftiness made me to feel alive, and strong. I'd no want to become feeble and fawning. We'd busied ourselves and had done much by the time the bell rang.

Breakfast was always filled with excited chatter. It was the time of plans. What jobs needed to be done, and who was going to do them; everyone there. On this morning, there was another at the table. As was the way, Declan had stayed overnight.

"I'll leave the cart here. I'll ride back. I brought my saddle. I have no keenness for driving a cart alone. It is fine when there is company and a need but I'd much rather ride. And to my good fortune, though my black has four white stockings, he is equally sound, as a mount or a carriage horse."

He cast a teasing glance in my direction. I felt the warmth filling my face.

"Oh, and I've offered to stable Orla's mare if she has a mind to bring her to Cill Ala on her next visit. Of course, she'll have to tie her to the cart for the journey, as I'll not sit upon a cart seat, and have Orla sit upon the saddle."

What laughter the thought of Declan O'Malley driving the cart with me riding alongside on my fine mare, brought to the table!

# Chapter Eleven

# WOODLAND

How easy I took up again the rhythm of life on the farm. Each day the same. My blessing, stable work, breakfast, more horse work, the midday meal, harp, the bell, the evening meal, more harp, then sleep. It was grand to be with my kin and Raven, yet I missed Maura and the tunnels.

I had parted from Maura with two tunes fully learned and committed to memory. One of the noble strain of Geantrai, for the joy and merriment, and one of the noble strain of Suantrai, for the soothing or sleeping. On most days the harp playing took me to another place, a place that closed out everything. Nothing entered but the sound of the harp. Granted the giving of time, being relieved of many chores, I'd made good progress. This granting was not a one for me to waste, though betimes it felt so.

There were days, I cannot lie, when to touch the strings was to make little more sound than the buzzing of a bee, my fingers not being able to clear the neighbouring strings. Times when my mind could not, or would not, share the tunes with my hands, secreting them away as some hidden treasure, not to be found at the whim of the seeker. Yet, these days were rare, and when they visited me, I spent my time working in the kitchen garden with the others, a pleasing distraction. Never would I sit idle, that was not my way.

Having been back at the farm for only two weeks, Clodagh told to me that Declan would be arriving the next day to take me back to Cill Ala, and that my staying with Maura, would this time, be longer. Though her words came upon me with a sudden-ness I was not expecting, and though shouldn't, I welcomed this news.

She spoke what I knew to be true. We both knew. It would be best for the young ones that I stay away. My comings and goings was hard on us all. It was unsettling. The coming together after all the years apart, then me leaving them. They understood well, why I went. We all understood well why it was I went to Cill Ala, yet this made the parting no less painful. Odd it was, that the learning of such a healing art, a calling of great importance, should cause such hurt and unsettle.

Leaving tomorrow! Staying longer! My mind muddled with emotion. Part of me eager. Part of me not wanting to leave. When would I return? I had things to make ready, yet, could think clearly on none. I'd thought little on Declan's offer to stable Raven not knowing it pressing, but now the decision was upon me. He said he could keep her safe. Was that so? Would she be happy and well taken care of, as she is here? When would I be able to see her? In

Cill Ala, I had not the freedom I enjoyed here, where I could walk to the stable whenever I had a mind to. That would not be so in Cill Ala where I hid most of the time, or skulked around as a boy. I paced back and forth across the small floor of my cottage. My footfall matching the thumping of my heart, trying to make some order of a mind that skipped this way and that. My cottage! No, it was not mine. What would I take? When would I see my children? Would I bring Raven?

The pacing slowed as I gathered myself. I took up the oilskin and laid it on the bed. I lifted my harp. Never had it felt so heavy. I slid it into its place of safety. I spread the contents of my crane bag on the table, checking and returning each. In truth, I had little to pack. A few clothes, including the new pair of frieze breeches made for me by Mary, my comb, not much else. All the while my mind chattered. I should be grateful. Others would be filled with awe and grace to be asked to do what I am being asked. I don't want to leave my children. I miss the thrill of not knowing what each day brings when I'm with Maura. I'll miss the farm. Be grateful.

The packing and scolding continued until finally all was made ready. Now the only decision to make was the one concerning Raven. I made my way to the stables, gladdened to find no other there. Pulling a bit of hay from a bale, I went into Raven's stall. As she ate, I brushed her. "What a fine mare you are."

I brushed her mane, it was long and glossy, reaching down passed her neck. I ran my hand along her broad back and down her rump. Her muscles and veins could be seen through her fine black coat. Her hooves, dark, were well shod. As I looked at her feet, the white stockings of Declan's black came to mind, the thinking on this still, even though alone, causing me to colour a little. I brushed her tail. Like her mane and forelock, it was long, reaching down to her hocks. Moving back up to her head, I asked, "Would you like to come with me?" As I asked, Raven rubbed her face up and down on my shoulder as horses are likely to do when they have an itch, but for me, it was more, it was the nodding of a yes!

D eclan arrived mid-morning. We were all working in the stables when he rode in. Dismounting, he unsaddled his black, and lead him into the empty stall next to Raven, removed the bridle, gave to him a casual pat and closed the lower door. We all greeted him.

"So Orla, is your mare coming with you?" Smiling he asked in the way of one already knowing the answer. Not waiting for my answer, he turned to Jarlath. "We'll be needing to take a saddle then."

Jarlath returned his smile. "You will, and all."

Declan then headed into the farmhouse to see Clodagh and bring her tidings from Maura. We finished our mornings work as Mary rang the bell for our midday meal, the last meal I'd have here for I didn't know how long. We all made a good show of hiding our feelings, and though a small event was made of my leaving the air was filled with a heaviness.

I collected my harp and bag and carried them to the stables. Declan, Seamus and Jarlath had Declan's black hitched to the cart, and were loading the saddles. I put my belongings near the cart, being careful to place them out of the way of the loading, then went to make Raven ready, there was no need. Someone had put on a halter and lead rope which was over her neck and loosely tied. She nuzzled me looking for the expected treat, today she found my hand empty. I rubbed her velvet nose, telling her quietly of our journey, not wanting my words to be heard by ears other than hers. "You are such a lovely girl, I hope we'll be together for all your days." Knowing horses don't live the span of a man or woman, it was likely Raven would leave this world before me though none could say for sure how long a harper would live in these times. But she was a young mare of only five years, so God be willing, and with luck on our side, our time together would be long.

The cart loaded, Declan lead his black out into the yard. Untying the lead rope from her neck, I followed with Raven, walking side by side. With the road being narrow, I knew she could not walk alongside the cart, and so, tied her to the back. It was a late spring day, a fair one. The air held a promise of the coming summer. Unlike the seasons, I knew not what lay ahead for me, yet it was made clear, that mine, was not to be a life on the farm with my kinfolk. Once more, my children and me would live apart, and though I cannot say why, nothing was said, there was something about this day marking me now only as a visitor to this place.

All came out to bid us farewell. There was much embracing as the unspoken ending hung in the air.

Paedar was most touched by it. I could feel an anger in his embrace. He whispered into my ear as he held me, he'd see my return to the farm, or die trying to make it so. I held him long, all the while my heart sharing his hurt. As was his way, Conor said little, but embraced me warmly, and Kathleen once more spoke with pride, and a hint of envy, of the duty I'd been charged with, and how it must feel to be the one chosen. As these words tumbled from her lips, I looked to Clodagh.

"You will be back to visit... often." She added with a true warmth, reaching for my hands.

Mary's was the face that I found most difficult to look upon as I stepped up to take my seat next to Declan. I saw in her eyes, an understanding of what it was that I was doing, leaving my children in her care once more. Mary knew well, betimes, we don't choose our fate. Hers was to raise my children, and mine decreed, was to play the harp. Back in Duleek if a one had told to me this tale, I'd have not believed it so, yet here it was.

My grandmother, the royal one, the decision-maker of us all had seen me as a harper in a vision, and who am I to deny the truth in it. When first told of this, I'd not a want of it, but now, much had changed. Clodagh Moran had granted me something different to what would have surely been death had I remained in Duleek. She had granted me the chance to see my children, given to me a harp and a beautiful horse. Never would these be mine without her. She had given me a new life!

A s the wheels of the cart turned to the steady beat of our horse's hooves, I turned and waved. I had a sadness, yet, my body thrilled with the unknowing. Both my harp and my horse, I had, where is it they'd be leading me? I looked up to see a Golden Eagle with its powerful wings spread wide, soaring on the warm air without effort. How must it be, to be free like a Golden Eagle?

Turning to me, Declan said, "Parting from loved ones is always difficult," his eyes following to where mine looked. "Ah, a majestic and powerful bird, the Golden Eagle. They're becoming few. They offer to some a great source of sport, and have been much hunted."

It came to my mind that this bird and I shared much. I did not shift my eyes from the bird, until it rose so high, I could no longer see it. I wondered aloud, "Will I be hunted, what will be my destiny?" Not knowing my voice had given sound to my thinking, Declan said, "That is a thing none of us can know Orla."

We journeyed on in silence. I had no wanting for the talking, and Declan made no effort to interrupt the quiet beating of our horse's feet. As we passed through marshland, his words of the land's willingness to kill the unsuspecting, made their entrance, yet, withered away as would the flowers of spring I now looked upon. I felt a strange kind of awe for the marriage of beauty and peril that could be found if one chose to seek it. It was akin to myself. For in my heart dwelt love, and its partner, hate. I carry both shame and pride, goodness, and with little falter, I'm sure, wickedness. Did the earth not just mirror, or us it, the two faces we all wear?

"Where are we going?" I asked, as Declan turned his horse down a way unknown to me. He explained this was a lesser travelled road, a safer one, that lead to his holding on the other side of Cill Ala. The place that for a time anyway, would be Raven's new home. He thought I might like to see where she'd be kept. Though it had come to me as a question, I was in no need of proof she'd be well cared for. Declan's manner and condition of his own horse showed to me this would be so. Yet, I was curious in seeing the place Declan O'Malley called home.

T he road wove its way through thick woodland. The ground was covered in lush green bracken, with the trunks of each tree wearing a dappled coat of lichen. The canopy of the trees grew over the road giving it a closed in feeling. A vague memory of trees such as these sat deep in my soul. Maybe from when I was a child, or when Seamus and me had ridden through some places like this when he brought me to County Mayo. I could not say for certain, perhaps it a dream!

Knowing a little of plants and healing herbs, I knew less of trees. Most around Duleek were cut down for cropping long before I was born except for the small woodland that sheltered Seamus and me as we watched the destruction and killing of our kin. It was plain to me these trees were not all the same.

Some, the oaks, were large with sprawling branches, a bark deep and rough covered in cracks in which the mosses and lichens found shelter. The shape of the oak leaves with their edges not clean and straight, but wandering like a path or a river might, bending in and around. These were like the oaks by Maura's. "What are these trees? Not the oaks, these I know, but what are the others?"

Declan laughed a little. "Always wanting to know, aren't you. The ones there with the bright green leaves, the ones with the ragged edges, they are the hazel, they have nuts when the season is right. The other, with the almost gone now, white flowers, that is the Quicken tree, though most call it the Rowan. In the summer it will be covered in bright red berries."

"Why is it called the Quicken tree?"

He laughed again. "I knew you would ask, but I cannot tell you. All I know of it, passed down to me through my ancestors, is that it is a tree highly prized, and much revered by the Old Ones. I think it much used in their rituals."

The ease at which he shared what he knew, I found pleasing. To me, Declan O'Malley was as a man who knew himself well, one who, though living in difficult times, took charge of his own destiny. When in his company, it was, falsely or otherwise, possible for me to believe, that I too, could one day be in charge of my own life. Those free to captain their own fate, mostly men, and mostly English, I think, do not value this liberty, seeing it as a birth right, yet Declan O'Malley, I was sure, was not one of these.

Though I wore the clothes of a man, I knew full well the freedoms enjoyed by them, were, in this moment not mine. As we moved along the road, one I thought would have been travelled more easily on foot, I found myself silently praying to the gods and goddesses. Struck by my own silent words, for in my past I'd only made prayer to one God, yet, in this place surrounded by these magnificent trees; a place where magical and mysterious beings might dwell, a place where rituals and offerings could be made in secret, it was to them I prayed, that I might one day be able to choose my own direction in life.

The trees, the dappled light, the shadows cast, the strangeness of the woodland, swelled my heart with wonder. Swaddled in this green covering, I felt, as I did in the tunnels with my harp. Away, and protected from the harshness that was life beyond. Here I could see myself living a quiet, simple life in a neat little cottage, with a few chickens, and a tidy kitchen garden.

Lost in this dream, Declan suddenly halted his black, thrusting the reins into my hand, he reached around producing a bow and a handful of arrows. The silent quickness of head and hand; better this man be friend than foe.

"What are you doing?"

"Be quiet," he snapped in an urgent whisper.

Stepping quietly from the cart as if a ghost, loading an arrow into his bow, he stood still as a rock, listening. Then, all at once a wild thing, bellowing a terrifying noise, a whistling from Declan's arrow, and a panicked squeal from Raven, filled the air. Throwing the bow down, pulling a dagger from the pouch he wore on his belt, Declan stabbed the thing that squirmed but a few steps away from Raven. She breathing hard, and snorting pulling back, putting as much ground between her and the monster the lead rope would allow.

"What is it?" I gasped, my heart thumping so hard, I could hear it between my ears.

"A wild boar. There's not many of them about these days. It is a sorrow to have to kill it but they can gore a man or beast, and if success is theirs, then feast upon their prey with little remorse."

I shuddered with disgust at the picture that shaped in my mind.

Retrieving his bow and scattered arrows, returning them to the cart, Declan began to shift my harp and belongings, and the rest of the load to the front of the cart. Still shaken, I asked, "What are you doing?" He laughed as if nothing had happened.

"Even when there is trouble, your questions continue. I'll take it back to my farm. I and my men will make good use of it. I would not have killed the beast if it were not necessary, but now that it has forfeited its life, I will honour it by making what use I can of its body. My men will welcome its meat."

"You have men at your farm?" He did not answer. All of his strength was needed to heft the beast with its menacing tusks into the cart; covering it with the large sheet of oilskin that was kept always in readiness to protect cargo from the often falling rain. He then moved to Raven who was still snorting and leaning back on her haunches. Talking softly, rubbing her nose and her neck, he gently coaxed her forward. As the rope slackened, she began to quieten. He made no effort to hurry this, talking to

her, rubbing and patting her. Only when her breathing settled did he climb back into the cart.

"Yes. I do have men at my farm."

## Chapter Twelve

# FARM OR FORTRESS

We took up our journey again, Declan, as though nothing had happened, me, thinking on the great ugly beast that had visited itself upon us. "You say, there are not many boars, why is that?"

"The forests and woodlands have been cut, and the boars along with them. I feel my own, and my forebears guilt in this. Building boats, requires much wood, and we have been building boats here for a long time. Many generations back, trees covered all of this land, but the building of houses takes wood, fires take wood and boats take wood."

Though I had travelled little about Cill Ala, I'd seen no trees in the town, yet, further up the lane where Maura's small house stood, there was the edge of a woodland, I wondered now, if this were part of that stand.

"Declan, ahint Maura's cottage, those trees, do they join these?"

He looked thoughtfully at me. "I wonder if you ever cease from the asking of questions," he said teasingly, but went on. "Yes, they do, and I have thought about you and your mare. It is through these woods, that I will get her to you, or you to her. It is not the best for riding, yet it gives good cover away from the eyes of those it serves us best to not have look upon you."

As he spoke, I heard what I thought must be the call of a bird ring through the trees. I realised as Declan answered with a similar whistle, this to be a signal. "Who do you call to?"

"Whissht woman! I'm going to have to call you the Madam Inquisitor... My gateman!"

Encouraged by his amusement, I asked, "And how many men do you have?"

He hesitated. "It takes a lot of men to build, and sail a galley, though, not all sail, and not all live under my roof. And before you ask, let me tell you, of those that work for, and with me, all are not Irish. Some are born here, yet, their forebears were Norsemen, and some of my men are English."

I could not stop the gasp that escaped my mouth.

"Not all English are bad, Orla, just as not all Irish are good. I employ my men because they are skilled at their trade, and because they value the same things I do. Those who do not, do not stay."

"Ní thuigim. I thought the English our enemy," I said.

"Mostly, that is true, though not entirely."

"I build galleys, fine galleys; the English want what I have to sell. Just as your own family produce fine horses. Horses that the English want. This is how we stay alive! This is how we hold our position, this is how we wage war, yet the enemy for us, is death. We do not yield to the English, nor do we kill them, and importantly, they do not kill us!

The English yeomanry of Cill Ala know I smuggle and trade, but they seek not to question my arrangements; what I do serves us all well. It is understood they could easily kill me, but what good would that bring? They would have no fine Cill Ala built boats, I would have no life. Some of my men would kill some of theirs, and theirs mine. So Madam Inquisitor, my question to you is, regardless of your allegiance, what service can one be if one is dead?"

When Declan O'Malley spoke in this open, frank way, which he had a mind to do when he thought it useful or important, it had a habit of unsettling me. I did not trust the English, not one iota! The thought of doing business with them, was to me, a brackish thing. I held inside me a loathing, that one day might be dimmed, yet with my body defiled, and a few short months ago, my parents and husband dead by English hands, that day had not come. Nor did I think it would, anytime soon!

"They killed my parents."

He sighed sorrowfully. "I know Orla, Clodagh told me. And for this I am sorry, but they are not all bad. It is unwise and unfair to damn all, because of some."

"You cannot know how I have suffered," I said with such venom that the words hissed from my lips.

"True, I cannot know Orla, but I think, perhaps, I understand," said Declan.

I wanted to speak no more on this, and the sight ahead on the road aided me. In front of us stood two great stones. On one, a grand gate was hung. Ahint the other stood a square tower. The gate was open, yet as we approached a man appeared, greeting Declan. Through the gate we went, Declan's black, the cart, Raven, and me staring with disbelief at what was before us. Men and women moved busily about a large building.

This was like no farmhouse I'd ever seen. It was a tall building. Not a low one like my kin's farmhouse or Maura's cottage. There were large windows, and many stacks with smoke coming from them. On the top, there were places, where, I was sure, men could stand to defend the great house. This surely could not be the home of Declan O'Malley! I thought on his relative Maura Bourke. The simple life she lived in her small house; this was a world away!

"You live here?"

O thers were now around the cart. I heard someone ask whether Declan had brought himself
another horse. Raven! I jumped from the cart and
rushed to her, untying the lead rope. I held it firm,
my knuckles white. Staring out at these unknown
faces, I tried not to show the fear that filled me.
There were so many! I was not at ease among them,
like my first time in Cill Ala.

I could hear a familiar voice, muffled by my own
blood sounding in my head like waves thrashing on
rocks, speaking of a boar in the back of the cart,
and care to be taken with the harp, and something
about saddles, and horses and stables. Yet I could
make no sense of it. My mind overcome by the
strangeness of it all.

"Orla, are you right to lead her? Orla!"

Hearing my own name spoken, I blinked and nodded. I followed Declan, no one followed us. Mute, I
walked passed the big house, among some smaller,
but equally grand outbuildings, to the stables. So
neat they were, with about a dozen or so stalls on
one side, most, with horses in them.

On the other wall were rooms, for tack and feed,
I supposed. We'd only walked a few steps in when
a man came to us. He looked to be about the same
age as Declan. He had a kind face and was wearing
a warm smile.

"This is John, he'll take care of Raven. He has a way
with horses, they take to him well," said Declan.

"Greetings."

My body became as stone. Was I now meant to hand over my most precious treasure to the English? He slowly reached out his hand in front of Raven's nose. He did not touch her, only to let her get his scent. She breathed him in, then nudged his hand. Only then, did he move to run his hand down her neck then gently along her back.

"Ah, you're a fine girl," he said quietly. "What do we call you?" Hearing no answer, he turned and looked to me wearing the question.

"Raven. I call her Raven." He turned back to her.

"Raven, that's a fitting name for one as black as you," he said, moving back to her head.

She nuzzled him, the way she did me. He laughed and reached into his pocket. Holding out his hand she took the small amount of loose feed he offered.

"You and I are going to get along just fine."

He reached for the lead rope still held firmly in my hand. I made no move to offer it.

"You know me not, but, I will take good care of her, that I promise."

Declan nodded to me. I handed the Englishman the rope.

"I'll put her in this stall," he said walking with ease, Raven at his side.

As Declan and I walked back to the cart, me still reeling from the ordeal of arrival, I said harshly, "Never could I believe, that you'd have me willingly give my beautiful Raven to the English."

Declan stopped walking. Looking deeply into my eyes in the way that caused me to feel awkward, he said with more than a hint of reproach.

"You did not hand Raven to the English. You gave her into John's care. That he is English, is of no matter. What does matter, is that he is skilled with horses, he will be kind to Raven, and that she took to him. That's what matters. John is a good man. His birth, and this is true of us all, is no fault of his own making. You would do well to remember that Orla. You have no cause for concern for Raven. John would give his life to protect our horses, never doubt that. No one could ask more of a man, whether he be English, Irish or Norse. Now, we best be getting you back to Maura, I have no desire to cause her worry."

Glancing over my shoulder many times, we walked back to the cart. With the stun having left me, I could see now there were fewer people than I first thought milling around in the yard.

When we drove in, I felt it to be like driving into a swarm of people, now I see I was wrong. My eyes had offered no deception though with regard to the size and grandness of the great building in front of which was parked the cart. From it, the boar had been taken and carried away to somewhere unseen by me.

Now with my mind more clear, I recall the delight and excitement in the voices of those unloading it.

As Declan had vowed, the dead boar would not be cast away to rot as a thing that disgusts might, it would be honoured as the true and mighty beast that it was.

M aura's cottage come in to view, when we had been journeying for only a little time. How different was the cottage from Declan's big house. Few words had been exchanged as the cart was steered down the track, too narrow to comfortably accommodate a cart, even a small one such as ours. As I spoke of my surprise to see the cottage, Declan told me there were many roads through the woodland. To those who knew them well, he said, one could enter and issue at many points, taking little time to do so if on foot or horseback; not hauling a cart!

"I will have to think on a way for your harp to be carried by horse, then we could save ourselves the displeasure of having to be so encumbered. I think too, that my black, though well behaved dragging us and this box, would be much happier to have his body free to move along without it."

Reaching Maura's door, she came out to greet us. I was never more pleased to look upon her face, and to be back in her small house. The familiar cottage in which I felt at ease. Though it was late in the day, she invited Declan to stay for a cup of tea. Taking down my bag, he thanked her, but refused, saying he'd take my harp to the chamber, and he had a number of things to attend to before the night was done. He told me we would sort out some arrangement for me to visit Raven. Embracing Maura, he took his leave. I took up my bag, and with Maura's arm around my shoulder we went inside.

"So, Orla, this will be your home for a while. I'm pleased to have you here with me, you are most welcome. Now, let us get you settled, then we'll have supper."

I shared Maura's pleasure to be back with her once more. She was the one person, with whom, I could truly be myself. I could talk with her about a great many things without fear. I could laugh, weep; I could even play the harp badly before her, without being judged. Yes, I was well pleased to be with Maura, and though I was at ease here, it being no fault of hers, I did not truly think of her cottage as my home.

As we sat by the fire that evening, we talked of the leaving my kin and the farm. As was her way, Maura, gave me another place from which to view the parting. She spoke of the ground that could be covered with greater speed in my becoming a harper, and she spoke of the freedom now given me.

I thought this odd for free I did not feel. On the farm, after chores, I was free to play my harp, also I had the freedom to ride Raven when I had the time or the want, now Raven was a woodland away. How often could I ride her? How often could I see her? Would I ever find ease in attending Declan's big house?

"Have you ever been to the place that Declan lives?"

Maura raised her brow. "Of course. He is my kin."

I followed with, "I thought you said he lived alone."

Maura looked at me, "Never would I have said that, for he does not. It is true enough he has no wife, and he has company aplenty, yet none are kin to him as I am."

Do you know Declan has Englishmen working for him? I wondered, but did not ask. I would choose my words, and the time with great care when I asked this question, for I had no want to cause a rift between the two. Thinking more on this, she must know. They were very close, Maura and Declan. She would know.

My mind was a whir with questions, so rapid they came, as the beating of a moth's wing when drawn to the flame. Why, when he had a house of that size, did Maura not live there? I believed with all my heart, that he'd have extended an invitation to do so.

I saw men and women at the big house. Did they all live there? If so, were they married? Or was there another union blessed, perhaps by the Old Ones, that was in place? Though Declan would not take a wife, was there a woman, or many, in that big house that warmed his bed at night? So many questions came to me as we sat, I asked only one. One a person taking a gentle interest might ask.

"Is the house as grand on the inside as on the out?"

"Did you not go in?"

I think I would not, even if I'd been invited so. "No, we just offloaded the boar, and took Raven to the stables."

Again she raised her brow, "A boar?"

I then told her of the charge the beast had made at us, the loosing of the arrow, the stabbing, and the heaving into the cart. Her response echoed the pleasure of those receiving it, saying that wild meat was rare these days, the flavour much valued, and with the number to feed at the house it would not only please Declan's men, but as fate would have it, would be of benefit to Declan. I told of the trueness of Declan's skill with the bow.

"It was Declan's grandfather, the string maker, who taught him the way with the bow. He keeps it up to honour his grandfather; to stay connected."

Until that day, I'd never seen a bow, so knew nothing of them, unlike Maura, who knew much of them. She told me there were two types, a short and a long bow. They could be made using different woods. Very few in our times were skilled in the art of bowmanship, particularly the long bow. Most still having an interest, choosing the more easily mastered, crossbow. A thing Maura said was like a bow mated with a gun.

She said it would never be the way of Declan to use the crossbow; he was much more drawn to the skill of a thing, than to the ease of it. She believed, as we were travelling by cart, and it being concealed, it would have been a short bow he used, probably made of yew; good for a fast, close kill.

"You should see him shoot the long bow. Now, that is a sight to behold. His favourite long bow is taller than he. It takes much strength to shoot, and he is deadly accurate over a great distance. With that he is a true warrior, no one has his match."

There was a deep love, and pride in her voice as she spoke these words, the likes a mother for her son.

B eing much interested in her words, and not wanting to take her from her talking, I listened eagerly, until she came to the place of her choosing and returned to my question.

"Tis a grand house, indeed Orla. You must see the furniture, it's the finest I've seen in all my days; heavily carved and dark. And the dining table sits more than twenty! In that room, the dining room, there's a big painting of a woman, she is our relative. It is she that joins Declan and me, and it is from her comes the house. It's the thing he treasures most in the house.

It's a grand thing that Declan has the house and land, it's worked out well for him, and many others. He has a lot of men, loyal men, some go back a long way, and being able to provide a home for them and their kin, if they have any, means much to Declan. We'll go one day, and I'll show you. Tis a grand house!"

All of my days in Duleek, I had lived in a small stone cottage. The walls we brushed with lime when we could; the roof was of thatch. It was forever cold and damp. Filled with smoke from the hearth and cots, standing wherever a place could be found on the floor of earth. Its face made up of two small windows that never gave much light, and a door.

Though modest, this face welcomed us home each evening from the hard days of work on the farm. Toil done for a landlord who cared nothing for us, one who constantly threatened to deny us the little shelter from the elements the most humble of cottages could provide. Yet, here was a man, Declan O'Malley, that cared so much for those who worked for him, that not only would he have them share his roof but also his table. How is this so?

"Declan's house tells me that he is a man of some wealth," I said in an offhand manner, trying to hide my keen curiosity.

"No more than any other squireen," replied Maura.

Not ever hearing this word before, I asked, "Maura, what is a squireen?"

It being late, and she tired, Maura sighed, "You've heard of a squire?" Not waiting for me to answer, she went on. "Well, that is what the English called a landowner, here in Ireland, a man who has a holding of land, not a big holding mind, we call a squireen. We only use the title in jest, him and me, yet it be true, Declan is a squireen."

Maura stood, saying it her time for bed. Telling me we had much harp work to do the next day, suggesting I do the same. Bidding her goodnight, I sat a while longer by the hearth, thinking on the day. What a strange day it had been.

Strange was the home of Declan O'Malley, and strangest of all, was that I'd placed Raven into the care of John, an Englishman. I thought on Declan's words, words tainted with anger as he chided me for marking all English to be of one mind, and of one kind; despiser's of the Irish. What cause had I to think otherwise of them? Not a one had I met, extended kindness or shown mercy to either my own self or my kin. That I had entrusted my most beloved Raven into the care of one born of my lifetime enemy caused me great concern, and disturbed much of my sleep on that night.

# Chapter Thirteen

# THE BROKEN STRING

G oing down the tunnels the next day I ran my hand along the rock walls as we walked. So smooth they were. I could not help but wonder at the care taken to shape each stone. It was as if the very being of the mason; his mark, was there in every one. As we neared the chamber of the harps, I began to feel my mind and body shift in readiness to accept the sound of their heavenly voices. Now I understand why angels were shown with harps in our own small church in Duleek; before we could no longer attend; before the destruction of it. There they stood, our harps, waiting for our hands to re-lease their notes. Today, Maura had told me, was the day we would begin work on the Goltrai, the strain of sorrow.

Before Maura played the tune, she told me the story of it. She said that it was of great worth to know the story of the music. To understand the heart of the tune helped with the learning of it, and over time, the recalling of it. The story was of a woman whose love had drowned at sea. I did not ask, yet, wondered if this was a tune made by Maura herself, for the tale was so closely likened to her loss of Liam. She did not call the tune *Lament for Liam*, though it would not have stunned me if it were so called. She called it *Lament for the Seafarer*.

When finished with the telling, Maura played. I sat, eyes closed, listening, thinking on the story, breathing in the mood of the lament. She played it through many times, and with each repeat my sorrow grew. I cannot say if it was the music itself that sorrowed me, the story, or my heart breaking for this woman I'd come to hold dear. Maura had spoken of the healing that weeping can bring, but on this day, I would not weep. I could not weep for fear I may be unable to stop, such was the sadness upon me for Maura.

When she lifted her hands from the strings I knew it was my time to try the tune. As was the way in the beginning the notes were fitful, but with Maura playing or humming the first part, it began to shape into music. Not smooth flowing music as Maura played, but notes that followed in a way one could hear the tune peeping out from its place of hiding. I struggled with the learning, my head muddled with emotion. By the day's end, I had only the first part, though Maura praised me with her kind words, assuring me I'd find it a more easy task on the morrow.

The following day down in the chamber, we tuned our harps. I played through the two tunes known to me then took to working again on the new piece, the Goltrai piece. Being a good pupil, taking much pleasure in the learning, I worked hard. Listening with care, returning many times to the bits where I could not make the notes tell the story well. I thought it like a wean learning to talk, first comes garble, then the single word, then slowly the words join and flow into a way that one can share with another; both being able to understand. At the end of the second day, I could sing all four parts of the melody. Three, I could play clumsily on the harp, as well as putting in a few drone notes. Readying ourselves for taking the leave of our harps, Maura spoke again of the steady work of the stonemason; we then sang our way out to the brambles of the abbey.

On the third day of working on the tune, with all the melody loosely woven into my fingers, we sat eating the bread and boiled eggs we'd packed when a loud thwack sounded. I jerked with a start. Maura did not.

"Ah, there goes a string. I think it be one of yours."

Rising quickly I went to my harp, sure enough, there was a gap where the string should be. The string hung down in a forlorn way across the sound-board.

"Well now Orla, you know what to do. You've done this many times."

I went to my crane bag, I had some spare strings Declan made. Given me when first I was given the harp. I took out the strings, yet none were the same as the broken one.

"I did not think you to have a string for that one. It's a thick one. They'll not often go, those low ones."

"Why would it break like that? I was not playing it. Nothing was near my harp, it was just stood there."

"This is a harp, Orla. Strings can go at anytime. They have no care of when or where. Sometimes they'll break while you're playing. We can never know when a string has had its life. We'll go home and I'll go to see Declan while you get our supper ready. Give to me your broken string, so he can know its size."

T wo more days passed before Maura and I set off on the walk through the woodland to Declan's house. "Are you not afraid that a boar might attack?"

Maura laughed, "Orla, I have walked, many, many times through this woodland, and never a once have I sighted a boar. I am surprised one would show itself, and surprised even more that it would charge at you. May be it was the horses made it to do so."

I did not think this the road Declan brought me to Maura's cottage in the cart, and on saying so, Maura said, as Declan had, there were many paths hidden in the woodland. The walking was easy, and much more pleasant than the lurching and twitching ride in the cart. "These trees are indeed lovely."

Maura looked around her. "They are that." A whistle sounded. "Ah, our arrival is announced."

Not much further down the road, I could see the large gate stones. As we neared, the same man that greeted Declan when we brought Raven here, greeted Maura. He told to us Declan would meet us by the house.

"Why is it, that the whistle is made when we come near?"

"It's just the ways it is. Declan has his reasons and these I do not question. A man has a right to work in his own way."

Embracing Maura, Declan turned to me. "You'll be keen to see your mare then Orla. Maura, you go in, there are many waiting to see you. We'll be at the stables. Come there if you have a mind. We'll be a while. I'll make Orla's new string after she has seen her horse."

We walked, the two of us. Declan telling me of a room in the stables where he makes the strings. I being very curious, looked forward to watching; having him show me. The making of a string was a thing I could not begin to know.

Stepping inside the stable there was the face of my beautiful Raven. Softly, she nickered her welcome. I hurried to her. Oh, how pleased was I to see her.

"She's settled in well," said Declan.

And from nowhere came another voice. "Yes, she's a lovely mare," said the Englishman.

"John" said Declan, "I know you've met her horse, but you've not been properly introduced. This is... "

Before he could say any more, I said, standing tall and lifting my chin, "Mrs. Connellan." Declan flashed a glare at me.

"I'm pleased to meet you Mrs. Connellan," said the Englishman politely.

"We'll leave you John, I've a string to make," said Declan wheeling. John nodded.

As I caught him up, Declan hissed at me, "If you wish it to be that you and I remain friends, then never, do you hear me, never, disrespect John in that way again!"

Just then Maura's voice rang out, "John, how good it is to see you. Are you well?"

Her voice held the same warmth in it as when she talked with Declan.

"Maura, you and Orla, best head off home. Something's come up I need to attend to before I make the string. She'll have to wait until another time to see how it is done," said Declan bluntly, not speaking my name.

I felt slapped.

Maura knowing Declan well, reading his mood, said, "Yes, I'm sure there'll be another time more fitting. Come Orla, it's time for us to be away."

Stunned, without returning to Raven, I walked alongside Maura past the big house through the gates and back down the road.

"I fear I've angered Declan." I then went on to tell her what happened.

"Ah, sure. That'll do it. His friendship with John goes a long ways back. They are as brothers. Each has saved the other's life more than once. He will cool. He's not a man given to malice, but I tell you, heed his words, if you do not wish him to shun you."

With the days passing, no news of the string from Declan, and my mind being troubled, Maura, said, "Tis not worth the walk to go to our harps. You stay here. I'm going to see Declan."

I was pleased to hear her speak these words, for I had been much unsettled by my last meeting with Declan. It made me to realise how beholden I was to this man. He had done much to aid our cause; my grandmother's vision. If he was to withdraw his support, all could be lost. Whether he chose to wield it or not, Declan O'Malley had great power over me. My future as a harper lay in his hands. Though unworldly, I'd gathered enough wisdom over my years, to know there is little gain to be had in angering one who stands in a position such as he.

Maura and me had gone to our harps each day since the breaking of the string. My work on the melody had continued. And though, it was coming along, since going to Declan's, no longer would my mind settle on playing, no longer could I pluck the strings without his stinging words invading the shadows of my mind. So greatly disquieted was my mind that try as I might, I could not keep attention on the playing. With Maura's vexation showing itself by way of her constant loud issue of breath, and Declan's words, *If you wish it to be, that you and I remain friends,* my heart nor my thoughts could stay with the music.

I did wish for Declan and I to remain friends. Though it be true, he held command over me, he'd made no show of might, He had always allowed and indeed, encouraged me to be the one I truly am. Just as the skitter of a horse the name he often called me by, Madam Inquisitor, came to me. Such is the way my mind had been since my clash with the Englishman, and Declan's scolding. Darting here and there like a rabbit through the briars!

I had no wanting to make an enemy of Declan O'Malley. He had treated me well. He'd done much for me, and I repaid him with my contempt and unkindness toward one he cares for deeply. This I need mend, for the sake of us all. To not do so would benefit none! And for Maura. He being her relative, and me her pupil and guest. This wrong is mine, and I must make it right!

On Maura's return I told her I wanted to go to Declan's as soon as could be arranged. I had thought on this and would speak with Declan. I would tell him I was sorry. I would also speak with John the Englishman and tell him of my regret for the way I had treated him. I would do what I knew to be right. I would thank John for his care of Raven. I would tell him, though it be difficult for me, I would try to not think of him as one of the English, but as himself, John, in Declan's words a good man. These words raced from my lips as a fox being chased by hounds, scampering out as fast as they could, so desperate was my need to make this right!

Maura, sighed. "I have never said this, Orla, though it has afforded me some concern when you have been damning the English. You could yourself be one of them. For I think you are towards them, as many of them are towards us Irish. Do not let hate rot your soul. There be good and bad in us all."

Maura's words pulled me to a halt. As an Irish born woman, I had no want to be filled with hate and bitterness toward anyone. Yet in my lifetime all the pain and misery inflicted on me was at the hand of the English. They'd even tried through oppressing us and making us to be fearful, to take away from us our native tongue. In Duleek, only in our cottage did we speak the Irish. To be heard by the wrong ears speaking the Gaeilge could bring maim or death to the speaker and see their kin cast out into the wilds. A risk my father would not take.

"Do not despair, Orla, the harp will take you on a journey. It will change many things in your life. Sure, I believe it has already. It can change the way you feel... and the way you see things. We're all flawed in some way, but the harp is truly a magic thing; it can do much for the healing and the bringing together of people. You'll come to know this in time."

I listened to Maura's words for she was surely a wise one, but could see no way for this to be so, yet

I spoke no more on it, my mind being set on making things right with Declan O'Malley.

"Did you see Declan?" I asked with an urgency.

"Yes. He's made your string, though it is not yet ready for use. Being a thick string it takes time to dry and harden. He says, if you'd like to see your mare, we can go today. He'll be going home shortly after midday."

Eager was I see Raven, and to make amends. I nodded my keenness to go.

"Ah, there's a squirrel," said Maura as we walked along the woodland path to Declan's.

It was down on the ground eating something it held in its tiny hands. Startled by us, it ran quickly up the tree nearest it. How lovely these little creatures are with their ginger red hair, big round eyes, and a tail that looks as one's hair after a restless night of sleep. He sat as still as could be on a low branch of an oak tree. His small pointed ears, capped with the same fluff of his tail; listening intently. We watched him, and he us, for a short while. Then as Maura and I continued, she told me, like the boars, there once were many squirrels, now their numbers were less as they were killed and the trees cut. She said the squirrels could be quite naughty at times. This I found easy to believe as looking on them made me to think them as a small spirited child, or the little people so often told in the tales to me by my father.

As was often the way, the gate to Declan's big house came upon us quickly. The walk being an easy one on such a fair day as this. The warm summer sun filtering through the thick treetops, birds fluttering among them in the dappled light, their calls mingling with the whistle of our arrival. As we neared the house, coming from the direction of the stables, John the Englishman appeared. He smiled.

Maura said, "You go to your horse with John. I'll find Declan. No doubt he'll be at his desk. We'll come over to the stables when we've a mind to."

Maura walked away from us toward the house leaving John and me standing there. Awkwardly, I said, "I have no want for taking you from your work." He smiled, and took a step in the direction of the stable, hesitating, waiting for me to move along with him.

As I did, he said, "It is no bother Mrs. Connellan, the horses are my work."

My face reddened with shame to hear him address me so. "Most call me Orla. I'd like it were you to call me so. Also John, I wish to beg your forgiveness for my rudeness last time we met. I have a long history with the English, and it's not a pleasant one. Yet, that does not grant me the right to treat you with the disdain I showed you, I am truly sorry. I bear the shame as mine alone, you've given me no cause to judge your ways as those of the ways of your countrymen. I can only hope your nature is such that you can excuse my manner, and there be no malice between us."

He did not stop walking, nor turn his head toward me as he spoke. "I understand your misgivings Mrs.

C...... Orla, and forgive you readily, of that you must not doubt. I know that many, no most, of those from my land of birth have persecuted the Irish, your people, and continue to do so. We each have a shame to bear, all I ask is that you judge me for the man I am, not the land from which I come. This, I think, a fair request, don't you?"

"Yes," I said as Raven called out her hello as we entered the stables. Whether she nickered to me, or John the Englishman, is unknown. What is known, is that we both took pleasure on hearing her call!

## Chapter Fourteen

# THE QUIET WAR

"She is of such a gentle nature, this mare of yours," said John. "It is a gift for me to have her in my care. She likes me well enough I think, but I see it is you she has the eye for. She misses you."

Rubbing her face, breathing in her smell, I simply said, "I am missing her also... very much." How odd I thought this exchange with a man I knew not, and an English one into the bargain.

"I'll get you some brushes," he said suddenly, as if it a new idea come to mind. "No. Come with me... Orla. I will show you where they are kept, then you will be able to use them when you want." I followed him.

Standing at the doorway of a room in the stable building, a room filled with saddles, bridles, spare stirrups and girths, I watched as John fossicked in one of the many bins. He was quite a tall man, similar in height and age to Declan. His colouring being more fair, and had I not known otherwise, though taller than most, he looked to me, much like an Irishman.

"These should do," he said, his voice low and well timbered, as he thrust an assortment of grooming brushes into my hands. "Oh, you'll need a hoof pick. I haven't done her feet today," he said, grabbing one that was hanging on the wall, passing it to me. "There's your saddle over there."

Looking to where he pointed, I saw my saddle with my bridle hanging above it. Strange, how in a room full of saddles, with them all looking alike, one can know theirs from the others.

"You should do well with that lot. I will leave you to spend some time with her." He walked toward the door, and I made my way back to Raven.

Entering the stall, I set to work giving her a brush down. I had little use for the hard metal curry comb. The weather being warm and the hand of another having tended Raven well, her winter coat long gone. In truth, the brushing was unneeded, something to do as a way of being close to Raven. I checked her feet. Important as Jarlath had impressed upon me this was to do, though like her coat, they too were clean. My joy, was being once more, in the company of the one, who I had no need to guard my thoughts or my tongue; to Raven the only word of sorry I need make was for my absence.

As I was passing the brush over Raven, paying more attention to her than the task, I heard the voices of men approaching. I turned my head to the sound. Declan and John the Englishman now stood at the door of Raven's stall.

"Would you like to take her out for a ride?" Asked Declan, to my relief, in his usual relaxed manner.

"I would."

Declan then asked John to get my saddle and bridle from the tack room. John replied, "I showed Mrs. Con... Orla, where her gear is. I'm sure she is more than able to get it herself. Besides, if I am to take... Orla out riding, I have my own horse to ready." With that, he turned and left.

Declan looked at me with a smile, and said, "You heard the man. Best make yourself ready. John has endless time for his horses, but less so for people." Then he too, took his leave.

Quickly gathering up the grooming gear, I hurried back to the tack room, hanging up the hook, I threw the brushes into the bin, and grabbed my saddle, its cloth and my bridle. As fortune had it, Raven was as eager as I to go out, taking the bit easily, as I slipped the bridle over her ears. I was just tightening up the girth when John the Englishman's voice sounded at the door.

"Not ready yet?" He said with a grin.

Though it not my intention, I found myself warming to this man. I liked that he did not do for me, but expected me to do for myself.

"Where would you like to go? We have a few choices. We can gallop in one of the open fields, or take one of the many paths through the woodland."

Though not expecting to be going out riding, specially not at the side of this English man, I felt at ease. If it was not for the sound of his voice, I could be preparing to ride out with Jarlath or Seamus, so was my comfort. "I do not know this area well, but would it not be unwise for me to ride in the open?" He looked thoughtfully at me. I could see in his hazel coloured eyes, that he did not think on my question, but more on my need to ask.

"You are safe here. We can ride where you choose."

I did not hesitate, having been given the invitation. "Can we do both? It would be such a joy to have a gallop, and the woodlands are so pleasant at this time?"

He smiled. "Yes."

A s we rode, though not kin, it was plain to see that John the Englishman and Declan O'Malley had spent much time together. They shared many of the same traits, much as kin might. The way they held themselves, each had a confidence about them as they might fear little; both sitting a horse with ease, as though man and beast were one.

This thought, brought my eye to the mount ridden by the Englishman. It was not surprising that it was a tall horse, but beyond that it was ordinary to look at, a bay with a black mane and tail. Well cared for, a little skittish, but plain.

"We'll warm our horses as we make our way across the field, and then have a gallop back. After that we can take them into the woodland," he said.

We walked, trotted, and lightly cantered our way from the gate in one corner of the field, to the far corner. Riding Raven again, filled me with much joy.

"So Orla, are ready for your gallop? I'll race you back. You go. You'll need a long head start on this one," he said laughing.

I sat up tall in my saddle, tilting up my chin, I said, "We'll see about that."

Raven needed little encouragement, and she was away. It felt so thrilling to feel the power of her. The wind, the freedom, she, in that moment my whole world. Then I heard it, the thundering of hooves on the grass, growing louder, and with no effort the Englishman, laughing loudly on his plain bay, left us ahint.

"He's fast, your bay," I said, breathless from the gallop.

"Yes, no other horse I know can run like this fellow. There is many a danger I have escaped due to his speed and his courage."

It was beyond my way of knowing the sort of scrapes this Englishman may have found himself in. As we rode from the field into the woods, I stifled my curiosity, resisting my desire to ask for details of such ordeals.

"You have known Declan a long time?"

"Yes, we have been close, and loyal friends now for near on thirty years. We have done much together, he and I."

I so wanted to know more, yet, kept in check the asking that was my habit, though spoke my thought. "It is a strange alliance, an Englishman and an Irishman. For most, this would make you enemies."

He hesitated, then said, "There are many ways to fight a war; to bring about peace. Some do this with gun or canon. Declan and I have chosen another way, a better way, we think. Our quest for peace, though no less determined than the man who uses the sword or gun, is through friendship. Ours is a quiet war!"

We'd been riding for a while, crossing from one path to another. I was beginning now to see the mighty web of paths held within the woodland. Glad to be with another who knew their way well, for on my own, I would have great difficulty in finding the way back to the place from where we started. Having an escort allowed me to look around and truly enjoy the ride and the surrounds. Watching birds flying with great skill among the trees, and Raven's ears twitching alertly listening to sounds new to her, and watching the Englishman. Though he rode with ease, he shared Raven's alertness. He did not speak as we wended our way quietly through the trees, so startled I was when he said it was time for us to be heading back. His low voice, warm though it was, had a tone not unlike Declan's, of one used to issuing commands.

"Lead the way," said the Englishman.

I could see from his face his words were truly meant. My heart began pounding. Now the paths were like a maze, they were in all directions! Why had he not spoken of my need to be the pathfinder? If he'd done so, I would have paid more attention. I would have looked for landmarks, bends in the path, lines where the paths crossed, trees that were unlike others. None of these could I use, none had I taken note of. The birds I had watched were of no aid, they had no need for paths and were now long gone.

I would have to once more bow to the English. I would have to submit, and give myself over to this Englishman, for without him I could be forced to sleep the night in the woodland. Small and with much beauty though it was, I knew I could with ease, become entrapped in its web.

"I do not know which way to go," I said, hoping my voice did not betray my feelings.

"I fear that playing the harp is not all you have to learn. I understand the importance of your calling, yet, unless you stay alert and alive all your learning will be for naught?"

Though I knew there was a rightness in the words he spoke, it was a truth I did not want to have fall upon my ears. I felt an anger towards John the Englishman. Was this his plan all along? Did he wish to show me the fool that I was; a mere helpless woman? Had he arranged this as an opportunity to mock me, was that it? My anger now extended to myself. How could I have been so blind to this? How could I, so easily, let myself fall into the trap of this man? This Englishman!

"Why is it that you gave to me no warning of my being expected to lead our return?" I asked with the venom that betimes tainted my words.

"Have you never been met with events in your life that have presented without warning?" He asked evenly in his low smooth voice.

At that moment I wanted to scream at him! If I were close enough I thought I might strike him! Of course, I'd been met with things without warning! Much of my life had been filled with suddenness. The calmness with which he spoke made me only more wrathful. If I could have stepped away from myself, I might have seen that my anger was driven by my own hurt and embarrassment, but I could not. I did not! Instead, I spat the words, "You have no knowing of the evil I have lived through! Mostly at the hand of the likes of you, the English!"

As the words flew from my lips, the recklessness of them struck my mind. What if John the Englishman, brother to Declan should share what was spoken here? Foolish again I had been, dull-witted I was not. "I am sorry John, my harshness towards you was not right. It's just I didn't know it was for me to become the leader," I said lamely, hearing the feebleness in my own words.

"I think my countrymen have offered you much hurt, more than I can presume to know. I see it will take time for you to forgive me as one born of a country that has caused you such pain. I can wait that time, yet, lessons for you on the art of path-finding cannot." He then added quietly, "There are many positions from which you can lead, Orla, always remember that."

There was no malice or anger in his voice as we made our way back. Him in the lead, explaining things I should be looking for. How the position of the sun was useful, though he noted with our unreliable Irish weather, it was not always possible to see. I should look for any outstanding features, keep track of how many paths there were and when they crossed, and how many did they cross with. Much of this I knew to be so but had heeded little. He assured me my skill would improve. One day, he said, I'd be able to watch the birds, the squirrels and the flowers, yet still know where I was, and make my way to wherever I was planning on going. As we rode, him pointing out what I needed to be looking out for, never once did John the Englishman effort to make me feel a fool. It was only me that saw me so.

The path we rode along, sheltered by the canopy of trees, ended with little warning. Suddenly, up ahead was Declan's big house. We didn't enter through the big gate, for it was not through them, that our ride had begun, nor was there a whistle announcing our return. When I spoke of this, all John had said was, they know well who we are. As we got closer to the stables, with each step, I felt more unsettled. "John, thank you for taking me out, and once more, I'm sorry for my unkind outburst. Betimes, the pain I've lived through, and the doubt

I have in myself, causes me to unleash a vicious tongue."

He laughed, and said with his usual warmth, "I think Orla, over time, our friendship will bring great skill to not only your way-finding but also to your art of seeking forgiveness. Already, in our brief acquaintance, I have provided you more than one opportunity to practice, and something tells me, with a spirited nature such as yours, this number will surely rise. Fortunate it is, that I am one who readily forgives, and you set to be in the need of that. I look forward with great interest to our future clashes."

I could hear in John the Englishman's voice, that my harsh words caused him no bother, and though he didn't say, in my soul, I had a knowing that what we spoke of on our ride would remain with us. Feeling this, gave to me comfort. The tightness in my stomach softened, as the fear of our exchange and its possible rending of my friendship with Declan O'Malley, waned.

"So, how was the ride?" asked Declan, as we approached the stables from different directions, he on foot from his big house, and us on horseback, by way of the field.

"It was wonderful to be atop Raven's back again," I answered. John smiled.

"Orla is quite the horsewoman."

As we dismounted, Declan asked John to unsaddle and put away the horses.

Mischief crept across the Englishman's face, curling the edges of his mouth and setting a twinkling in his eye.

"I will not! As I said before, if Orla wants to ride, then she must do her duty to her horse. She can unsaddle, brush her mare down, and give her water, and a feed. That is the way it is for you and I, Declan, I see no reason for it to be any different for Orla. If she were not capable, then I may oblige, but she is, and I refuse. She can do for herself."

He slapped Declan on the back. They laughed as brothers. I too, laughed a little glad to be considered in a small way, their equal, then set to tending to Raven.

"If that is the way of it then, when you are done, Orla, come to the house. The door is open. Someone will show you to Maura and me." With that, Declan turned, and walked back toward the house.

John the Englishman, said nothing. There was no need. He passed a look to me. In his eyes, though I knew him little, there was an honesty. Perhaps, even though it caused much strife in my mind, him being English, that like Declan, one day I might come to trust John the Englishman.

# Chapter Fifteen

# GRACE

Though I did not see John the Englishman again on that day, I heard him moving about within the stables going about his work. The words spoken on our ride, and his look, stayed with me, and were with me still as I walked unsurely toward the big house. To think on opening the door to the house, another's house, and just entering was not a thing that gave to me any comfort. Standing in front of the door, with a strong burning to turn and walk away, it suddenly opened, and I found myself looking on the face of a woman of about thirty years. Upon sharing a look of surprise, I told her I was after knowing where I might find Maura. I did not speak Declan's name.

"Come on then," was all she said.

Stepping inside, all around me was a grandness unlike anything I'd ever seen. Everywhere I turned were things of beauty. I had a great want to stand and take in every bit of it, but did not. I followed the woman, who walked with much haste into the room I knew from what Maura had told me, to be the dining room. Declan and Maura were sitting at one end of the long, grand table. In front of them were many papers, and a large wooden box. I thought them to be talking business or the likes.

Ahint them hung the painting of a woman. This must be the woman, the one Maura told to me. It was much bigger than I'd been thinking it to be. It was the biggest painting I'd ever seen. Much bigger than any of the paintings in the church in Duleek. The painted woman had the same commanding look about her I'd seen in Declan's face, and though she was finely dressed, there was a wildness to her, an untamed, almost fierce look to her. This too I'd seen in Declan the day he shot the boar, and the day he'd spoken harshly to me. Recalling this, made me to feel unsettled. I'd no want for him to revisit upon me words akin to those.

With no waiting or politeness, the woman I followed, said, "Thissn wants Maura," pointing to me with her head.

I understood her well, but I found her manner odd.

"Thank you, May." The woman nodded and hurried off.

"We've had a bit of good fortune," said Maura, waving her hand toward the box near her on the table. "We've found a string for you among some others Declan remembered he'd put away. He's not yet finished the new one he's making for you, it needs more drying, but we think this one will do for now."

She handed me a coiled string held firmly by the wrapping of its own end. As I took it from her hand, she stood.

"We'd best be taking our leave. You know I'm a one for getting settled in before the evening comes."

I'd not spoken a word since entering the house, and still did not. I nodded to Declan and followed Maura out through the grandness, out through the big front door.

O ur woodland walk back to the cottage, was for me, more enjoyable than the walk to the big house made earlier that day. My peace had been made. The burden that weighed much on me had been cast off by my setting things to right, though I'd almost undone my peacemaking on the ride with John the Englishman. As we walked, I told Maura of the happenings on our ride.

Understanding my reasons, she showed me no ire, yet, advised me I'd do well to guard my tongue, given as it was to the spitting of venom. And as Declan had already told to me, I should judge more by the actions of a man or woman than by their look, or the place from where they come. While walking quietly along a woodland path I knew these words to be wise words, and ones I should heed. Yet, forty years of ill-treatment for being Irish, and a woman, make fervent emotions quick to rise and colour the thinking, and the words that spew forth.

I was glad to have spoken to Maura of my run in with the Englishman. Whether aware or not, she'd become my confessor. With her I shared most things, not all though, as I believe there are some things, not for the sharing. Unseen treasures meant only for the self to know. A touch or a look given from one to another that needs not be spoken of. A look to be held as a dear secret in the hope it would never be stolen away as is often the way when one has a precious thing. Always is there another keen to covet it, only too willing to use evil or devious ways, to steal it for their own.

We walked quickly to be indoors by suppertime, with Maura's chickens safely locked away, and the fire well alight, as was her way. Preparing for the evening, she said, made her to feel a comfort, one she looked for to help her sleep well.

Fondly, I was thinking it a plan that worked well for Maura, her soft but reassuring nightly snoring, telling me so. I was not so lucky, and did not sleep easy. Being given to the constant thinking. The going over of words spoken, notes on the harp, things that happened, feelings, mine and others, sights, seen and unseen. These things whirled in my mind most nights as I lay in my bed. The rare times when sleep came quickly, on these nights, I was truly grateful. This was not a one! My outburst at the Englishman, and the woman in the painting my companions, as I waited for the drifting off.

I was eager next morning to fit the new string to my harp. Too many days had I been troubled by the guilt of my own manner, and the delay of a broken string. These both now being put right, it was time to return to the work of the Goltrai strain. Odd to me was it that the strain of sorrow, a thing well known to me, should be the strain to give me the most trouble in the getting to of the learning. I could not bring to mind the intention or thinking, needed for the work of the harper, due to the burden of wrongness carried in my own heart. In this, I found a learning, not from the lips of Maura, but from within.

It seemed to me, though there may be much going on around, and some the harper may not have a bearing on, that the mind of the harper must be free of bad thoughts and the thinking of self, to be able to work with a heart that is true.

I spoke of this with Maura. She said this was so. The harper, she said, can only work for the benefit of others with a trueness when their thoughts are pure and their intentions are focused outwards. Though quickly added, the harper could, if needs be, work for their own healing but still the intention must be clear, and only for good. Never, should the harp strings be played with a wrongful intention, for to do so, would not only be of harm to the one who is hearing the music, but also to the heart of the harper. I could not in my mind, think of why a one would want to use the beauty of the harp to bring about harm to any, though Maura told to me, it can be done.

I t gave me much pleasure to be back playing my harp, free of the troubled thoughts that had plagued my mind in recent days. The lessons given me by Maura on the changing of a string, though I'd not changed one of this thickness, placed me well for the task. The string, though not as easy to work as the thin ones I had practiced changing, was manageable still. Maura told to me to keep my tuning key close by as I would be much in need of it as a new string, would stretch until it found its home. As I worked on the Goltrai tune, using the new string often in the playing of the drone, it took little time in the stretching, coming true, and holding.

Maura gave to me, encouraging words as we made our way home that afternoon. She said, most would not have, in the time I'd been learning, have three whole tunes. Though, I could not say my playing of the three, was yet solid, her words heartened me.

We did not spend a long day in the chamber, as was usual. Maura had a want to go to town for the buying of some things. Now I was living with her, our time together, and ways of life were more settled. The urgency of my lessons, though still busy and constant, were now felt as less pressing.

The order of this day was restful for my mind as a harper, yet, my wonder and curiosity of Declan's big house found no ease. I had a want to see more of what it offered the eye than I'd yet been afforded. When I spoke on this, Maura, told to me this could easily be remedied. We had not the time for a tour on our last visit, due to the lateness of our setting out from her cottage, and my lengthy horse riding wanderings. Her words were true, so too, was my curiosity. We'd see to that sometime, Maura said.

As we sat in the evening, I told to Maura, that I could see a likeness in the face of the woman in the painting, and Declan. "She looks a strong woman, what do you know of her?" Maura said there was a great deal to know of this woman, one unlike all others of her time, a wild and fierce woman that few had a yearning to cross. This is what she told to me.

"She was born more than one hundred years ago, around 1530. She shares the family name Declan has; O'Malley, she is Grace O'Malley. The story told, is that she was known as the queen of pirates. Her family, our family, were seafarers of hundreds of years. Gráinne, her Irish name, with it in her blood, had a strong desire to put to sea, though being a girl, her father refused to allow this. So determined was she to not be hindered by her womanhood, she disobeyed him and followed her heart. Whether it be due to her being a woman, it is not known, but she became ever so fierce, ruling the waves along our rugged coast for many, many years, trading and raiding, earning the title the Pirate Queen."

Maura went on. "Like her forebears, Grace gave no quarter, she was ruthless! Terrorising and demanding monies from fishermen in the form of a tax. It is told that she was as good a leader as any man, afraid of no one, not even her sworn enemy, the English. Indeed, so fierce and powerful was she, and so highly regarded, that during the time of the English Queen, Elizabeth, Grace went to England and demanded to meet with Elizabeth. So formidable and well known was the reputation of Grace, the Queen agreed. Proud she was! She even refused to bow to the Queen of England, saying that Elizabeth was not the queen of Ireland, not her queen!

"Grace, it seems, had a way with men, as not only did she command the loyalty of so many on the seas, but she also wed a number of times. It was through one of her marriages that the sharing of blood between Declan and myself comes to be. It is known with many loyal followers, she moved the seat of her business to Clare Island, and is buried there, dying around the same time as Declan was coming into this world. Declan has inherited the O'Malley love for the high seas, and shares with Grace a good many traits, though I like to think him a little less ruthless than she."

I could not pretend to know Declan O'Malley well at this time, yet, I could know already some of the traits passed through time from his forbears. The value he placed on loyalty, I knew well, and like Grace, men followed him and stayed with him. Maura I recalled, had said he was a trader, and a smuggler. This, I think, though perhaps by using different means, is not so far from the life of a pirate. Declan surely was a man in possession of much cleverness, with little to no fear of the English. Yes, I believed Maura correct in her reckoning. When I looked again on the painting, I would now better understand the wild woman who looked back at me, and what she meant for Declan.

"When can we go again to Declan's?"

"I'll think on it. Yet, for now, my bed calls to me." Maura said.

That night I was visited by the mare of the night, the one that brings fitful rest. My mind was filled with raging winds, and high seas. Boats with men being cast overboard by the wild weather, and a woman's voice, bellowing out orders, wielding a cutlass, screaming above the noise like a wild banshee. Two galleys banged together, the wild woman leapt from one onto the other, and as she swung the cutlass to separate the head from the shoulders of a man, I awoke.

Trembling, I sat up in my bed. So real was the picture in my mind, so frightening, so fierce was the woman! I was want to wonder if that look lived in Declan's eyes? Whites gleaming, shining with the thought of drawing blood. So disturbed was I, that sleep did not return. I lay there waiting for the light of day to arrive.

Relieved was I, when I heard Maura beginning to stir. I rose quickly, needing to shift the awful visions from my mind. I gave my blessing for the day, dressed, and made ready for a day of harping. Sitting at the table, as we ate, a loud clap of thunder sounded, so sudden it was, that we each shrieked. Looking to each other we laughed. Heavy rain began to fall.

"Such is the way of our fine Irish weather, one moment fine; the next the heavens open."

We laughed at the truth of it, yet continued with our readying for the day.

"We will make our way to the tunnels with haste. Rain and wind, I do not mind, and indeed am much used to, but I have no liking for the lightning, and I fear on a day as this, there'll be plenty of it about," said Maura.

As we ran, our heavy woollen brats covering our heads and bodies, Maura said, "Glad I am that our harps are already in the chamber, for running with a great lumbering thing is not easily done. I have, many times in my life, been forced to do so, and it is a burden I am happy to be without."

Running with a harp was unknown to me, so little did I understand her words. In time this would change. On entering the tunnel, pulling back the hoods on our brats, I struck the tinder and lit the lamp. How peaceful it was in the tunnel, the quietness of it, odd, when just moments before, we'd been pelted by heavy rain, and serenaded by claps of thunder and the cracking of lightning. Yet here, nothing but welcomed silence.

We stayed long in the chamber that day, leaving with only enough time to make ready the fire in the cottage and our evening meal. I worked through the three tunes many times, now they were beginning to sit well under my hands. Maura, made certain before I began playing each strain, that time was given to clear my mind, and focus well my intention.

"It be better to play a wrong note with good intention, than to play each note perfect with no heart. As a harper, it's your duty to bring light into the darkness of the hearts of those you play for. This you cannot do, without being sure of your own intention," she said.

As we came from the tunnels back into the light of day, the sun, though low in the sky was shining. Everything about us sparkled in the newness brought to it by the washing rain. We did not tarry; our boots becoming heavy with mud as we tramped our way home. So used to it we are. I once heard someone say, we cannot have such an Emerald as ours without an abounding amount of God's tears to make it so. In these words there is as much truth as there is rain that falls in the making of our land's beautiful cloak of green.

Not wanting to be bothersome, yet eager, I asked Maura again that evening when we might go to Declan's house. I was more than curious to see inside the house, and keener still, to see Raven. Maura said we could tomorrow, as it would do me good to have a day away from the tunes. This would help them to settle into my head.

She also said something that made me to feel a bit unsettled. She said when we walked tomorrow, I should take note of the road, as soon it would be that I should go there alone, Maura having tasks of her own interest to seek. The thought of walking the road alone troubled me. When I said this aloud to Maura, she laughed and told me to think on the boldness of Grace O'Malley.

"You are not having to sail the wild seas, or command a hundred fighting men... it's just walking!"

And true enough it was. We laughed. How fond I had grown of this sprightly, dear woman and her wise simple ways.

# CHAPTER SIXTEEN

# THE BIG HOUSE

"Does Declan know we're coming?" I asked, as we walked down the path.

"Whissht, woman! Are you learning your way? That should be where your mind's at."

Maura's pretending to scold me set me to laugh.

"What is it that brings you to the laughing then? That you know your way is a serious matter. You needs to know. I have things other than yourself needing my attention."

The seriousness of Maura's words made me to laugh all the more. Though she knew not why, not being able to stop herself, Maura joined the laughing. Soon we were holding our sides with tears rolling down our faces. That she did not know what set me to the laughing, yet was so lost in the laughing herself, only made me to laugh all the more, and Maura to follow. When after a long while, with our laughter quietened to only small snickerings, Maura said, "Now tell to me what that was all about."

Trying hard not to fall into another fit, I said, "It was the whissht woman! And the way you said it. Declan said those same words to me, plumb in the same way as yourself."

She did not think the words as funny as me, yet spoke great praise for the benefits of a long hard laugh. I too, though my sides were sore, felt my mood much lifted; my heart and soul filled with a joy that rarely visits one.

"You have not yet given me an answer. Does Declan know we're coming to his house, or is it we arrive unannounced?"

Maura gave a small snort, "I am not skilled so, that I can talk with sense, while I roll about with the laughing you have brought on me. Do not fear, Orla, we'll never arrive at Declan O'Malley's gate unannounced, you'll be hearing the whistle as sure as day follows night."

Would Declan be there? I wondered to myself. It would be likely not, for he had the building of the boats to oversee. And, his skill in working wood, skill that only comes to one who's spent much time at the craft, told me he was not a one for the standing and watching while others be doing the work. I think Declan a man, who finds joy in the crafting of a thing; taking something raw, and bringing out the beauty hidden within; the skill of it.

Just as Maura had said, the whistle sounded as we neared the gate. Had I given enough attention to our path that I could find my own way here? Of this I felt unsure. The thing I was sure of, was that I had little want to travel through the woodland alone. I'd spent much time on my own, and liked it fine, yet it was always in a protected way. There'd always been others not far from me. In truth, I'd done little on my own, truly on my own! I'd thought about how good it would be to be free to do whatever I had a wanting for, but now it was being expected of me to do for myself, I felt afeared. Of what, a boar, getting lost, of myself? I cannot say.

"**W**ho'll be here?"

Maura looked to me. "It matters not. The house is here, your horse is here, these are what we came to see; and... for you to find your way. May be Declan will be here, and if he is, I will be pleased, but it is not for him that we came. Now, which is it you want to see first?"

I thought on this briefly, as the house neared. Last time, it disappointed me not having the chance to see more of the house, robbed by the lateness of the day. The woman with the strange tongue had taken me directly to the dining room, a room I'd like to see again, along with other parts of the house, such is my curious nature, and today we had the time.

"The house."

My answer and the doorstep arrived together, without knocking, without hesitation, Maura opened the large front door. As the door closed a voice said, "'Ow do Maura?" It was May. Maura smiled. "Hello May. I've come to show Orla the house. I'll come and have a cup of tea with you when we're done. Orla's going to see her horse." May smiled, nodded, and scampered away.

"Does she live here?" Maura looked unsurprised at my question.

"She's the wife of one of Declan's men. A nice girl, friendly and kind. Now let's get on."

The front door opened into what Maura called the entrance hall. There was a large heavily carved dark piece of furniture. Maura said it was called a sideboard. It was beautiful with small figures carved into the doors, and a top of stone that Maura called marble. Beyond the entrance hall was a big stair-case, it was so grand. Never had I seen anything like this. When I looked up, the roof, Maura said they called it the ceiling, was white with fancy work all around the edges, and in the middle hung a huge light Maura called a chandelier. It took around a dozen or more candles. Maura pulled on a small looped chain; it was as magic, down it came. Maura told me, this you did to light or replace the candles.

We went up the stairs. I ran my hand along the rail. Maura called it the bannister. Oh, how smooth and warm the wood! There were chandeliers and carved wood panels, and fireplaces with beautiful carved mantles. I felt faint with the splendour of it all! And the windows! Some with seats where one could sit and look out. I thought if I lived here I would never want to leave. On the walls, hung large mirrors that brought the outdoors into the house, and paintings, and carved cupboards that Maura said were called cabinets. I heard a lot of new words that day!

N ever could my mind have shown to me what my eyes now saw. Every so often, there was a metal holder on the wall that could take two candles. Even these were crafted with little people, their arms up, holding a cup for the candles! Knowing how rare and precious candles to be, when I spoke of this, Maura said in an offhand manner, "Declan is apt to come by things that aid one to live well."

She said also, some of the wives of his men keep bees and were much skilled at the making of candles.

We walked along a hall with doors leading off on each side. Maura said these were bedrooms where Declan's men and their families slept. When we came to the last of these, she said the door on the left lead into Declan's private rooms. She made no move to enter. I was much relieved. As to think of entering his room with him not here to offer invitation, was an act, the very thought of made me to feel unsettled. As her words on this ended, Maura took from about her neck, a chain. On this chain hung a key. This she said was the key to the room now on our right, her room! A room that was kept only for her should she be in need, or decide to stay overnight. Maura, turned the key, and opened the door.

In the center of the room, with its head against one wall, stood a large bed. The foot of which was heavily carved. Over it hung a canopy of the most lovely crimson coloured tapestry. The furniture numbered few pieces, but it was clear they were of high quality. Everything was beautiful! One chair with the same coloured cloth as the canopy. A mirror on a stand. Two sets of matching drawers, and a writing table with a simple wooden chair. All carved, and as heavenly to the eye as is nectar to the tongue! I wondered aloud, "Why is it that you do not live here?"

Maura, simply said, "I like to come here, even to stay sometimes, as it bethinks me, yet, I am much happier and more at home in my cottage."

M aura closed the door, turned the key in the lock, and put the chain back around her neck. Retracing our steps along the hall, we went down the stairs. Yet, instead of going into the dining room, Maura turned through a doorway to our left. This way she told me, lead to the kitchen. I'd be in need of knowing this, as this is where she would wait for me while I spent time with Raven.

The kitchen room like the rest of the house, was grand. Copper pots and pans were hung above a large cooking hearth. There were baskets of vegetables along one wall, and a big worktable, around which sat a handful of women, all nattering and preparing food. As we went in, their fondness for Maura was made clear by the warmth shown her in their greetings. Maura, introduced me. I felt awkward. I nodded my greetings and made good my escape; heading for the stables.

Quickly I covered the ground between the big house and the stables, great was my eagerness to see Raven. In my hurrying, as I rounded the stable doors, looking to see Raven's face, and not the way I was going, I walked with some might, into John the Englishman.

"In a hurry then, are you?" He asked with a laugh.

"I'm sorry," I stammered, startled by the unexpected meeting. "I'm going to take Raven out for a short ride in the field."

"I'll let you get on with it then. You know where everything is. Oh, I haven't checked her feet today, not being aware that she'd be going out." He walked away.

Hearing my voice, Raven whinnied loudly to me. I called back to her as I went into the tack room to gather my gear, and the hoof pick.

Carrying the saddle and cloth over my arms, with my bridle over my shoulder, I gave thanks for my strength, and good health. Many others of my years, through hunger and poverty, had been rendered frail and ailing. I was glad to not be among them. Entering the stall I took little time in getting Raven bridled and saddled. She was as ever gentle and obliging. Eager as me to be getting out and about. With the thought of cantering on her across the field, I put my arms around her neck, burying my head into her mane, I said, "How I love you, my dearest friend." As the words left my lips, I heard a shuffling of feet, and a quiet walking away, though no one did I see.

# CHAPTER SEVENTEEN

# BROTHERHOOD

I lead Raven from the stables out into the yard. Throwing the reins over her head, grasping the front of the saddle, I placed my foot in the stirrup and swung onto her back glad to be wearing the breeches Mary'd made me. So accustom to them I was, that the thinking on wearing a skirt was now rare. The breeches suited me well. Being atop Raven's strong broad back, was wonderful. It was as though being in another world, lost to this one! It was like the way I felt playing my harp in the cottage at the farm or down in the chamber. Yet journeying with the harp was one of quiet, with Raven there was a wildness about it. I walked her to the field, and following the stone wall, I rode to the corner where John the Englishman and me had raced;this time I'd gallop alone.

On our getting to this place, I had spoken all the while to Raven, telling her about what I'd seen in the big house; the beauty and the awe. I told her of my harp playing, and of my fear of having to walk to Declan's alone. I felt unburdened as I spoke aloud my feelings, holding nothing back, for there was no need. Raven did not judge me! Not as a woman, a harper, a pathfinder. May be this is what it is to be truly free. May be freedom lives more in the mind than the body.

We turned, I gave a nudge with my legs, though Raven needed little urging. She broke swiftly into a canter, lengthening her stride to the gallop. Holding the reins lightly, I let her have her head. As we galloped the wind whipped through my hair, though still in plaits, free of the cap that now lay on the straw in Raven's stall. The pleasure of the ride never lessening!

We slowed as the corner of the field grew closer. Patting her neck and shortening my rein, Raven snorted as though casting out any stale air within her, and prancing about, as to let me know she shared my thrill of the run. Not wanting our ride to end, I stayed on her back, bending low to ride into the stables, and not dismounting until her stall was reached.

Leading her into the stall, I closed the half-door, and set about unsaddling her. As I undid the girth, John the Englishman's voice sounded.

"You've had a good ride then... both of you?" He asked, knowing he had no need. I nodded running up the stirrups. "You are a fortunate one. I think her the loveliest mare to have ever crossed my path." I smiled and nodded my agreement. "You will freshen her water and mix her a feed before you leave?" Though he asked as a question, I knew he was offering me an unneeded reminder.

As I hung the saddle over the door, I said, "I will, and I'll give her a brush down." He smiled, and went about his work.

D iscomfort came upon me again as I approached the door of the big house. The feeling of strangeness at entering another's house without invitation weighed upon me. It was not my way. I readied myself. I'd taken careful note of the route that lead to the kitchen, this I would take quickly, and most directly. I turned the handle, opened the door, yet, as I began on my way to the kitchen, Declan's voice came from the dining room.

"Is that you Orla? Come in here. I have your string ready."

I stopped for an instant, making myself tall, trying to appear more bold on the outside than I felt within, I entered the dining room. Declan was seated at the head of the table, a place I thought must be his place at the table, as it was where he was sat last time with Maura. Before I had time to curb my mind, I thought on how handsome a man he was. It was not only the look of him made him so. Though it could not be denied his long dark hair, tied as always, back off his face, his green eyes, straight nose, and warm smile were easy to look upon; it was more than this. It was the ease of himself, made him so.

He stood and walked to one of the cabinets in the room, pulling out a drawer, he took from it a coiled string. His tallness being made all the more so by his clothing. The loose linen shirt, over which he wore a long green vested jacket, and dark brown trousers, showing his striking height.

Looking directly into my eyes, as was his way, when he spoke, he said, "The string that you fitted is old, it may not last well, but now you will have this one if it is to go."

I thanked him, looking him well in the eye, hoping that mine did not give away my thoughts or my thumping heart, and said, "I've come for Maura. She told me to collect her when I was finished with Raven."

"You know John is so taken with that mare of yours, I swear if your claim on her was not so strong, he would take her as his own." Then added, "And one would not show him blame for the wanting of her."

On the way back to Maura's, she reminded me to be most alert, as the next time I came on this path, I'd walk it alone. I had no want for this, and my lack showed.

"Sometimes, we have to do the thing we do not want, yet, if we can overcome this fear, we can grow stronger. I do not know where the doubt for your own strength comes from Orla, for many times you have proven yourself. It is as though it is in plain view to others, but hides itself from you. I ask that you do something for me. You, with a great fondness for questions; look within, and ask why it is you are so blind to your own courage. Will you do this for me?" I nodded. "Good. Never fall to the voice of doubt. Now watch where we are walking!"

Maura, had the skill of speaking of serious matters, then lifting one's mood, by ending with words
that kept the learning, but in a playful way. A skill
she used with much profit. I'd come to know well
the value of Maura's words. Heeding her advice, I
turned my attention back to the landmarks of note,
the ones that would be my guides next time I used
this path.

M aura said as we clambered through the brambles of the abbey, "I have invited Declan to
come and eat with us again. It's selfish of me I know,
but I enjoy having his company and not having to
share him with all his household. Good and fine
people though they be."

I did not think on this, as I had no want for my
intention to be tainted by the thoughts of anything
but the music, and Declan O'Malley found the way
into my thinking easier than most. On this day, it
was only music I allowed in. After our work that day
on my three tunes, Maura spoke to me of giving the
tunes life. She said what I had learned of the tunes,
so far, had been the bones, and now it was time for
me to put some flesh on them. It was time for me to
learn some ways to make the tunes more my own.
Though many harpers played the same tune, this
she said, was the way, each gave to it their own seal.

Maura then played the Geantrai tune, the one I
was most familiar with, it being my first learned. She
played it through the way she had taught it to me,
then again, using different drones, and including
some ornamentation. The tune sounded beautiful
to my ear, both ways. The skill of the harper, she

told me, would be heard by the listener, through thoughtful use of these. The drones could include an extra note, or be played in different parts of the harp, or mirror or blend with the melody.

Particular attention must be given to the use of ornaments. She said, often was it, that those new to the use of them on the harp, would subject a tune to overuse of the ornaments, dulling the beauty of the queen; this was always to be avoided. Maura then taught to me, the cut. This was a fast light note. A note that came from above the more strongly played melody note. She told me that it could also come from below the melody note, and this she called a tip. Though I did not find it to be too difficult, the playing of the note before the melody, getting the note to sound light, and softer than was the melody, proved to be much more troubling. When I lamented this, Maura said, "Think on the young lads learning to choose and shape the stones."

A few evenings later Declan came to take the evening meal with us. Gifting us again another bottle of fine mead. As we sat by the fire, my unquenchable curiosity urged me to ask, "How is it that you and John came to meet?"

Declan laughed. "I was wondering how long it would take for the Madam Inquisitor to join us."

Maura, too, laughed. I joined them to be polite, yet not knowing, in truth, the cause of the mirth. Declan said, they'd met on the continent, both fighting in an army, but on opposite sides. They were young, around twenty years. His reason for being there, like many young men, a fondness for the coin. Such was Declan's desire for the coin he'd do almost anything to gather as many as he could. Being a mercenary jingled loudly in his pocket. For John, it was his fore- bears brought him to the field of war on that day; he came from a long line of soldiers and thought it his duty to follow.

Declan said they'd come upon each other among some trees, when most of the fighting was done. They wrestled hard and long, the two of them be- ing of equal match. Finally breaking free from each other, both pulled pistols from their belt. Pointing at one another, John spoke. Declan said, as they stood there, neither with the desire to pull his trigger, John said, he could think of no good reason why their lives should be forfeited for another who sent them into battle for the greed of land and power, of none, would be their share.

John said, that I knew not him, nor him me, yet, if my desire to kill was so great as to end his life on that day, so be it. Nothing though, would force him to let loose from his gun a bullet directed at me. On saying this, John lowered his pistol and asked me to think on his words, then decide if he was to die my enemy or that I might grant him life. John also said, perhaps out of the misery and destruction of this bloody war, a brotherhood might grow. And so it has.

His words hung heavily in the air and after a long silence, I asked, "What stopped you from shooting him?"

I could see Declan searching for an answer. "The truth he spoke."

Shifting the talk, Maura said, "Orla is going to walk the woodland path to your house on her own when she next visits her horse."

Declan raised an eyebrow. "And when might that next be?"

Before I had time to answer, Maura said, "She'll come the day after tomorrow."

"Will I?"

With a poor attempt of wearing her stern face, she said, "Yes, I have things to do, so will have no time to give you a lesson."

Declan looked to me. "Will you come then in the morning Orla?"

With no lesson and the prospect of spending the whole day with Raven, I nodded.

"I'll be at the boatyard, but I'll tell John to look out for you."

After Declan left, I asked Maura a question. One, that I had not wished to ask Declan for fear it might show my unknowingness, yet, one to which I was in need of an answer. "Maura what is an inquisitor?" Maura embraced me.

"Do not fear, child. It is meant kindly Orla. An inquisitor is one that simply asks a lot of questions, or makes inquiries, a searcher of answers, and that you surely are. Now, take your sleep." She kissed lightly my cheek.

## Chapter Eighteen

# WALKING ALONE

The day of walking alone to Declan's came. The thinking on it had troubled my mind and made me much unsettled. All the days of my life had been ruled by happenings, or by others, now being offered the charge, I was greatly troubled. What if I was to take a wrong path? Never having to lead the way for myself I doubted my skills of knowing how a right choice was to be made. These I could make for the good of others, but for myself, I was less sure. Had I taken enough note of the way? With such a web of paths among the woodland, what would happen, if I, without knowing, was to place my foot on a path other than the one meant for me?

Those who lead us would know. Men would know. They make most of our choices; for them this would be no cause for concern. To men, they would see my task as one of ease. That is the path, they would say, and if so said, I would take the one told. That is the way it has been for me. Now I must choose!

My grandmother, Clodagh Moran, would know. Many times, she had been the one to lead; indeed, I was here, due to an order issued from her lips. She would not be hesitant or filled with the fear and doubt, as I now was. And what of Grace O'Malley? She, I thought, would take charge. I so wanted to take charge. No! What I truly wanted in this moment, was for Maura to have a change of heart and walk with me as she had always done. I wanted to feel safe. I knew this a thing for which I could not ask. In my mind, I had claimed a want to rule my own life, choose my own fate; here was the first step on this path, and I was afraid. This thing I would do. This walk I must do. How timid the choice of others had made me. I am sure a wean is not born into this world with such a fear. I am sure I was born with courage, yet, the events of life have locked it away. I would not allow that which has befallen me, to keep the key to my courage, hidden!

Maura made no motherly fuss, other than to advise me to pack a little food, and a flask, such as the like we would take to the tunnels. She, herself, was going into the town, and would expect my return by nightfall. Wishing me well, she walked out of the cottage. Now, the time had come! Now I must make my first footfall. I slung my crane bag over my shoulder, leaving my tuning key, and spare harp strings on the table for fear of losing them. Standing myself up tall in a bid to feel all the bolder, I set off.

The beginning of the path, I knew well, and my tread on this part was confident. Though the quiet, a peace, many a time I had looked for, on that day brought upon me a strangeness. No sun shone, and the canopy of the trees which I had welcomed in the past as shelter, now cast over me a blanket of gloom. When my fear urged me to turn back, I thought on my grandmother and Grace O'Malley. It was the braveness of them that walked with me on my journey and kept my steps moving forward.

My confidence shattered when it came to mind I'd been walking for longer than was usual to reach Declan's. Looking round me, no trees were known to me; this part of the woodland a stranger. My eyes widened in the hope of seeing something I knew. I recognised nothing. My heart set to banging. Retracing my steps, I came upon another path, the one I knew to be the one that lead to Declan's big house. How had I missed it? Relief flooded my body. I'd not been long on the path, when ahead coming toward me, I saw two horses. They came at a walking pace, one being ridden the other lead. As they got closer, I recognised the ridden horse as the bay of the Englishman, and the horse being lead, my own dear Raven.

"I thought you might like to ride the rest of the way," John the Englishman said calmly as he neared me.

It seems my arrival was expected earlier in the day, and now it was after midday. Though greatly relieved to see him, I had no desire, for him, or anyone, to know that I had lost my way, I told him my starting out had been delayed attending to some pressing chores. Fortunately, he did not ask of what nature, for had he done so, I would have been forced to lie, a habit to which I was not inclined. I mounted Raven, turning her back toward the big house.

"Did you have somewhere in particular that you wanted to ride?"

My mind raced. I needed to complete my journey, so as to be sure of it for my next time. "I thought we might begin with a good gallop across the field again. I so enjoyed that," I said, hoping my utterance of want, would take us to where I needed. He offered no argument.

"As you'd like."

So comforted was I by his agreeable manner, I began to settle on Raven's back. How thoughtful it was for John the Englishman to come and meet me, and to do so with Raven in tow, saddled and ready for me to swing my leg across her back. I wondered if Declan, or somehow Maura, had brought our meeting about. Did they doubt I'd find my way? Though I could not say truthfully, that my route had been direct, I did, as the large gate came into view, however, consider my first lone walk, a triumph.

A pride swelled within me that I had journeyed, though not without flaw, to my wanted place. No one but God could know the strength it required of me; so great was my fear, beaten down only by my determination. God! I hardly thought much on him now. Was it he, who had brought John the Englishman, or perhaps the Old Ones?

"Do you know of the Old Ones, John?"

"I do," he answered. "Declan and Maura have spoken much on them to me. I had not heard of them, nor thought in truth, much on those who have gone before us before the weaving of Declan and Maura, into my life. Yet these days, though it has taken time, I have come to feel the Old Ones' presence around me, and often call for their counsel."

After we galloped, once more Raven and I being left well behind by John and his bay, he said in his quietly assuring voice, "As you do not yet know much of our woodland, I will take you to a place I think you may like to see." Then with a laugh, he went on. "Before we set out, to save myself from the wrath of your tongue, you must know, I will lead us there but it will be your task to lead us back."

Every now and again, John would point out a strange tree, or draw my attention to another path leading off the one we rode, or mark the position of the sun as it now shone through the trees. "I know what you're doing, you're like Uncle Jarlath" I said.

He made no apology. "Yes, I am teaching you. As I said I would. The important question is, are you learning?" I nodded. "Good, then my work is not in vain." He smiled.

"We are here." John said dismounting and leading his bay in off the path.

Following him, I did the same. Opening out in front of us lay a clearing with a short avenue of stones opening out into a large circle. It too, ringed with stones. "What is this place?" I asked.

"We, Declan, Maura and I, think it a place of the Old Ones."

It was most beautiful with the white stones, the rich green grass, and a smattering of bluebells and buttercups. As we sat in silence on the soft grass, in this place, this holy place, though unsure, I felt we were not alone. "They are here, aren't they?"

"Yes."

With the holiness of the place having restored us, my stomach made a loud rumbling sound. I'd not eaten since early that morning. I took the bread, cheese and the flask from my bag, and offered some to John. He did not speak, yet, ate with me. We sat there, we two, sharing the food, sharing the other-worldly wonder, around us.

"I got lost."

"No, Orla, you did not get lost. When I came upon you, you were on the path leading to Declan's. That you took an unexpected way of getting there does not matter. You were finding your way."

I do not know why I made this confession to him. All of my days I had feared all men other than kin, and yet, now I find myself fully at ease with this man; and he being an Englishman making it all the more strange.

"I think it is time for us now to see how well you have learned from my teachings." He was right I knew in saying it was time to leave, for even when we reached the stables, I would need to attend to Raven, for though he did not say, I knew John would not do for me what I could do for myself. This he had made clear. Then there was the walk back through the woodland. A walk I feared less than I had this morning, knowing now what lay before me.

I have found fear often lurking in the unknown. Yet, once a thing is known to me, the fear is weakened. That is the way it has been for me. This I hoped would be true now for my walk back. Though wishing we could stay longer in this green haven, I had no want for the making of my return home late for supper knowing Maura would be waiting, so gathered my belongings and mounted Raven.

"You have done well," said John as the galloping field came into sight.

I breathed a little more easy, though I felt confident in my leading as we rode. I unsaddled Raven, getting her fed and watered as quickly as I could. I did not stint any task. Brushing her down, checking her hooves, putting my gear away. These I did, though in a hurrying way. I bid farewell to John and was soon making my way through the gates. I do not know why it is, but heading home appeared a much easier path for me. I took no detours, making good time, delighting both myself and Maura, arriving well in time for supper!

# Chapter Nineteen

# Always With You

Though my days were well filled, my mind taken up with the learning, and little time for much else than an every now and again ride on Raven, at night, when I lay in my bed, waiting for sleep, my thinking was set to wandering. I thought much on my children. After them being gone from me for the past ten years, being with them again, and now I gone from them. This was hard on my heart. I was comforted on coming to the farm, seeing them grown and well cared for, yet now, almost as before, we were apart.

I missed them. I missed knowing what they were doing on the farm. I had such a short time with them. Only long enough to begin the knowing of them again, now I was away. This new life was rewarding and I liked it well, but to hear some news of them I would gladly welcome, but nothing came. It was as though when Declan and I left the farm the last day, a knife had severed us once more. I missed too, Mary and my cousin Seamus, and Jarlath. I missed my uncle's kind and patient ways. I missed the glint of his eye. And I missed my grandmother. I prayed, though these days I was unsure to who, for Jarlath to come knocking at Maura's door, and bring me my children, or at least some word of them.

Next morning as I put on my cap in readiness for our day in the chambers, we heard the footfall of a horse. Looking out the window, Maura said, "It's Jarlath."

Rushing out to greet him, this time with no risk of reproach, as I was, as instructed by him, dressed fully as a boy, clad in breeches, hair plaited and tied up, hidden well beneath my cap. How pleased I was to cast my eye upon him. "Uncle," I said, throwing my arms about his neck.

He stepped back, but smiled. "It does not do for a lad to be seen embracing another man with so much vigour; this is the greeting of a woman. Watch yourself lass. Remember what I told you. You best watch your way at all times. Let us go in the house."

I nside, I removed my cap, and threw my arms around Jarlath without worry. He smiled his usual smile. I was so thrilled to see him, my words could not come fast enough. Then a dark thought came to mind. Was he here bearing bad news? Had something happened? Was someone ill? "The children, are they all well?" I blurted.

"They're well. Everyone is well Orla. You have no need for concern."

The thrilling of seeing him came back to me. I listened with a keen ear as he told me in turn of each, and Mary, Seamus and Clodagh, my grandmother.

"And of yourself Uncle, what has occupied your time?" He looked deeply at me.

"There is little in my life worthy of being considered news. I work with the horses, organise the sale of them, clear the land of stones, and think on things. Nothing has changed since your leaving."

There was something in the way he spoke, that made me to think he'd come on this day with a particular thing in mind. "Uncle, what is it that brings you here today?"

He glanced at Maura, then looked back to me. "I wanted to talk with you both before going ahead with an idea I had. I think it would be grand if you'd both come for a visit to the farm. It's been a while. The young folk miss you. We all miss you. Maura could stay in the farmhouse, and you, Orla, in your cottage. If Declan hitched up a cart for you here, we could do the same our end for your coming back. Maura knows the way well enough. What do you say?"

"Well Jarlath, I think we do not need to hear Orla's words. Do her eyes not answer for her? And for myself, I would dearly love to spend time with Clodagh. I did not come to visit last time, so yes, we will come!"

"Grand, I'll set things in place."

We did not go to our harps that day as Jarlath stayed a long time with us. He took many mugs of tea, shared our midday meal, and talked much of my kin. My dear Uncle Jarlath! How grand it was to spend time with him. There was a bond between us two. I think he thought more on me as a daughter than a niece. Perhaps, he was thinking if his wife Niamh had not died in childbirth with Seamus, he might have had a daughter the likes of me. I could not explain my own feeling, nor would I ask of him his reason for this bond, bonds often being fragile in nature. And I have learned well the lesson that betimes we do not need to know, it's enough that things just be!

If all was to Declan's liking, it was arranged that Maura and I would go to the farm in one week. After Jarlath left I told Maura of the prayer I'd made the night before. Unlike me, she found no strangeness in his coming to visit. Doing the chores needing to be done before the closing in of the night, Maura spoke to me of things I found both strange and thrilling, things I wanted to know more of!

M aura told me that when we put our thoughts and words out into the air, they fall on the ears of those we cannot see. She said this is surely what'd happened when I made my prayer asking for news of my family. She asked me to think on a time when someone had spoken of another, perhaps someone who had for a long time, been absent. She told me simply thinking on a one, or speaking their name was enough to call them, or news of them, to the one who uttered their name. Maura, said of herself, living for seventy years, she'd seen this many times. I thought on this. I could not in truth, call to mind a thing of this nature, yet, recalled my own mother speaking so of this many times.

When I asked why it was that I did not have accounts of this to offer, Maura said she was sure I had, but had not listened, had not noted. Maura said our voices, our thoughts, the things we dream of, or desire, are heard, though we may not be aware, unless it is made so. When I asked how this might be done, she told me it was a simple thing to do, yet a thing that most do not. She told me one must open their heart and mind to the world, seek the wisdom from within, and without. Feel what is real, though you may not see it with your eyes. Feel what is right and true for you with your heart, for then, one can act with thought rather than rashness, and in this peace there is great power.

Had I called my uncle to me? Is this what Maura was saying? When I asked this, Maura told me that this was the truth of it. I'd sent my desire out into the air, and it'd been heard, and work was done to make it so. Work was done? There was much I did not understand and told Maura so. She assured me that in time I would come to know my world fully, yet for now, all I needed to do was open myself up to it; listen with my whole being. You will hear much she told me, some things will not be for you. I would know this, Maura said, I would feel this.

"Who is it that has done the work for me?"

"Not done for you, with you; the Old Ones. They are with you always."

Maura's words did not leave me. If my mother had known of this, why is it she had not spoken of this with me?

When I asked Maura, she said, "Perhaps your mother was afraid, or knew you not ready to open yourself to all that you can be. Perhaps it was your own fear that she protected you from. Perhaps she had a knowing of the power that lives within you, and knew the time for you to accept this had not yet arrived."

"I have no power."

"Ah, but you do."

"My whole life has been shaped by happenings and others. Do you not see that?"

"I see much Orla, and in time so will you. It will come. You do not have to seek the knowledge. You do not have to look for it, as it is not through the eyes, but, through the heart, that the knowing will make its path."

The morning after my uncle's visit, as we neared the abbey, Maura said she would go into town to talk with Declan, and I should make my way to the chamber. We both knew without words, that this unsettled me. I had not gone through the tunnels on my own. It seemed to me of late I was being tested in many ways, not all of them made me to feel easy.

Maura spoke of this as a chance to become a better, stronger, wiser woman. How, when asked to do things that troubled me, to ask myself, what is it makes me feel so? To use the answers to prise open, little by little, my heart of knowing. And if fear should rise up to do battle with me, then I should put out a call for guidance, and if my heart was open, it would be so. Reaching now the abbey, as Maura continued on down the lane, I made my way through the thicket growing among the crumbling stones to the brambles hiding the doorway, the beginning of my small, though daunting quest.

With hands less steady than I was used to, I took up the tinderbox and made a nest of some threads of jute. Holding the char cloth firmly on the flint, I struck it quickly and sharply with the striker. With little coaxing the char cloth began to glow. Placing it in the nest, I blew gently until the life of a flame came into being. I held a fine twig in the flame and lit the lamp that would show the way down to my harp. Once the lamp was burning, I stamped out the jute, it being useful for another light, then began along the tunnel.

With Maura by my side, I'd enjoyed walking along these passages. Today, I thought being alone, I'd like it less, yet, once I began on my way, this was not so. I still found great beauty in the stone slabs, my awe for them, pure, and my steps were made with ease. I'd walked many times to my harp following Maura, chattering and without much thought, and on this day, though I walked the same path, in the quiet, it was not the same.

I'd expected to be afraid, and indeed working with the tinderbox, had told to me the truth of it, yet now, fear did not travel with me. I did not feel alone! Was it the Old Ones who walked with me? I did not ask for help. Deciding firmly though I felt fear, I would not be hindered by it, or give any of my thoughts to it, that was all! Of this I would speak with Maura.

M aura did not come to the harp chamber as I thought she would. It mattered not. I attended well to my playing. First tuning and playing through my three tunes, practicing the ornamentations shown to me by Maura. I had not tried them in any of my tunes, as I could not yet get them to flow evenly in a sure way.

I enjoyed the time on my own with my harp, this was something I'd not had since my time on the farm. There, I had a lot of time to be with my harp, time I welcomed, now that time was gone. And when Maura and I went next to the farm for our visit, we would not take my harp. A visit of two days was too short a time to warrant the bagging and carrying of such a lumbering thing. This time would be spent with my kin. I so looked forward to be seeing them.

My hands on the harp were now beginning, for the most part, to work smoothly with each other. Though I still played only simple drones with my left. When Maura played, I noted her doing much more with her drone hand. Moving around and playing strings that became part of the melody or gave to the melody in some way. This was yet beyond my skill and a thing I hoped one day to be able to do. I passed the morning doing my set study, then took some rest from it, eating a little and drinking from my flask. When I sat back at my harp I played with my harp, rather than on my harp. The way Maura had told me to do in the days when the harp and me were new to each other.

I played small phrases with my right hand, my melody hand, then my left. Well, if the truth be known, I tried to. I found my left hand to be sluggish, awkward and contrary. Glad was I, to only have to contend with three fingers and my thumb on each hand, with the little finger being too short for the playing, having nothing to do but trail along. I tried a rising scale with my right hand, crossing my fourth finger under as Maura had shown me, playing eight notes, being what she called an octave, then playing back down crossing over with my thumb. This, I'd done many times with my melody hand. It knew the way, though when I tried with my left, my attempts were clumsy and awkward. If I was to get better at the harping, my drone hand would need to get quicker, stronger and more nimble.

On my return home, I spoke of this with Maura, asking her to give me some tasks to help both of my hands. Though knowing one hand to be the 'queen' and the other the 'ground', I could well see the need for both to be deft.

"Clodagh made a good choice when she named you to become the harper to bring peoples together and heal the spirits; you are a good pupil. Already you begin to teach yourself. Already you seek ways to improve your playing. I am blessed Orla! We are blessed, all of us, to play a small part in your becoming so!"

I felt humbled by the words Maura spoke. Yet, and though I did not say, the joy of the day was dimmed by the reminding of the burden that was mine to bear.

T he days of that week passed in the blink of an eye. I walked twice to Declan's, making my way there and returning without upset, though the truth of it, hearing the sounding of the whistle signalling my approach brought me great relief. I rode alone on Raven mostly in the galloping field, only one time going a short way down the path John the English-man had taken me the first time we rode together. I talked with him on my second visit, telling him of Maura and me going to the farm of my kin for a few days. I also spoke of my wanting to return to the place of holiness where he'd taken me on our last ride together. John gave his word he'd take good care of Raven, as was always his way, and that I should let him know when it was that I wanted to visit again the grove in the woodland, saying he'd gladly accompany me. Adding, that he welcomed any excuse to visit there.

Maura and I rose early on the morning of our leaving to ready ourselves and make sure the few chickens we kept had plenty of water and extra food to tide them over until our return. Though, Maura said with fond humour, they'd probably eat it all with little regard, being the gluttons they were and having a small brain! Back in the house, I packed a few things into my travel bag including a skirt and a shawl. I would not take my crane bag. There was no need. I'd travel as I always did, as a lad. Maura thought it best, saying we'd attract less attention travelling as perhaps, mother and son. I gave her a wink, saying that if I continued to dress as a man, perhaps one day, I might enjoy the privileges of one.

She replied, "And their woes."

J ust as we were finishing our packing, we heard the steady walking beat of a horse and the crunching roll of cart wheels on the earth. Maura opened the door for Declan. He came in wearing his handsome warm smile. Without our asking, he gathered our bags from near the door and carried them to the cart. Maura offered him a cup of tea, he refused saying he had work to do, and besides, we should begin making our way, it being a decent journey. Maura agreed, and we three went out the cottage door; Maura locking it ahint us.

I drew a loud gasp as I looked upon the horse hitched to the cart, quickly turning to Declan, wearing disbelief. He knew what had brought the look of shock upon my face, yet smiled, saying "I could hardly pack you off with an untried horse; this one will do you well, even though he has stockings of white." He winked a teasing eye.

Knowing Declan's love for this horse, I was troubled greatly. "But Declan," I began.

"No buts, Orla. Maura and my horse both well know the way, and I have trust in you enough for both of us. Now be on your way."

With not another word, he kissed Maura on the brow as was his way, and headed down the lane, leaving me to take up the reins of his beloved black.

# Chapter Twenty

# WAIFS

Though I held the reins, in truth, there was little for me to do. As Declan said, his black well knew the way. It was always a slow journey to the farm. We walked when we had to, and trotted where we could. Rocking and bumping along, Maura and I chatting, she, always good company. I'd often wondered how Maura had come to know my grandmother, they were bonded in a way closer than most. As we travelled, I asked. Maura told me the story of how and why this was so.

"One day, as I walked back from the town to my small house, I was drawn to the abbey, I know not by what. I walked by there often with never going in, only to enter the tunnels, and at that time, this being around fifty years ago, when the burning of the abbey was still fresh in our hearts, and an assault on our eyes; this was seldom. Though, I not being overly fond of religion of any sort, the wasteful destruction of the work of many men's hands disgusts me to this day. The seeking of power and greed can urge a man to do awful things... back to your grandmother.

"On that day, the building being not so forlorn as it is now, I walked in through the doorway and found huddled ahint a wall, three waifs; two women and a young man. They were dirty, starving and covered in scratches and sores, the younger woman of the two, was with child. As I approached, the young man attempted to shield the women, yet, so weak, he could barely lift his arms. I spoke gently to them, looking as I did, into the older woman's eyes, she placed her hand on the shoulder of the young man, telling him that they were in no danger. She was right to do so, for my only want was to help them. Though I knew nothing about them, I could feel a power living within the older woman, a woman though only known to me for moments, I felt strongly connected to her. I could feel that she too shared this knowing.

"I took them into my small house, and with me they stayed until they were repaired. Though the younger woman, Niamh, never regained fully her strength. I learned much of Clodagh during those weeks. She is a most remarkable woman, and one that I have much love for. She told me a vision had brought them here when they ran from Duleek escaping death. In the vision there was a farm, a farm for sale, one she would purchase, and they would begin their lives again. I knew well the farm she spoke of. Round here in those days, everybody knew everyone's business. It's not so these days with the coming of more English... anyways, the sale was made with no time lost; Clodagh having the money, and the farmer a great desire to be rid of the property.

"The farm was very run down, so the three stayed on with me, though Clodagh and Jarlath spent most of their days making the house fit for living in. When this was done, all three moved. They'd only been gone a few days, when Jarlath came running, saying the wean was coming, but it was not going well for Niamh, and would I help. We ran as fast as we could; no horses in them days. When we arrived the wean was already born, yet, Niamh was weak and suffering. Jarlath cradled her, and as their wean took his first breaths, Niamh took her last. And that is the story of my meeting with Clodagh!"

As her story came to an end, so too, did our journey. We were greeted with much excitement. Paeder, always first to my side embracing me and kissing my cheek, saying how he missed me. Kathleen, though less awkward with me nowadays, kissing me too, yet quickly stepping back. Then came Conor, with his quiet way. Smiling, saying nothing, only embracing me with a warmth I felt in my very heart. Then Mary. Dear kind, round Mary, embracing me, kissing my cheek, then stepping back to stand with Seamus. As she did, he placed his arm round her shoulder. My mind ran to thinking this was the life Jarlath once hoped for him and Niamh? One that never was. Jarlath, just nodded and gave to me the smallest love-filled wink.

Conor took our bags from the cart, as Mary bustled us into the house with much exciting talk of the food she'd prepared, and telling us of Granny's waiting to see us. Her tumbling words speaking her pleasure in having us come to stay. Mary set a pot of tea to brewing as Maura and I made our way to my grandmother's room. There she stood, awaiting our arrival looking as she always did. Upright, earnest and proud. Try as I might, I could not see her in a bedraggled state, such as a one Maura described her to be on their first meeting. Though there was nothing about Clodagh Moran's appearance marking her from any other woman, there was an air about her, telling her to be sharply different! As Uncle Jarlath had said, she was a rare one.

Glancing first to Maura with her love for her fellow woman clearly showing, then stepping across the room to me. "Orla, dear granddaughter, it is good to see you," she said, embracing me. "I trust my dear friend Maura, is proving to be a good companion, and a fine teacher." I cast a look to Maura, nodding. "Come, let us go to the kitchen, Mary has been fussing for days. I am certain we will be treated to a grand fare."

Before we left the room, my grandmother moved to Maura, placing a hand on each of her shoulders, she looked into Maura's eyes, then placed a long kiss on her cheek. Maura did the same.

As we sat at the table, all my living kinfolk, and Maura, feasting on Mary's lovingly prepared food, Niamh came to my thoughts. I knew little of her. No one spoke of her, not even Jarlath, yet, on that day, I felt her there with us. I looked to my grandmother, and the look she returned, without words, told me she knew what it was I felt.

Suddenly Paedar's voice fell upon my ear. "Mammy, you must be well in with Declan to have him trust you with his horse. Never a once have I known him to surrender his fine black to another."

My face flushed at his words. "I think it his concern for Maura having more to do with his decision for sending us with his trusted horse, rather than his trust in me." I said quickly, trying to cover my discomfort. Paedar did not appear to notice my lack of ease, and went on.

"Tell Declan he was much missed at our table, and it is our hope he will soon pay us a visit."

"Mary, you've done yourself proud once more," I said in an attempt to shift the talk. "What have you all been doing while I've been gone? How is the garden, and the horses? I'll be looking to help with the chores while I'm here. I didn't bring my harp, this visit being a brief one, so I'll be looking to having my hours filled." I was wanting it to be known, especially to Paedar, that Maura and I were on the farm for only a short time, for he was always the one to find my leaving most hard.

Our meal over, I asked Conor where he put my bag. Collecting this, I walked across to the cottage that I had, all too briefly, considered my home. Opening the door, glad I was to see it just as it was on my leaving. I put down my bag, removed my cap and hung it on the hook, looking forward to once more spending the night under the roof of this small room.

That first afternoon, I spent working with the young folk in the kitchen garden; so much had it grown. Being with my children, working in this way with the plants and the earth, had been missed by me. Though Maura had a small kitchen garden we tended, such was its size, with two people to do work, it took little effort to keep the weeds at bay, and pick its produce. Being so far from the town, this garden providing most of the food for the household, was large, and much sweat ran from the brow of those who toiled for its harvest.

In the evening, it was planned I'd work in the stables the next morning, though the afternoon, my grandmother made clear, I would spend with her. Paedar, as was his way, offered protest to the sharing out of my time, saying this should not be needed, and I should be back to living here among my kin. This I quickly quieted, assuring him of my comfort living with Maura, shortening the time for my learning to become a harper. Also, I reminded him that it was not far from here to Cill Ala, and visits in both directions could be made with ease. This satisfied him.

Laying in my bed that night, I thought on what it might be that my grandmother would speak to me of on the morrow. With Clodagh, I was never to know what was coming. The wise sage with a hint of mischief and adventure; I fell to sleep with the wondering upon me.

# CHAPTER TWENTY-ONE

# THE SPIDER'S WEB

It was most pleasing to be in the stables. The smell of the horses, the straw, and the steaming of oats; a smell that foretold the selling of horses. It was the way Jarlath had in readying them for sale, giving them this special treat a few times in the weeks before their leaving. Having such a liking for the smell of it, and it not being a regular thing, I thought myself fortunate to be working here in the stables on this day.

The dry oats were put in a large pot, and placed atop the fire that Seamus and Jarlath used when fashioning shoes for the horses, or creating or mending a tool for the farm, or the making of char cloth, though for the oats the fire was a gentle one, not fierce as it was when used for forging metal. The pot was only filled one-third with the dry hard oats then covered with water. Once they got hot enough the smell would rise. An odd smell, a smell once known, was to remain always known. Though being made of the same grain, the smell was nothing like porridge. It had more of the smell of bread on a fork held above the embers until it turned golden, a comforting smell.

The first time I saw Uncle Jarlath cooking up the oats, I thought it odd to use such a big pot and put so little in, but once they were covered with water and on the heat, the grains swelled filling the pot. Then came the understanding of why the pot was to be only a third filled. When cooked and cooled, the steamed oats were mixed with other things, such as bran and molasses, and shared among the horses being sold. Uncle Jarlath told me that by cooking the oats in this way, the horses would gain condition, yet, not be made too lively as they were when given the dry oats. Being new to the caring of horses, whether this be so or not, I cannot say. All I can say, is the horses very much enjoyed this treat, and to cast an eye over them, the horses bred and stabled by my kin, was to see the most glorious of beasts. That be the truth of it.

As everyone milled about doing their tasks, I was struck by how fit and strong they all were; the heavy work keeping them so. For myself, this was not so! The many hours spent sitting at my harp, plucking its strings, had found me less strong than when I began the journey of the harper. I knew when waking on the morrow, my muscles would be sore from the carrying of buckets of water, mucking out stalls, and the hay carting, yet tonight, I also knew that sleep would easily find me, rewarding me the toil of the day.

"Come in my dear! Maura has been telling me all about how well you are doing with the harp. She says that over the past few months you have made much progress. Indeed, Maura tells me you play as well as one who has been at the learning for a year or more. When next you visit, I ask that you bring your harp, and play for us. We would very much like to hear you."

Though I knew the purpose of my learning with Maura was to someday play for the ear of others, I did not think it to be so soon upon me. Unsettled by the thinking on it, I was glad to have not brought my harp on this visit. Glad too, was I that Maura was in the room with us, thinking her being here, would make the knowing of my mind a harder thing for my grandmother.

Taking a seat, I looked from one woman to another. So different they were, and so different was I from each! Clodagh, my grandmother, though sharing blood, I did not know well. I'd spent so little time with her, and her having the knack of knowing, was to me, unsettling. This, I did not think her meaning but a burden that comes with being blessed with the second sight, a gift I think most would not look upon with much joy; the knowing of a thing before its happening. Though at times allowing for some readying, it must I'm sure, be most terrifying, and cause much troubling to one's thoughts.

And Maura, the one these days I was with most often. The wise woman who gave to me counsel in many more things than the learning of the harp, the one who always had a way to advise, comfort, and put me at my ease. Looking at these two women sitting together, it was plain, how close they were. I did not think if a choice be given, though not bonded by blood, that either would choose another to be their friend and companion. Though I know it wrongful, I envied their union.

"You will be leaving for Cill Ala in the morning, so I wanted to share a vision visited upon me. I do not know when this will be, yet, as it involves you both, I believe it right to tell you of it together."

My grandmother's words were of no surprise to me, for there was always a cause to her bidding. Maura, with their friendship being over many years, would too, be well used to the utterances of Clodagh. And in them even more than me, I'm sure, would find no bewilder!

My grandmother spoke of a journey that Maura and I would take. The details of which were scant. Of where we would go or when this would be, she could not say, only that it would take us to another land. She had seen a boat, harps and many trees. As these words left her lips, Maura and I looked to each other, then back to Clodagh. Her face told us, this was where her vision had ended. For now, that was all she had to tell, yet, assured us, this was often the way of the visions. They made their way in bits and pieces. She would tell us more when she knew more.

With our cart hitched to Declan's black, our goodbyes bidden, this time made less painful in the knowing we'd return, and visits by my kin to Maura's cottage always welcome, we set off on our return journey. At first Maura and I spoke of the vision shared with us by my grandmother. Yet, with knowing little of this, Maura advised it not wise to wonder what might be involved, saying that the mind often had a way of making up awfulness or dangers, that in truth, may not be the way of things. With the only thing really told in the vision being that Maura and I would some time travel across the water, my interest shifted to the other thing my grandmother Clodagh Moran, had spoken of.

"Did Clodagh speak with you of my playing the harp for my kin?"

Without blinking Maura told me it was at her prodding the request had been made. The fear I felt caused me to tighten my grip on the reins, the black responded by trotting a few steps. I spoke quietly to him and pulled him back, for to go faster on this part of the road could end badly, perhaps tipping the cart. Or worse, us and Declan's fine black, being made prisoners of the marshy bog that made its cruel way up to the edge of the road.

Not feeling ready to play for others, I asked. "Why did you not talk to me? Why would you do such a thing to me Maura?"

"I did not do it to you Orla, I did it for you! Such do you doubt yourself, if the decision to play for others be left with you, then never would we hear your music. This is the way for you to begin, and you are right, at this moment, you are not ready, we will make you ready. We will prepare both your music and your mind. This is the way it begins. First, you will play for your kin, the ones who love you. We will, you and me, make certain that your first outing goes well. Then we will choose with care the next ears for your music to fall upon. You must trust me on this Orla. I'll not be asking more of you than I know you can give. Know though, you may sometimes find things troubling as the life of a harper becomes the way of your life. Such is the way of it."

There were long silences as Maura and I sat on the bench of the cart, following the rump and long flowing tail of Declan's black. He was a tall handsome horse, well muscled and reliable. I blushed as I thought on him having the qualities of his owner. Checking myself, I returned to think on what it might be like to play my harp for those other than Maura. Dearest Maura, I did trust her! Always had she been steady and kind to me, offering sound advice, whether asked for or freely given. And her skill and teachings as a harper had seen me make progress more quickly than ever I had thought. Much more than the plucking of strings did this woman teach me in her wise and gentle way.

Her high regard for the music was solid, and sown into me was the value of knowing as much as one can of the story of the music. A tune was not a thing to be treated with coldness, no matter how small, or with what lilt or noble strain it be from. They were all to be prized. For Maura, all music was an offering made to this world, and the otherworld, the place where the Old Ones dwelt. I believe myself truly blessed to have a tutor of such quality as Maura. One who understands the pain I carry, yet one who can bring forth the joy and laughter that lives within me, that until more recent times rarely showed its face.

"Turn down this path."

Maura's words brought me back from my thoughts. I did not know this path, yet, did as told. Maura had lived here for many years. How long, I did not know. Yet, I knew it to be longer than my lifetime. My hand light on the reins, hardly moved, and the black turned as if to know as well the way.

"We'll go directly to Declan's, he can come with us and take the cart back."

The black now trotted as if knowing him nearly home. The steady beating of his hooves giving an assuring rhythm in harmony with the passing trees and flashes of sunlight falling between them. Looking up, I noted the position of the sun. I was not only fortunate to have Maura. There were others that had shown me kindness and a willingness to share their wisdom and skills, and in whose company we would shortly be.

The whistle sounded well before the gates came into view. The black lifted his head a little. Pricking up his ears he quickened his step, slowing only when the gate was reached. Greeting the gatekeeper, and he us, we made our way toward the big house, stopping by the door. I was more used to the people milling about now having been a few times when coming to ride Raven. I waited in the cart while Maura went in to tell Declan of our return. She came back alone saying we were not expected so early in the day and he was working at the building of a boat.

"Wait here. I'll see if John's around. He'll take us if he has the time."

She was not gone long, coming back with John the Englishman at her side. How tall he looked beside Maura! As he gave me his greeting, I began to make move thinking I'd ride in the cart and he would drive. Raising his hand, he sprang into the back of the cart.

"You're in charge Orla, drive on."

Taking up the reins to the disappointment of the black, I turned him around, his step now not so sprightly. I, not being used to driving the cart, made it clear that though willing to hold the reins, I was re-lying on my two companions to be the pathfinders! All three of us knowing why this was said, laughed.

As we journeyed, I asked of Raven. John, laying back in the cart, looking to be most at ease, told me, that between himself and Declan, she'd been well cared for. John added that he thought Declan in missing his black, though not riding out on her, had treated Raven as he would his own horse. These two men, unbeholding to me, had treated me with a kindness that might be given only to kin, and for this and the care of my horse, I was indeed grateful.

Following their clear directions, it was little time before we were stood in front of Maura's small house. John jumped down, grabbing our bags, he placed them by the door. I stepped down from the cart, and handing the reins to John, thanked him. Maura embraced him, as was her way, and readied her key. With it being so few months since I left Duleek, never would I have thought to feel a comfort to be in the presence of an Englishman, yet with John, this was the way of it.

"Ah, it matters not how long one is away, it's always good to be home, don't you think?"

I did not answer, for I had no answer to give. This was not my home. Though it a place where I felt a comfort, I did not yet think of it as my home. I did not think anywhere, anymore, was there a place for me to call home. I thought it once the cottage at my kinfolk's farm would be my home, yet, that was not to be. And here in Maura's house, it was just that, Maura's house. I felt a comfort in returning to a place familiar to me, though still, I could not call this place my home. One day, perhaps my want to be settled and live a safe, quiet life might be realised, but that time had not come, and my grandmother's vision had told me, it would not come, at least for a time.

After taking a midday meal together, Maura and I unpacked and went about the few chores needing to be done. With the wood brought in, the chickens fed, and the evening meal seen to, Maura asked, before heading into the town, what it was I might be up to while she was away. I told her I'd go to my harp for a few hours. Though, not keen in the beginning, I'd now come to finding my way, and being in the chamber alone, a pleasing thing.

We walked together as far as the abbey, Maura continuing along the lane to town, and me going among the brambles to the tunnel. As I walked within the fallen walls of the abbey I thought on which wall it'd been that Maura had found my grandmother, Jarlath and Niamh huddled by. How odd it was to think on my kin as hungry, frightened waifs! How luck had shone on them to be found by one with such a kind heart as Maura. Poor dead, fragile Niamh; unknown to me! And Jarlath my uncle, though well hidden from most, forever bearing the constant hint of sadness. Not a one of us can truly know what will come to us in life, or death!

In the chamber, I played most times that day, the lament. Drawn to it, I was. I did my tuning, and played my two other tunes, yet kept returning to the lament. On thinking on Niamh, it was the one most fitting. I offered the tune as my way of honouring her. A kinswoman I had never met, yet, would forever be bound to by a silken thread from which the web of life is spun. A web that none can understand. The making of it a mystery. The ensnaring ways of it a mystery; a gleaming magic work of nature, both at once beautiful and deadly, and one from that none can escape.

# CHAPTER TWENTY-TWO

# THE UNSEEN

"Today we'll begin preparing for your first time playing out," said Maura, striking the flint to light the lamp.

Though there be a small amount of light at the end of the tunnel by the brambles, it only took a few steps to be veiled in blackness, a solid blackness where not even a trace of one's own shadow could be found. Down in the tunnels was an otherworldly place, so quiet the only sounds being footsteps and breath. A place, when on my own I could hear my heartbeat; how peaceful was this dark, silent place.

On this day, on any day, I would have rathered be alone with my harp, not making ready to show my skill, or lack of, as a harper. Had I not the trust in Maura's counsel and the binding of my duty, I might have tried to put off the playing. Though never was I a one to be beaten by my own fear!

Tilting the harp back, feeling the light balance of wood on my shoulder, the stretch of the strings as my fingers pulled and let go in the readying, the smell of the timber so close to my face and the quiver of the soundbox against my body as the harp began to sing, these days, gave me much pleasure. Gone was the awkward discomfort that was mine the first time I sat at the harp. Now with my feet on the ground, and notes of the harp softly ringing out into the air, I truly believed myself to be at once, joined to both the earth and the heavens.

"P ut up your harp, Orla. The work will not begin with playing. First, we must make your mind ready. The playing for others can see the mind become a trickster. It will try to speak in a way that will feed the doubt you already have in yourself, so we first need to put that rogue in his place."

I never was to think that making me ready to play the harp for the ears of others, would begin with me not playing. I thought it to be, playing over and over the pieces, yet Maura told to me this a mistake many have made. Playing out must begin with the head, not the hand!

Picking up her stool Maura moved it away from her harp, asking me to bring my stool to sit beside her.

"Close your eyes."

I did as she bid. She then asked of me to bring a thing to my mind, an object, something I valued, something that meant something to me. One would expect it be Raven, yet it was not! Instead a big oak tree, one I'd seen with Declan, came to my mind's eye. The wind was blowing through its branches, waving and bending with the force of the air.

"What do you see?" I told her of my vision. "Good, that will be your anchor. Now each time before you play, close your eyes, see the tree, and breathe it into you, deep into your belly. And call to the Old Ones, they will help you. They will give you strength."

I did not touch my harp again that day, but practiced bringing the vision of the tree to my mind's eye, and calling in the Old Ones. This was strange to me, and unsure I was of my way. Yet, Maura spoke of this being bound by trust and intention. So long as these were present, then all would be well.

That evening Maura asked what it was the tree held for me, why it was I'd called it in. At first, I could not say, but with her urging, I came to know. It was its bending, the way it could yield to the wind, yet not break. It was its strength, the way it could stand tall against the destructive gusting; that it could endure, for me it represented myself, my land and its people.

It was three more days before I put my harp to my shoulder. I spent those days going through the closing of my eyes, visioning my tree, calling in the Old Ones, and thinking on why I was becoming a harper. When Maura asked the question of why, unlike the visioning of the tree, for me the purpose was clear. The words of my grandmother rang loudly in my ear.

*The people of our land need you to do this! They are divided! Their hearts and spirits are broken! Only you and the harp can bring about the mending!*

I truly know what it is to suffer as many in our land have suffered, yet, in my new life I had begun to know the early buds of healing. Raven, friendship, and the playing of the harp had softened my pain. If my music could, even if only in part, do this for others, then when the time came for me to go to my grave, I would go content with my effort.

"Take your stool back to your harp Orla. Bring your harp to your shoulder, but do not play." I did as asked. "Now, close your eyes and bring forth your oak. Do you see it?"

"Yes."

"Now breathe in the Old Ones. Good. Now tip your harp away and open your eyes."

This was the work we did on that day, over and over, broken up by talk of my reason for taking on the harp. Maura, told to me this work was as important, perhaps more so, than the plucking of the strings. Trusting Maura, I did not question her wisdom, for never a once had she given me bad counsel. And her playing of the harp, being so powerful and moving, gave me a knowing she would do what she could to make of me, the best harper I could be!

Day after day the work continued. Walking in the tunnels, we talked of my reason for harping, setting it deep in my thinking. This was never done in such a way as to make it stale, Maura was much too wise for that. It was told to me through stories.

Interesting, and rousing stories, making my wanting to learn grow strong. After a few days, though still not playing, I did place my hands. I sat at my harp, bringing it to my shoulder, closing my eyes, visioning my anchor the oak tree, breathing in the Old Ones, then on Maura's word, opening my eyes, I raised my hands to the strings. This we did time after time throughout the day. Some may have found it tiresome, I did not. I kept in my mind the work of the stonemasons. Slowly but surely laying one stone atop another, with faith in their hearts that one day a fine building would come into being.

E ach day Maura would have me build on a little. First, it was the placing of the hands on the strings, next came the plucking of them. Then I would take my hands away and do it again. When Maura thought these stones laid, she had me lay another; the beginning of one of my tunes. The tune she chose was the one of the noble strain Suantrai, it being the one I knew least well. This she said would serve me best. Her knowing the bones of the Geantrai tune, being my first, and the Goltrai, being my best liked, were well under my hands.

She was right; I struggled. She offered little help, saying it be better for me to search inside myself to find the notes. Little by little, I found the tune. Each time I stumbled, Maura would tell to me to close my eyes, vision my oak and breathe in the Old Ones, then begin again. This she said was giving me the doorway to a place where I could play from the heart with a knowing of peace and confidence. I cannot say in the early part of this learning, I felt either. Though, I believed her words to be true.

As the days wore on, it slowly came to me. As I tilted back my harp, my eyes would close, my tree was there, and my breath came deep and full. Doing this taking less time and effort than in the beginning. Maura, told to me, that it would, in time, just become part of my playing.

We went on like this with me playing all three tunes, breaking in between to do the visioning. When I could do this with ease, Maura, said it was time to choose the order the tunes would be played. She gave me the task of choosing if the Goltrai or Suantrai was to be first, saying there'd be no choice needed for the last piece, as this would be the Geantrai. It would not do, said Maura, to leave those I played for in a state of sadness; much better on my first outing to leave those who gave their ears to my music, to be left with joy in their hearts.

I chose the lament to be my first tune, as it was the one I played well, and the one with which I was most akin. Maura laughed knowingly. Once the order was decided, we spoke of the ornamentation. I had a love for the bones of the tunes, caring much less for the fancying up of it. Maura said, my own style was developing, and I should only use the ornaments when I believed them to bring something to the melody. In truth, I found few places where I had a want to play the ornaments. Maura let me to be on this, saying for the most part, such was my touch on the harp, little else was needed. Some, she said, when harpers were more widely found in Ireland, were not of this thinking, with some taking from, rather than giving to, the melody... the queen!

With all choices made, and my visioning, and breath growing stronger, Maura made sure that now after the tuning, I practiced my three pieces as I intended to play them. Betimes Maura, would clap when I was mid-tune, or speak to me, perhaps asking a question. When first she did this, I stopped playing. Like most things with Maura though, she had a reason for doing what she was doing. She told to me, no matter what she did, I was not to stop playing. This was not an easy thing, for she had a great many tricks. She coughed, spoke to me, walked about me, played her own harp, all as I was playing. It was most unsettling! When I could keep playing, paying her no mind, she was most pleased. Maura told to me that when playing out, these things I might meet, and best to be at ease with them now in the chamber rather than being met with them for the first time in someone's parlour.

Playing in someone's parlour! This was not a thing I'd given much time to the thinking on. Maura said it was best I began the thinking on it, and I should begin the thinking of learning more tunes. Three would do for the playing to my kin, but for the ear of those I'd play for in time to come I'd be needing more, many more!

I n these past few weeks, there'd been little time to go to Declan's. Much did I miss Raven! Maura's wisdom though was such that she knew when the learning became too much, and we'd have a brisk walk, and short visit. Sometimes, she'd send me on my own. Knowing the way well now, on these times, I'd run parts of the path such was my eagerness. One time, in those few weeks, Maura had business to attend to at the big house, and we stayed long enough for me to have a ride in the field, it filled me with such joy! I knew John was taking Raven out when I could not, and for this I was grateful, though a little jealous. He was kind to her, and she fond of him, so when I could not stretch her legs, there was not a better person could stand in my place. Though, he be an Englishman.

As we walked back through the woodland that day, Maura told me she'd spoken with Declan about when we'd go next to my kin. She said Declan would take us, and my harp. My stomach tightened.

"So Declan will come to hear me as well?" I asked.

"He will. We'll be going in five days. You'll be playing for those who love you Orla. They've a wanting for you to do well. And you are ready! They'll be kind, and not expecting more of you than you can give. You be playing nicely! And if your heart is good, your intention clear, and you think the music more important than yourself, all will be well. You'll be grand!"

Glad I was knowing this with time to prepare. I cannot tell why, but it was important to me that I'd not be making a fool of myself in front of Declan.

I did not go to visit Raven in those five days, instead devoting all my time to working at my harp. I spent long days, visioning, breathing, calling in the Old Ones. Much did I call in the Old Ones! Help me! Give to me courage! Make me strong I would pray to them as I closed my eyes in making myself ready for the playing.

On the second to last day before our leaving, as I did this, a voice came into my head.

*All you ask is for yourself, yet, you pay little heed to what you've been taught. Where does your intention lay? Remember why you're doing this. It is not for yourself. You're not the important one. It's the music and what it brings to those who listen that's important. You are only the one who places the hand on the strings. It's the music that touches the heart. You are only the bringer of this. Do not forget that, never forget that.*

I swear, so loud and clear was that voice, a man's voice. I opened my eyes looking for the one who spoke those words. No one could I see, yet I knew them to be there!

The day arrived, and after midday, so did Declan with his fine black and my harp. As we went, me sitting in the back of the cart with my bagged harp for company. I thought much on the playing I'd be doing that night. The words and the question, asked to me by the unseen in the chamber staying with me. What was my intention?

My wanting to be worthy of the duty given me, my wanting to be of good service to my people so strong now burdened me. I'd allowed the weight of it to steal from me the joy of playing. A joy I knew well when I played alone in the chamber. I'd done what Maura had warned me against, I'd let myself get in the way of the music! If I am to be a harper that can bring the healing, then I must step aside. I must work truly from heart to harp reaching out to the souls of those who listened, bringing joy and healing to them. On this, I must remain clear, for this is my intention!

A s we arrived into the farmyard, my kin there to
greet us, Declan stepped down from the cart
coming to the back and giving me his hand to help
me down. Though I was in no need of his help, I took
his hand. His touch though brief, rose in me such a
warmth I'd not known for many a year. A warmth
that in the first years of marriage I'd known with my
own dear, dead husband. I turned my face to allow
the heat in it to cool. As I did, Declan pulled my harp
from the cart.

"Where do you want it?" he asked. "I can take it to
the house, or your cottage."

To think of eyes on me as I battled it from its cover,
gave rise to a tightening in my belly. "Leave it here,
I'll take it to the cottage for tuning, and bring it over
after we have taken our meal."

As I lay the harp on the bed removing the cover, I
thought on the feeling that Declan's touch had given
rise to. I knew it well to be that of desire. Though
alone, thinking on this caused a thrill to flood my
whole body. My bosom rose, and my face blushed,
my breath grew deep with longing. I shook myself.
This was not the time to be thinking on this. I was
here as a harper, not a woman!

And Declan had given me no cause to think him
giving me his hand was anything more than good
manners. I knew well from his own lips he was
bound to remain an unmarried man, and when he'd
chided me for my curt treatment of John the Englishman, his words were, *that if we were to remain*

*friends.* A friend is the only way he looked on me. To want or expect more, would be foolish, and I'd behaved foolishly before Declan O'Malley already more times than I had a want. I would not do so again!

With the evening meal done I went to the cottage to collect my harp and stool. Giving my harp a check for the tuning, I carried them to the farmhouse, down the long hallway to my grandmother's room. This was a large room, taking us ten, and my harp with ease. I stood my harp in the only bare corner of the room, just inside the doorway, and placed my stool ahint. I was glad of the chatter going on as it made me to feel less that the eyes of all were on me. As I took up my seat, Uncle Jarlath gave to me his look. The one that always brought a pleasing to me, a look of both mischief and affection.

I closed my eyes for an instant, and breathed in the Old Ones, hoping they would come, though still not certain of how I might know. Opening my eyes, I began to tell of the piece I'd play. Maura had taught me to first tell of the music, if known, before playing so people would better understand from where it came. Closing my eyes for an instant, breathing deep into my belly, I opened them and with my heart beating loudly in my ears, I raised my ever so slightly trembling hands to the strings. Now I knew the value of Maura's teachings.

Aware of my beating heart, it offered no distraction, and though my hands trembled throughout the piece, I knew it well enough for this to neither hinder, nor take away from the beauty of the music. The first piece was always the most difficult Maura had told me. Once this was played, the trembling grew less and the thumping of my heart grew quiet.

I told of, and played my other two pieces. Though not without flaws, they were such that no one seemed to notice them imperfect, except Maura and myself. Being taught through Maura's distracting ways, and her ordering me to never stop playing in the middle of a tune, I had already the skill of being able to get on, if an unexpected note should ring from my harp, and to pretend it part of the music. A skill I'd only to use few times, but was yet glad to be in the having of it.

With my playing over, I could now rest easy and enjoy the being with my kin. Declan had brought some of his fine mead, which had been keenly shared by all during my playing. Having refused the offer before, I now accepted a glass, sipping and swallowing the sweet nectar that Declan seemed to have an endless supply of.

My grandmother came to me, taking up my hands in hers, she said, "Orla, your playing is just as I knew it would be. Not gilded, mild, with a power from the very first note that touches the heart. You have done well child! I knew you to be the one for this task, and you have seen me right."

With that, she embraced me, her lips close to me ear, and before placing a long kiss on my cheek, she whispered, "Choose wisely the one you give your affections to."

There was much congratulating me that evening. I swelled from their kind words, yet only a little, remembering it was the music that was important, not me. My uncle, giving to me his look again, and my sons embracing me, saying they couldn't believe how quickly I'd learned the tunes. And Kathleen, my dearest daughter, spoke as she had before, "I am so proud that you do this for your kin and country, I wish it were me."

In this moment, there seemed little but pleasure to be found in the learning of the harp, yet, I and others knew the danger these times could bring to those who chose the life of a harper. For this, I rathered it be my task, and not one of my children. Though I did not desire death, I had lived at least some of my life, theirs was yet to come.

# CHAPTER TWENTY-THREE

# UNTOUCHED

Making our way back to Cill Ala, sitting in the back of the cart, I thought on many things. I thought on the feelings Declan's touch gave life to in me, and my grandmother's words. Were they spoken because she knew what I'd felt, or were they just a grandmother's words of advice to her granddaughter? And why was it I had risen to Declan's touch in such a way? Had I, without thinking, grown drawn to him? I could not deny I found him to be a handsome man, no one could deny this, for one only had to look upon him to know him so. True, he'd shown me kindness, yet no more than that. Was it that his touch caused me to rise simply because, for so long, I had not known the touch of a man?

My husband, being older than me, had shown no interest in me as a woman for many years. Perhaps this was due to the constant weariness brought about by the hard work in keeping us from the threat of starvation, lining our unkind landlord's pocket, the one who menaced us with eviction ever given the slightest cause. Was it, the man I married, though in the early days of our marrying told to me I was his treasure, had no longer found me so? Or was it the veil of shame thrown over us all the night the English soldiers came calling? We'd never spoken of his reasons, and him now being dead, never would we!

With him newly dead, to think on matters such as these was foolish and wrong. For now, I would only give my heart to Raven and my harp, having been charged with the becoming of a harper. On these, and nothing else, would I place my concern.

Aware now, Declan urging his fine black to a trot, that our journey would soon be at an end, I turned my thinking to other things. I thought on the night before. My playing had gone well, for that, I was pleased. And the joy of seeing my kin swelled my heart, yet, I also thought on why it was that Declan had not made any approach to me, or spoken any word of my playing. Was it not to his liking?

No! This was not a place for my mind to go. Maura had warned me against this. As a true harper, I must not use my playing to gain the favour of another, the music was always to be the more important. I closed my eyes and let the steady beat of hooves quieten my mind. The warm summer sun shining down on my face made me to be dreamy; in my mind's eye, Raven came to me, how I missed her lovely dark eyes. Only to her would I ever speak my secrets.

The visit, and playing for my kin now over, life returned to a more even pace. Maura began the teaching to me of a new tune, saying the lament was not a tune to be played for all. Now it would be best I learn two more Gentrai tunes before I played for others again. This caused me no bother as I was still able to play the lament down in the chamber. The new tunes were both of a pleasing nature and the learning of their bones now came more easy, though the singing of them I enjoyed less.

I was once again able to make more regular visits to Raven. Mostly, I rode her in the galloping field with short rides down the path now becoming more familiar to me. Each time I went a little further along, getting to know the trees, and the turns of the path. I never went too far though, riding alone as I was. The fear of the unknown, and of losing my way still with me, though not so much now as I practiced the watching of the sun, and the noting of landmarks. I also watched Raven's ears. Always alert, she'd let me know of things moving in the trees, mostly birds and squirrels, sometimes a fox. Mostly liking to ride quietly, one day I saw a vole skittering about collecting nuts and mushrooms; such joy!

On my visits to Raven, I rarely saw John the Englishman. The care and exercising of many horses taking up his time, much of it outside of the stables. Betimes I would encounter him in the field working a horse on a long rope or riding one of them. We'd exchange a few words, but mostly only a few, as he busy, and I there to spend time with Raven. I did one time though, ask him if he might have the time to take me again to that lovely green grove, the one to where he'd taken me before the getting ready for my playing out had taken up most of my hours. He said he'd be delighted to accompany me as this was one of his most favoured places. We could go in three day's time if the weather was kind.

The next two days, it rained without stopping. It mattered not. Maura and me being sheltered by our thick woollen brats, spent most of our hours down in the dry agreeable chambers, or within the warmth of her small house. I now had the two new tunes under my hands, though not smoothly yet. But with each day, and much practice, my playing was improving. Maura said soon, we'd begin on some ornaments, as the noble strain of Geantraí lent itself most readily to the having of these. Maura was mindful to add, these would be few, respecting my now budding way of playing.

With the weather being so unkind, I thought it unlikely that the planned ride to the grove would come about, but, as we slept the rain stopped, and we awoke to a clear day. When I'd told Maura, on the return of my last visit to Raven, of my wanting to spend the whole day riding she'd been most agreeable. For now, my learning filled most of her days, leaving little time for her own self. Though, she was most gracious about this, never complaining, not a once, like me, her life was now very different to the one she had known before my coming. We did our chores, and with enough food for two, and a flask packed in my bag, I set out.

My going was slower than usual with the path, though always damp, being now very muddy and in places found me needing to walk among the trees alongside its edge. Never did I recall so many birds as that day. Singing and flying as if to be rejoicing in the clear air. Like us, perhaps the past days had seen them huddled in their nests, taking what shelter they could among the leaves.

Eventually, I heard the whistle and saw ahead the large stone gate posts. I stopped now, and finding a stick, scraped my boots. They, from the walk, were now heavy and ugly with the mud. Not boots fit for placing in a stirrup, or pressing to the sides of a fine mount. Once scraped, to finish the cleaning, I gathered up some wet leaves, of which there were plenty, and rubbed them over, glad that the road at the end of my walk was a firm one.

It was mid-morning and John was working in the stables when I arrived. He greeted me, remarking on the kindness of the weather, and we set about readying our horses. It was little time before we began on our ride, John as eager as me to visit the grove. There'd be no galloping on this day with the ground in the field being made boggy by the heavy constant rain. I gave it no mind, glad I was just to be sitting atop Raven, looking forward to reaching the grove. We spoke little as we rode along, both content to take in the beauty of the trees, with their dark bark and their leaves glistening, made bright by the washing they'd had.

When we arrived at that special place, we tied our horses to the branch of a tree, far enough apart so they could be company for each other but not tangle. John who always rode with saddle-bags, took from one of these a nose-bag filled with a small feed for a horse and handed it to me. Then from his other bag took out one for his own horse. Never having put on one of these before I watched him, following his lead. With the horses happily chewing their feed, John then took an oilskin that was strapped to the rear of his saddle.

Unrolling it and spreading it with a throw, he said, "The grass will, without something between it and us, be too wet for sitting on."

How kind this man, the one on meeting, I'd looked upon as the enemy. A man with a heart as good as Declan's, though a less fiery nature; a thing I was glad of, as it put me more at ease. I was not always watching my words or my ways as I was with Declan. John the Englishman had over the months of knowing him, shown himself to be a man of great patience and generosity. And more important to me, he'd given to my horse Raven, the care and love equal to that of my kin and myself.

Sitting there in the quiet, John spoke with his low, smooth voice, "Do you feel them?"

I knew without the need to ask he meant the Old Ones. In truth, I'd not thought on them, only taking in the beauty of the place. "When last we were here, I thought I did, but now cannot. Perhaps last time I was wrong."

John rubbed his chin as he slowly looked around the grove. "That is the way of it, Orla. It takes time and attention to know them, and the nearness of them. Do not trouble yourself and do not try too hard. They will show themselves to you when the time is right, or if you need them. They are always near."

I did want to feel them. I did want to know them. Yet John, like Maura, had given me only true counsel, so I would not be hasty in my quest, I would be as John was, patient.

"I brought us food again." My words, and even food seemed dull against the wonder and magic of the Old Ones. He smiled and nodded.

As we ate, John casually said, "Declan tells me you are quite the harper, he was most impressed by your playing."

I didn't say, but, on the night of my playing, Declan said nothing, and having seen him a few times since, he'd never once talked of it. "I've been working hard at the learning of it, and Maura has given much time to the teaching of me. I'll never be able to repay her."

He rubbed his chin. A thing I'd come to know him do when his thinking was deep. Not looking at me, he said, "Your playing is her reward, she will expect no more."

We then fell back into the silence, me thinking on his words of Declan's praise for my playing, knowing that earning his favour mattered more to me than it should.

When it was time, we readied to leave. I having put the flask in my bag threw the scraps of our uneaten food into the trees for the birds and animals to find, while John rolled up the oilskin and strapped it onto the back of his saddle.

As I slipped off the nosebag from Raven and handed it to John, he casually said, "I am very much looking forward to hearing you play. Declan tells me that will be soon. Occasionally we are treated to

Maura's fine playing, yet that is rare these days. It will be lovely to hear your harp in the ballroom. The room is built for music."

I clenched tightly my teeth. Saying nothing! Swirling ire around in my mouth! Giving an untrue smile, I mounted. Had my life gone back to the old ways? The way where others chose what it was I was to do! My body warmed with the anger. I rode, holding the reins with a grip firmer than needed, not uttering a word. Not seeing anything, my thinking blinding my eyes. John did not ask me to lead that day, and neither did he make any effort to draw me into the talking. He seemed to have a knowing now his words were new to my ears. Having learned when unsettled or fearful that I was likely to spit venom, he was careful not to vex me; that venom swirling in my mouth! Not talking, let me to keep in the anger, and by the time we'd reached the stables I'd cooled enough to mind my manners and thank John the Englishman, telling him I hoped we could soon ride again to the grove.

Having seen to Raven, I took to the path home. Alone, I let the embers of the anger in me rise again to a fire. I began to run. Hating the rain, the mud, the path, and Declan! As I ran, I was not a woman of my years, I was a spoiled child! I wanted to stamp my feet, bellow, thump my fists against the one who denied me getting my way, telling me what to do! I wanted to inflict hurt upon the one who thought it their right to determine my life; the one who caused me to hurt!

I picked my way as fast as nature would allow, taking to the trees when I needed. On I went, cursing, fuelling my own anger. How dare Declan, the one who'd not even the good manners to speak to me of my playing, now think and tell to others that I'd come to his house, his big house, and play for him and his people. Did he think me nothing but a chattel? Was this the price exacted for the housing of Raven? Did he think that gave him the right to think on me as his property? Was this my lot, to be forever under the control of another? As I made my way, I spat out these words with hot angry tears running down my face. Much troubled by my own thoughts! Reaching the cottage, I burst open Maura's door.

"Orla, what has happened? Have you been attacked?" said Maura, quickly coming to me.

"Its Declan," I sobbed.

Her brow furrowed, and a puzzlement came to her eyes. "Declan? What has happened? Has he hurt you?" Her face wearing a look of disbelief.

"John said Declan has decreed that I will play for him and his people, in his big house." I sobbed out the words.

Maura's face softened. "Ah, I see." She took up a cloth, wetting it from a bowl of water on the bench and wiped my face before saying, "Orla, it was not Declan who said you would play there, it was me."

I was frozen, as though I had been dealt a blow of betrayal. "You!" Now it my turn to wear the face of disbelief. "I thought you my friend. How could you make this so, *again*, without speaking of it first to me?" I asked, my voice filled with the hurting.

"I am your friend." She said trying to place a comforting arm about my shoulder. I turned out from under her arm and moved away. "I spoke with Declan and asked that you might play at his house, he agreed readily. It is a wise next step for you as a harper. I did not want to tell you until I spoke first with him, and you were ready to hear. It was from my lips you were meant to hear of this plan. I'm sorry this is now not so. Yet, it does not lessen the value of it. I know your trust in others is shallow still, and I am sorry you have been upset, but I am your friend, so too is Declan. Never doubt this."

Taking up a bowl she went quietly to the big pot hanging over the fire, and into it served some stew. A small serve, then one for herself. Placing them on the table, she said, "Come now and eat. It will do no good to be drained by your feelings, and weakened through lack of nourishment. To have you so will serve none of us."

I spooned the food into my mouth, raising and lowering my arm, opening my mouth, chewing and swallowing; my body there, but not my spirit. After eating I washed up the dishes. Spent, and needing to be alone, I went to my bed.

Next morning the quietness stayed with me. Maura made no effort to press me into talking but as we walked to the abbey, she asked, "Did you have words with Declan?"

I knew my habit of being wary and quick with my mouth sat ahint this question. "No. I did not see him."

Glad I was of this, as had I laid eyes on him I knew well I'd have uttered my anger, and issued him many curses for treating me in such an uncivil way. Wrongfully, would I have accused him, this I knew now!. Yet yesterday filled with anger, I did not. Had we met, once more my foolishness, and quickness to lash out with my unruly tongue would have been on show. In that moment, as we walked I gave thanks we had not encountered each other. This I did with the sincerest of heart.

"I'm sorry Orla for my lack of speaking to you about your next foray as a harper. It was always my intention. Perhaps, I should have asked of Declan not to speak of this with another, though at the time I did not think it necessary. I know he would have spoken with John only because of their close-ness, and the true pride he feels for your playing." Without allowing the space for me to speak, she then asked, "How did you behave when John told of this matter?" I knew by the way she asked, the uneasiness in her voice, she expected me to have issued a fiery reply.

"I spoke not a word of it."

"Ah, you *are* a quick learner," was all she said.

When we came to our harps, my playing suffered due to my mood. Maura asked me to step away from my harp. I did not play again that day, listening instead to the wisdom offered by Maura on ways that as a harper, I might be unsettled, or meet with a sudden change of plans. These things she said,

I must be ready for. She spoke again of the times we're living in, where the life of a harper was a powerful, yet dangerous one. I needed to be nimble, and learn to take the unexpected in my stride.

"You did well, Orla, to keep your words to yourself. To do this, I counsel you, will prove a much safer and less troublesome way to do your work. To allow your feelings to blaze unbridled, has in my long years, been seen to yield the most troublesome of results. Heed my words."

# CHAPTER TWENTY-FOUR

# THE KNOCK

M aura's talking of how quick things could change, expecting the unexpected, could not have been spoken truer! That very night when we were in our beds sound asleep there came a loud, urgent knocking on the door. Half in a daze, Maura grabbed for a shawl, and wrapping it quickly about her went to the door calling out, "Who's there?"

"It's me Declan." As Maura opened it, he rushed in. "There's trouble. You need to move your harps, and quickly. I have them ready, but have no time to do it myself. My men and I have much to shift. Take them to the tower." And he was gone.

The lateness of his call, and the pressing in his voice, spurred us into action. "Get dressed," said Maura, as she was pulling on her clothes. It was clear, from the way she acted, she knew well what had to be done. We ran by moonlight to the abbey, glad of its rare shining face when so often it hid ahint the cover of cloud. With her usual ease, Maura lit the lamp, urging me to follow her with haste. I'd seen the nimbleness with which Maura could move, yet, on this night, though calm and deliberate, her feet were sped along by the trouble that came from a threat still unknown.

Halting only briefly for the lighting of the lamp, like rats we scurried along the tunnels. We reached the chamber and there were our harps, bagged and ready. My cleverly fashioned stool stowed in its cover, the one I used in the tunnels, gone. Maura's still there sitting beside hers, would need like our harps, to be carried. Each slinging the strap of our harps over our shoulder, me taking up Maura's stool, her as pathfinder, needing to carry the lamp, we set off back down the tunnel the way we had just run. Though now burdened with the weight and awkwardness of lugging our harps, our way was made much more slowly. We did not emerge at the abbey that night, but turned down one of the tunnels we usually passed by. So many tunnels there were. Like the paths in the woodland; a spider's web. I had no knowing of where we were or where we going, only that Declan said we should take our harps to the tower. Breathing hard, we stopped a few moments to rest.

"What tower? Where is the tower?" I asked. Maura, laughed weakly.

"Whissht woman! You truly are the Madam Inquisitor. You will have your answers soon enough. We're close now."

It was not much further that the tunnel came to an end. In front of us, a door. Maura held the lamp to the door, she found the handle. Stiff from not being used, it would not turn.

"Help me Orla, it will need the strength of us both. You turn and I'll push. It will come loose with a bit of working." We tried until Maura's hands could work the handle no more, then I tried the turning.

"I think it moved. Just a little. But I think it moved."

"Keep at it lass, we'll be getting in. It's like me, just a bit stiff with the old age and lack of use."

Maura's joking had not left her. Of that I was glad. The handle moved a little bit at a time, then with a start, the mighty door gave way to our efforts.

Maura was right! As she stepped through the door with the lamp, I knew the place we'd come to. I knew where we were! This was the great tall tower I'd seen on my first visit to Cill Ala. The one my Uncle Jarlath told me was very old and built of limestone like the stones on my kin's farm. The one that no one knew why it stood. Some thinking it a bell tower, some thinking it for religious worship or for the keeping safe of treasures. Others thinking it to be something to do with the making of war, or for people to lock themselves away from the attacks of Vikings. We were stood inside the round tower of Cill Ala!

From the outside it was a strange big building, but now being inside it, its mysteries were even more marked. It was a great tall building, yet here inside above us was a wooden roof. It was not more than two tall men if one stood on the shoulders of the other.

"Will I push the door to?" I asked. Maura did not answer, her thinking on something else, walking round holding the lamp up, looking for something.

"Ah," she said.

I could not tell if she was pleased or relieved, maybe both. She pulled on a rope hanging close to the wall, and the roof above us gave a creak, and from it a wooden ladder made in pieces came down. With each pull it slowly inched its way down toward us; only when it could reach down no further, did Maura stop yanking on the rope.

I asked again, "Should I close the door?"

Maura who seemed to be enjoying all the excitement, turned quickly to me, saying "We're first here. The others will be along soon enough... if the luck be with them. We'll leave the door for them. Can you climb up there with your harp?"

"I think so... yes. If I put the strap over my head. The same as when we were running. But will my harp fit through the opening?"

She looked up. "It will fit. I've done this a few times now. The trapdoor is bigger than you think. You'd be stunned at what we've taken up. We'll wait for the others. When they get here, we'll take our harps up. That way there'll be more light. Ah, there. I hear them now. Good."

I held my breath still heavy from the running, and could hear the voices of men flowing down the tunnels, sounding like they were being carried on the wind. Time had slowed since Maura and me had reached the tower, and the slowing stayed. For though we could hear them, it was some time before the men began spilling into the tower. They came lead by men with lanterns, carrying what they could. Barrels, chests, ropes, guns; all churned up! Some, like Maura, rising to the thrill of it, laughing and joking, others wearing the worrying of it, just wanting to get the job over with.

I heard Declan before I saw him, barking out commands; his usual calm voice sounding annoyed. "Stack the biggest to the back and leave the way to the door and the ladder clear."

Now with more light, Maura nodded to me to take up my harp. Shoulder it, and make ready for the climb.

"I'll go up first, then you can see your way," said Maura, grabbing the hem of her skirt and tucking it into her waist.

Leaving her harp stood next to me, up the ladder she went with the lamp in one hand, using the other to steady herself on the ladder. Leaving the lamp at the top, she came down for her harp. Shouldering the awkward thing, pushing it round to her back, she climbed again. This time though, and needing them both, she had two hands to hold the ladder.

When she got to the top, Maura called to me. Following her lead, I climbed as she'd done. She made it to look such an easy thing, it was not! I was not afraid of climbing but I'd never climbed with a harp, and the heaviness of it threatening to pull me away from the ladder made me to be unsure. Slowly I climbed, placing one hand above the other, steadying myself when I needed to, trying to keep myself close to the ladder for fear of being dragged off it by my harp. Though only a short climb, it did not seem so. Rung by rung I went. As I neared the top Maura reached down and pulled the strap;

leaden on my shoulder it was. Having her take up the weight of the harp freed up my moving, letting me to finish the climb with less burden.

As I stepped up on the floor, I saw another ladder leading up. I looked to the ladder.

Maura following my eye, said, "Do not be troubling yourself Orla, we're not taking them any further. Our harps will be safe enough up here, without having to worry for them being knocked over by Declan's men. They have much to do, and not all are given to the taking of much care."

Looking down I could see the room filling up with all sorts of boxes, coils of rope, barrels and bottles of liquor. Men passing things, passing each other, feet shuffling, voices; such a din! I was glad to be up on this perch away from the bustle. I could see Declan and John the Englishman among the rabble. For a moment looking down, I thought unkindly on Declan. Why would he not carry Maura's harp up, or mine? Then John's words came to me, *she can do for herself*. Thinking on those words brought to me a proudness. Yes, both Maura and I can do for ourselves. And we have!

Taking up the lamp, Maura said, "We'll be heading home now. It'll be good to get back to our cosy beds. These men, I fear will be some time yet. We've done our part."

Betimes the bluntness of Maura's words stunned me. She, like Declan, offered no helping hand. She showed no sign of wondering as to the cause of all this unsettling, just the wanting to leave. We climbed down. Untucking her skirt Maura walked towards the door, passing Declan, though the room be filled with action, he kissed her brow as was his way, saying "I'll come tomorrow and tell you what this is all about." She nodded.

B ack along the tunnel we made our retreat, briskly, though without haste. The walk being made all the easier for not being burdened by the load of our harps. Glad of this we were too. For men were still lugging in stock, at times needing Maura and me to press hard against the wall to make room for the passing. When we got to the place where the tunnels met, we went our way towards the cottage, though the voices and actions could still be heard, the fuss was no longer with us. Nearing the brambles Maura blew the lamp out. It was better for all, she said, if no one's eyes be on us moving about in the dark of night.

Maura poured us each a glass of water, then in her no nonsense manner, said it was time we took to our beds. Not a word did she speak of what we'd done, what we'd seen or where we'd been. In no time at all I could hear the breath of her sleep. How blessed was she to be visited so readily by the hand of sleep. This was often not so for me, and on a night such as this with all the scampering about, I knew it would be some time before I entered the otherworld where the mind and the body find peace. The running, the climbing, the bustle of the men all hurried about in my thinking, and the ladder leading to somewhere up there! Where was that going to? What was to be found up there in the round tower of Cill Ala? Wondering this, I drifted away.

As was his way, true to his word, Declan visited us in the early afternoon of the next day. He spoke of the reason for the upheaval. One of his men, a young lad, had gotten himself unwisely tied-up with the wife of a yeoman. The woman, older than him, had been taken by the look of the young boy and worked hard at finding every chance to draw him into her bed. For a time, it seems, he resisted her lauding of his looks and her teasing touches, but, finally the lust between his legs overtook the wisdom of his mind. What had happened though, is the lad finding a love of his own, no longer wanted to keep on the folly with the yeoman's wife. But she's not a wanting to end the tryst. She's threatened him, saying she'll tell her husband that the lad forced himself on her unless he continues to service her. The boy's gone to Declan, much troubled, telling him of his situation, seeking his counsel, not knowing what to do.

Though displeased by the foolishness of the lad, Declan resenting the woman trying to wield her power over one with a smaller voice, urged him to call her bluff. The woman's threats may be just that and come to nothing. A risk Declan believed worth the taking to see her back in her place; yet he would not risk his lot. He well knew that what was spoken of in the act of coupling, when a man could be weakened with desire, or charged with rapture, could bring his business undone; affecting the lives of many. With much shame, the lad could not recollect if he'd talked of the treasures stored in the tunnels. Though Declan believed that none of the yeoman had knowledge of the tunnels, he was no fool, and would not risk his gains, ill-gotten or otherwise, or the work of his men. He'd support the lad, even hide him off-shore for a time if needed, but for now, best to be safe than to risk all.

Until it was settled, Declan said Maura and me should live quietly, not draw any undue attention to ourselves or our actions. "Stay away from the tower until we know how this will go." Maura nodded in agreement.

Turning to me she said, "You'll be able to get in a bit more time with that hairy love of yours." We laughed.

Though knowing I'd have to be specially alert if the yeomen became active, Maura spoke the truth. This unsettling had given to me a chance to spend more time with Raven. A thing I welcomed!

# CHAPTER TWENTY-FIVE

# THE CHILD WITHIN

For the next few days the weather kept us prisoner in Maura's small house. We mended, cleaned, sang through my harp tunes, and talked by the fire. Taking turns to run out when needed, sheltered only from the pelting watery sheet that fell from the sky with no hint of slowing or stopping, by a woollen brat. Chickens did not lose their hunger to rain, neither did nature suspend the need to relieve oneself, yet all outings were done with much haste. Until now the weather had been kind, we'd been treated to many soft days. For this, one should give thanks, though precious time with Raven being denied me, found me cursing the blasted rain, praying keenly, though these days I knew not who to, for it to stop. Finally, my prayers were answered.

I knew when I opened my eyes that the day was clear. The light let in by the window was clean and bright, not like the shadowy dimness of the dark greyness that had come uninvited and overstayed its visit. Joy! Travelling the woodland path would be slow and muddy, this I knew, yet the prospect did not lessen in me the thrill of seeing my beautiful Raven. I gave my blessing for the day, a practice I did whether bleak or pleasant, glad still to be alive; shared the morning meal with Maura, packed my food and flask, and set off eagerly.

As I picked my way along the muddy path I was glad of Maura's wise counsel to wear my brat, for the trees I was often forced to walk among, hung heavy, dripping with the memory of the sky's shared tears. Touching upon them and treading among the bracken dampened my clothing, though not my spirit, not on this day! I saw a way off in the trees, a fox. As we each stood eyeing one another, I thought, though his ears dry and his eyes bright, his coat like mine, bore the bedraggled look given us by the charity of the damp woodland.

When I heard the whistle, a sound now well known to me and welcomed, I took an account of my dress. As I'd done before, I scraped the mud from my boots. There was less on them this time, whether because I walked more among the trees, or that the earth being mixed with more rain clung less due to it being more like soup than porridge. I cannot say I was overly presentable, but on this day as I quickened my step toward the stable, I did not care. Only the face of Raven filled my thoughts.

Entering the stables I took off my brat. It being very damp and though good for keeping me from the cold and wet, would be another thing be-tween Raven and me. She nickered when she saw me. A sound that brought a smile to my lips, and caused John the Englishman to leave what he was doing to check what roused her so. We greeted each other. Me telling him I was there for the day, and would welcome some stablework if he had need of an extra pair of hands.

I had no wanting to become weak. My own parents, though tired, were always strong, and my grandmother too. It was hard work and being active that kept them so, and saw me looking ever for ways to keep my brawn. John said on this day he would not call upon me, this being my first full day to spend with Raven. Yet, if I was to visit regularly during this break to my harp learning, he surely would.

He looked to my brat, "You can hang that in the tack room. It's warm in there." I thanked him, and soon did as he said.

Before I went though, I fossicked out from my bag the carrot I'd brought for Raven. I broke it in half, giving her the bigger half of the two. In the tack room, I hung my brat and my bag, knowing if I took it into the stall that Raven would be nosing it, wanting to eat not only the carrot but my food as well. This made me to smile. I gathered a few brushes and a hoof pick, and made my way back. Raven still grinding on the carrot, nudged me as I ran my hand down her neck. She was in fine condition, John cared for her well.

As I began to brush her, breathing in with pleasure the smell of horse, she turned her head to me; those lovely dark eyes and that face showing a hint of the fine veins running through it. I whispered to her as I brushed. I did not hurry. I had no want. This was a brushing of love. Not a chore. Not even needed.

A brushing as a mother might do for her child. A brushing filled with the pleasure of being in one another's company.

After a long time, and cleaning her feet, I returned the brushes and pick to the tack room. I didn't take up my bridle and saddle, instead choosing a halter and lead rope, and my bag. Today, I had no mood for riding, rathering to walk with my friend, quietly and tenderly. Such was the call of my being; a one-ness with my horse, just Raven and me.

As we walked I spoke aloud my thinking. Rarely, was there a time when my mind was quiet. Always wondering, always questioning, or going back over the last few days. It came to me, and I told of this to Raven, that I was not a one for thinking much on the past. Mostly my thinking was about now, or on what was yet to come, but hardly ever did I think on what had gone long ago. Is this the way of most people's thinking?

As before, I heard the voice of the unseen, saying *this was my way of walking through life, and my way was never the way of another, neither theirs be mine.* I gave much thinking to this, and to the voice. Where had it come from? I could not say for sure, yet, I had a notion. These were the words of a wise one, and in them I found a rightness, a truth. They fit me well!

We stopped every once in a while. Raven chewed on the lush grass, and me on a boiled egg and some bread. I did not sit, the ground being sodden from the rain. Wandering along the path on foot was different to being on horseback. The woodland seemed much quieter, more peaceful. It was as if Raven and me were the only two souls among the trees. Without warning a bird screeched as if to let me know that we were wayfarers, and far from alone. Treading our way through the homelands of the mostly unseen birds and animals who dwelt mildly among the trees and bracken.

After a time, with the position of the sun telling me it be mid-afternoon we turned and headed back. Such a pleasant time, I had. Back in the stables I fed and watered Raven, kissed her velvet whiskery nose, telling her that if the weather was fine, I'd be back in the morning. Having collected my now dry brat from the tack room, I left the stables feeling in that moment, all was well with the world. I'd only just passed the big house, not going in; I never would unless with Maura, when I heard Declan's shout.

"Orla, wait up." With his long stride he quickly covered the ground between us. "I thought you and Maura might like to come and spend a few days here. You could ride, and the women would very much enjoy spending time with Maura. She has her room which is plenty big enough for the two of you. It's not yet wise for you to go to the tower. Speak with her on this. You'd be most welcome."

I thanked him for the offer and took my leave. How strange it would be to sleep in that big house! Thinking on this was both unsettling and enticing. As I walked, I thought I'd leave the decision to Maura, then checked myself. Is it not the decisions others make for me, I'm wanting to be rid of?

By the time I reached the cottage, I was a sight. My hair was mussed and damp from the branches that had tugged at me when I was forced by mud and water to leave the path. My boots and the bottom part of my breeches were heavy with wetness and splattered with mud. I was not cold, though glad to see that Maura had a small fire burning in the hearth.

"I've heated some water. I thought you might be in need of a bath, all this mud."

How like a mother was Maura to me; always ahead of things. I hung my brat in its place, and took off my boots, trying, though without luck, to get as little mud as I could on my hands.

"Get undressed where you are. I'll ready the bath," said Maura.

I did as she said, sharing her wish of not wanting to be treading any more muck than was needed. Piling my soggy threads, naked I crossed the room and stepped into the bath. It was a small tub with little water in it, yet warm, and enough to wash the grime from my body. Maura had set it near to the fire, it was a comforting way to end my heavenly day.

I told Maura of Declan's offer, which she considered for a time, then asked, "Would you like to stay, let's say, for two nights at Declan's?"

I did have a wanting to be near to Raven, but had an unease about sleeping in a house as grand as Declan's. This I told to Maura. Maura agreed it was a big house, and grand, but it was a house still, nothing more. She told to me how newness was like a cousin to suddenness, something I should get used to, and one day, may be instead of finding it troubling I might come to welcome it. These were things I would surely meet in my life as a harper. To comfort me, she said in the staying at Declan's, I'd not be there alone, she'd be with me. Though we spoke of the visiting we made no firm plans.

"Well, will we go then or not?" Maura asked the next morning as we sat eating our porridge.

My belly tightened. I wanted to go, but I felt fear. Odd the way others think of me as brave and having courage, and yet I do not. I have a wanting to be brave, but if I truly was then I'd surely be bold. I think if left to myself, I might cosset away, and allow life to drift along like some quiet meandering river.

*Do not lie to yourself*, came the voice, the unseen's voice. *Never have you been one to sit mildly. You have too much spirit for that!* Startled, I looked around.

"What is it?" asked Maura.

I could not say nothing, for that would be untrue, so instead, said, "I thought I heard something. Have no mind."

Having made ready the day before, we set off early. The sky was heavy with clouds threatening to unburden themselves. We made our way with as much haste as the path would afford, still often taking to the trees. I'd made the offering of making the walk alone to ask Declan to bring the cart for Maura. In that, she would have no part, saying, when the day came she could no longer walk through her own homeland, that day would be the one when she returned to its earth in a coffin. Though smiling, I knew in my heart that no man or woman held a firmer belief in the truth than she, on speaking these words.

Just as the whistle sounded, the heavens welcomed our arrival with a teeming downpour. With nowhere for shelter save among the trees, pulling our hoods over our heads, we accepted our fate. There was nothing else for it! To stop and huddle would be meaningless, we would be soaked still, and no closer to the place we were going. We didn't run, for to do so would have guaranteed a fall. Better to arrive bedraggled and wet, than with our faces telling the tale of a meeting between ground and body.

The greeting at the gate, usually unhurried with much news being exchanged, was in the pouring rain not so. The salute matching our quickened steps towards the house. With a rush Maura opened the door and we stepped in. Eyeing each other, our laughter began. It was as it had been on the woodland path, laughing until we could not speak. Tears mingling with the rain on our faces, ending briefly with an unguarded embrace, only to begin again; an awareness of Declan's eyes upon us. Looking on his face, though wearing a smile, told us he had no notion of what had brought such mirth to us, and this unknowing, causing Maura and me to laugh all the more. Amused, and with patience, Declan waited for our chortling and gasping to subside, only then did he say to Maura, "It is wonderful to hear you so full of life and laughter."

Then turning to me. "Thank you Orla."

I gulped down the rising lump in my throat, and blinked away the tears, pretending they were tears left over from the laughter. How humbling his words of thanks were to me. I knew pain, suffering, humiliation, cruelty, death and many more sorrows, so had we all. Yet, in that one brief striking moment our spirits were lifted so high, filling us with a joy, body and soul, such that caused our sides to ache, words to be silenced by the laughing and gasping, and I was being thanked! Without speaking it, Declan's words told to me it was a long time since he'd seen Maura so filled with the living. It was this that wet my eyes!

Glad I was that mirth had not forever deserted us, and dwelt still within. Others in our land were not so fortunate. For them, joy had withered and died with their hopes and dreams, and their love and loved ones. Why some can stay afloat on the ocean of life, while others sink and drown is a mystery. I'm glad to be one of those not so easily drowned, to still know the rise of joy, its explosion into laughter, and best of all, for that joy to be shared with another or more. For this I give thanks to all gods and goddesses, whether they be the God of the Christian church, the Old Ones or any other; so blessed am I!

After the calm came back to us, we hung our brats and I followed Maura up to her room, such a lovely room! Placing my bag down I walked to the window. The view took the breath from me; so far could I see. And the room, so big! You could sleep easily three or four families in such a room. Without thinking I whirled about. Round and round

I went, then suddenly catching myself, I stopped. I turned to Maura, my face red, that a woman of my years should behave so.

"Orla, Orla! With me, you have no need to behave in any way other than your true self. That a child lives within you still, is rare. Treasure the little one. It may not be wise for you to let her out for all to see, but with me, don't hide her away, not from me. You have brought such life into my life!"

There was such love in her words, my fondness overtook me. Flinging my arms around her, I embraced her with a little more vigour than is womanly.

She laughed saying, "You've lost none of your strength then, my girl."

In that moment, Maura and me were as kin, and slipping from my mouth came the words. "I love you Maura. I truly do."

Rolling her eyes, she touched my hand. "Whissht woman."

After unpacking the few things from our bags, we went to the kitchen. May, and a few other women were there making ready the evening meal. There was a large pot of soup hanging over a low fire in the hearth. May told us to help ourselves.

"There's always a pot going here," Maura said with a smile.

That was the way of it at the big house. The evening meal always the main meal. With most of the men down working at the boat building during the day, sent off with food that could be carried, boiled eggs, cheese, bread, and some ale, the evening meal, a big hearty meal, not a fancy one was a one that would stick to the bones. I ate only a little of the soup eager to go to the stables, gave my thanks to the women, and took my leave.

Walking within the stables, my eye set upon Raven, I was surprised to hear Declan's voice.

"Ah, Orla, you've arrived then."

I turned towards his voice to see him and John coming from the room where I was thinking the strings to be made. John greeted me. How striking these two. Tall, strong men, both with comely faces. One fairer than the other, one more mild of manner than the other. Yet, both a quality about them, though unspoken of protection, a knowing if needed, they could and would, fight. A fierceness not on show, yet, there. Raven nickered to me as the colour began to rise in my face. I quickly turned and walked towards her, whispering my thanks. Such a regard for these men, I have. Betimes, I am fully at ease in their company, yet, both can make me to feel foolish, awkward and rattled as a young girl, as I felt now, though through no one's doing, but my own!

# Chapter Twenty-Six

# ALL TO THE GROVE

After spending the afternoon with Raven, I went back to the big house. Expecting to find Maura in the kitchen, I made my way there, only to be told by May that Maura had gone up to her room. Thanking her, I climbed the stairs. Unsure of myself, I knocked lightly on the door. Maura, opened it. Seeing me, she frowned.

"There's no need for you to be bothering me by knocking. This is your room too. I want you to know that. Just come in if you have a want. Now change your clothes and make yourself tidy for the evening meal... and wear your hair down. Such lovely hair."

I knew well what Maura meant by get tidy. She'd bade me to bring, what she called the clothes of a woman. This was not a thing I was going to do. For having always to wear breeches, I'd grown fond of them. They were much to my liking, and far more sensible than a skirt. Yet, to please her, I'd done as she asked.

"Ah", said Maura with a note of triumph. "Now, your hair."

As I unplaited it I felt the weakness creeping in. When I wore the breeches I felt bold and strong. Now the position of a woman, the wearing of a skirt, brought back to me the lesser standing of one born a girl.

What is it," asked Maura. "What causes trouble to cross your face?"

I spoke openly of my thoughts to Maura.

"Ah, yes I see," she said, then went on. "There are always more ways to look upon things than only one. Yes, you have been poor, with little choice and no voice, but this is not how it is for you now. You are lovelier than most with your dark hair and eyes as rich and green as our land, with a spirited disposition, you are honest, and you are a harper. These are grand qualities, and more than enough for one. Do not think being a woman makes you weak. You might not defeat a man in battle, still, there are many ways to win a war. And here in this place we are equal, men and women alike. This might not be so in the eyes of all out there beyond, but here it is so." She then stood me before the large looking glass. "The gods have blessed you well, do them the honour of wearing your beauty with pride."

I looked on myself in the glass. Though a small woman of now forty years, I was comely enough. My long hair released from the plaiting had a wildness to it that was becoming. My features, softened by age, were neat and well placed. My eyes, green, though a different shade than Declan's, were edged with long, thick dark lashes. My nose small and straight, my lips full and well coloured, framed my white and even spaced teeth, my breast full, and my waist and hips slim. Though I did not feel a pride in myself as Maura suggested, my look was fair, and for that I was pleased.

Walking into the dining room with the hope of quietly taking up a place was lost when May's voice sounded clear above the hum of the babble. "Ooh, ah. Thissn scrubs up awright. Don't she?"

All eyes turned to me. There was much laughter. Though, not at me, at May's words. The room filled with men, women and children, smiling and nodding their welcomes, and chattering away. Declan came to us, kissing Maura's brow, showed only his amusement for May's outburst for he'd seen me dressed this way before. I think him a man more interested in the deeper part of a person than the seen part. I thought the same of John. Though he did, from across the room, raise a brow, and with a small tilt of his head, give to me the smallest smile of approval.

I stood against the wall for a time, watching and listening. I could hear voices of people that came from other lands, yet here together, they did not clash. They did not judge. One was not better than another! Women, though they wore skirts, did not turn their faces to the floor but looked into the eyes of the men as they spoke. A thing, except for with kin, I had been discouraged though without success, from doing. I desired to look into the eyes of one I spoke with and have them do the same. This I thought a way to overcome the dimness of doubt. This is where one found the truth in another's words; in their eyes. It had not always served me well though. Well I remember the steadfast look I cast into the eye of an English soldier earning me the parting gift of a hard slap across the face. Yet, still the eyes, are the place where I search for truth.

The evening passed quickly and with much ease. I'd never before been in a room with so many, yet it took no effort to be among these people. They were kind, and good humoured. The food, though plentiful was simple, served with ale; despite many being there, the gathering was modest in nature. When I spoke of this to Maura, she reminded me, that this meal happened every night, and needed to be as it was; not a banquet, not grand, just a meal shared by a household larger than most.

As Maura had said, everyone here was treated justly. I was regarded as though I'd always lived in this place. Never had I fitted so well. Never had I felt so at home; belonged! Yet, as I waited for sleep in that lovely room of Maura's, I knew this was not my home. I had no home. In times gone I'd have been troubled by this, but now in this moment, that was not so. Determined was I, to make the best of my being here with Raven.

I rose early. Quietly, not wanting to disturb Maura. As I went down the stairs I could hear others moving about. With so many under one roof, no matter how big the house, there was bound to be others up. I went by the kitchen, May was there.

"Porridge?" She nodded towards the pot, as her hand reached out to me a bowl. I took it from her and served myself. As I sat down, she looked at me and smiled.

"Back as yerself t'day, then is ya?"

Returning her smile, I nodded, and said, "Yes, May, I'm back to myself today." We laughed together knowing that I was, as I'd always been. The only thing different last night were the clothes I wore, and the way I tied my hair. It was a comforting amusing quip that closed the space between us, and in an unspoken way, declared our freedom to choose who we were, despite our womanhood.

I felt light that morning, and leaving the big house, ran my way to the stables.

"What's the rush?" said John the Englishman.

"There's no rush. I just wanted to run. Do you not betimes want to run?"

He squinted a little. "Not by choice, no! I run to catch a horse, or to escape an enemy, or to save a life, but I cannot say that I run save no other reason than that of running. No!"

How sad. When I run, I feel alive. Perhaps, as Maura said, the child I was, has never left me. "You should give it a try John, see how it fits. You might find it as I do, a thing you have a liking for."

As I moved towards Raven's stall, John called after me. "Orla, Declan is coming back early afternoon. He thought we all, yourself, Declan, Maura, and I, could go to the grove."

I supposed he meant walk, but unsure I asked.

"Walk there?"

"No, ride."

Having never seen Maura on horseback, her always travelling by cart or walking, I thought her not to ride. "Maura rides?"

"When she has a mind to. She has a very well-mannered gelding. A grey, called Paddy. That's his head poking out, two stalls down from Raven. He lives mostly in one of the fields. I brought him in last night after Declan spoke of going to the grove. I've given him a good brush down. He was a bit shaggy, but, now I think he's quite presentable. He'll enjoy the outing."

I looked to the grey face staring back at us. Waiting, it seemed for all the world, for something to happen. *Why else am I in here?* Was the question the grey pony wore.

It was before midday when Declan walked through the stables. I was returning some grooming gear to the tack room.

"I've been to the house and spoken with Maura, she's keen for us to ride into the grove. Did John speak with you about it?"

"Yes. I think it a grand idea."

"Good. We'll have our meal early, so we can get on. Maura is readying herself. John, come on. We're going to eat."

The three of us walked to the house. Maura was in the kitchen lining up our bowls on the table. "I've filled some flasks, and packed some of May's brack." She said with much excitement.

We wasted little time with our meal, all of us eager to start out. John was first to leave the kitchen, having offered to saddle up Paddy for Maura. Amused, I raised a brow. He returned my look with a knowing grin. As Maura and me made our way to the stables, Declan went to speak with a couple of his men. How odd it was to see Maura wearing breeches, though she wore them with the ease of one used to the wearing of them.

"Ah, there's my Paddy," said Maura, then turning to me, said, "He's a bit of a plodder... suits me well!"

I looked along the stalls at the grey face looking out, now wearing a bridle. Collecting my gear from the tack room, hurrying with my own bridle slung over one shoulder, looking down at the saddle cradled across my arm, I was stopped suddenly by two hands on my shoulders. Looking up, there was Declan with his long arms holding us apart.

"It's always wise to look in the direction you're walking. Stops you crashing into things unexpectedly," he said with a warmth, and a touch that caused my body to thrill as it had back at the farm.

He dropped his hands as quickly as he had placed them on me and went about gathering his gear. With a flush on my cheek and my heart banging with desire, I scuttled away.

As I bridled and saddled Raven my heart still pounded from Declan's touch. Had I been alone with Raven I might have whispered my secret to her. But I was not alone, and my feelings were my secret, not for the ears of others! I settled as I worked. Doing up the chin strap on the bridle, throwing the reins over the saddle, tightening the girth, stretching Raven's front legs, one at a time to give her ease, pulling down the stirrups. With each task the pounding grew less, and the blood that had coursed its way to my face went back to the places it belonged. Unbolting the stall door, I lead Raven out. Maura was already outside, sitting astride her broad backed Paddy looking very much at home.

"He's a nice big pony, your Paddy, and you're right Maura, he does suit you well."

We passed the time waiting for the menfolk. Once we were all gathered and mounted we started towards the grove. It was a steady ride. John up front, Declan at the rear, and Maura and me in between. Our journey was about half over when John halted. Looking back at Declan, he nodded towards the trees. There was a man running among them, coming our way.

"He's one of mine," said Declan, seeing the fear on my face.

As he got closer, the man panted, "Declan. It's the yeomen. Two of them. At the house. Looking for Darragh."

None of us were expecting this. There'd been little bother since the night of shifting everything to the tower. No yeomen on the paths, no visits from them, we all thought maybe the slighted woman had made only empty threats to see her own pleasures satisfied. "They won't find him, I've made well sure of that. You three go on, I won't be long," said Declan in an easy, untroubled manner. Offering his arm to the man, he swung him up ahint; they cantered away on the fine black.

"On we go then," said John, speaking as calmly as Declan had.

Though just for a moment, a concerned look passed across Maura's face. She said nothing, and with John again leading the way, we continued on to the grove.

We tied our horses apart on a long rein made by unbuckling one rein from the bit, giving them plenty of grass to eat. I watched as Maura walked down the avenue of stones, then began to walk the circle. Several times she walked the circle.

"What's she doing?"

John said plainly, "What she always does. She calls to the Old Ones, honouring them, giving thanks for their guidance, and asks that they eternally attend her and those she loves in this world, and in death, in the otherworld. Never have I been here with them, when she, and Declan, have not performed this rite. Sometimes, they seek guidance on a given troubling. Sometimes, words are spoken aloud other times not. Yet the intention is always clear. They come to talk with the Old Ones."

Intention! Maura had spoken many times to me of the worth of intention, mostly having to do with my harp playing, though not always. And here in this place, she was doing a ritual using intention as one might use a prayer, though not in a church, but here in this place. A place that felt truly holy!

After a time Maura left the circle of stones and returned to John and me. Since my leaving Duleek, I'd come to see how little is my knowing and understanding of the world, natheless, my desire for the knowing always strong.

"Maura, can you teach me about the ritual?" I asked. She looked from me to the avenue of stones.

"It's not yet the time Orla. Remember, the stonemasons. For now, it's enough that you know of the being of the Old Ones. Little by little, you will come to know them. Come, let's sit."

S itting on the soft green grass, we drank a little from the flask, yet none of us ate. Though we did not speak of it, all our thinking was of Declan. Did all go well for him? Would the yeomen bring trouble? Would Declan be able to come to the grove as planned?

Without making a sound Maura touched my arm, and nodded to just beyond the stones. She'd no need to do the same with John, his eyes were already on that place. There stood watching us was a red stag. The beast standing proud, his dark eyes set in cream fur, same as the cream fur on his muzzle and filling his ears, were on us. The hair of his neck coming down to a point on his chest, a lordly mane! And his huge many pointed antlers worn as a noble crown. Boldly, he stood! Still as stone, we watched the kingly creature. When he'd had his fill of us he faded back into the woodland, the only trace of his well-muscled, chestnut majesty, was that held in our mind's eye.

The coming of the stag changed the mood strikingly. Where worry had been, now comfort was. I did not understand this, still I could not deny it being so.

"What has happened?" I asked.

Maura smiled at John and me. "The Old Ones have sent us a messenger. All bodes well for Declan."

How can this be? A stag comes. The mood lightens. And all is well. "How can you be sure?"

"Ah, Orla, you will come to know. The trust takes time."

John then said, in all the time he'd been in Ireland with Declan, living in the big house, riding in these woodlands, coming to this grove, he'd seen few deer, and never had a beast such as the one who visited us, made itself known. "I believe Maura is right, the stag has been sent to us," he said.

At that very moment as if by the wave of an unseen wand, the horses called out in answer to the light cantering of hooves and Declan appeared. He told us the yeoman's wife had not spoken of the tryst between her and Darragh, but accused him of not showing her the respect a person of her station deserved. Wisely, to please his wife, the yeoman had agreed to censure the young man formally, and so it was he dutifully made a visit official in nature. Plainly he was more troubled by his wife than the misdeed of the lad!

Having been informed by Declan of Darragh's absence, the two men agreed that on the lad's return, he'd make an apology in person to the yeoman's wife.

"I know that will be awkward for both Darragh and the yeoman's wife, but may be too, there will be a learning in it for them," Declan said with mirth.

"Now that you are here," said John, "I have nosebags for the horses. Will you help me put them on Orla?"

While we did this, Declan and Maura walked the stones. I could hear them softly murmuring, though, could not make out what was being said. So at ease were they in their ritual, I fell to envy. In Duleek, when I had gone to the church, I'd known the ritual, yet here I did not! Though here in this place, I now better understood the words Declan had spoken when he told me of his church. This is his church!

# Chapter Twenty-Seven

# THE TOWER

W e told Declan of the stag. Disappointed was he not to have seen the royal beast. When Maura spoke of it as a messenger, he gave a small nod and a look of understanding. Great, was my want to share the deep bond they have with the Old Ones. For Declan and Maura, the Old Ones had always been known. And through them, John was coming to know the Old Ones, yet for me, I was like the wean, my knowing was only at the beginning. I wanted much more!

As we rode back from the grove, we spoke of the getting of our harps. It was agreed the day after tomorrow was a good day to go to the tower; the four of us. Declan and John would come, not to help with the harps, but to show me proper, the tower. Declan offered to lead me on what was, in his words, a decent climb. John on hearing this and having only made the climb a few times, agreed the returning of our harps to the tunnel chamber, a worthy excuse to once again climb the round tower's ladders.

All the eagerness of what was to come, and the excitement of the news delivered by Declan's man on our going to the grove, seeped out of us as we made our way back to the big house. Both the going and the coming back were pleasing but each in their own way. Riding home we were more quiet, more settled, a calm fell over us as a shroud. To me it was, as it had been on the day I'd walked with Raven, all was well with the world! Maybe, it was the coming from the grove, itself a place of peace, or seeing the stag, or the slow ride. I cannot tell what or why, but I had not the chatter in my head, neither any thumping in my chest, only a stillness, and the sounds of the land; Declan's church.

We still had this hush on us as we rode up to the stable doors. It shifted slowly as we tended our horses. Maura did not stay to unsaddle, John offering to take care of her pony, yet, the three of us, John, Declan and myself, worked quietly as if none had a wanting for the breaking of the spell. Even the horses were quiet with the knowing.

The meal was as it had been the night before, a rowdy good humoured feast. With the eating over, I rose to help May and some of the women clear the table. She tried to stop me, though I was having none of it. These women were not my servants. I was not raised to have another wait on me. It was enough that they'd prepared the food, for this I was grateful, and as my thanks I'd do my share in the kitchen. It being only right. How else would I find my place here, even as a visitor, if I did nothing to make it so? I was well mannered in my ignoring their griping, and took up my station at the washtub. Many dishes there were in a meal for such a lot! Once looked on well as another pair of hands, the women jostled me and included me in their joking. It made the work to be quickly done. The ways of the women showed to me that the doing of the chores were as pleasing as the readying or the eating of the meal. The peace of the grove still with me as I drifted to sleep. Not having a home, on that night, troubled me nowt!

The next morning Declan, Maura and me met in the dining room. It was odd for Declan to be in the house. As Maura had told me it was his way to leave for the boat yard well before the dawn. He stayed on due to Maura and me leaving in the afternoon. He wanted to make a time for us to go to the round tower. This, it was decided would be just after midday on the morrow.

As well, Declan wanted to know when I would bring my harp to play. I looked to Maura. Folding one arm across her body, resting her other elbow on it, she propped her head with her thumb beneath her chin and her finger across her lips. Staring in a faraway manner, after a time she said, "Six weeks. She'll be ready in six weeks."

"Do you really think I'll be ready to play for all those people in six weeks?" I asked as we walked along the woodland path towards the cottage. My stomach churning at the thinking of it.

"I am not one for the telling of lies, as I've told you before. You must trust me. I'll not set you to fail Orla."

My need was to trust myself. I did not doubt Maura, my belief in her was strong, but faith in myself, this was less so. Walking, I straightened my back and raised my chin.

"I will need two more tunes. If I am not to play the lament, then I will need two more tunes. I will not play at Declan's unless I have six tunes. To have less, I think insulting. Those who live there, all of them, have treated me well. To show my thanks, I'll be wanting to give them six pieces."

Making this decision myself, strengthened my pledge. My words ringing with a promise made!

Maura, nodded. "Six it will be then."

It was good to be back at the cottage, and keen was my want to get my harp from the tower. I knew I had much work to do to ready myself for playing at the big house. My mind raced with the urgency of the task and charged my want to begin the work. Declan and John were early so instead of meeting us at the tower, had come to the cottage.

"I'll not climb," said Maura. "There are too many ladders for my skirt. I only have one pair of breeches, and them I've left at your house Declan for the riding of Paddy. The climb today is for Orla. The climb will be easy for her. She has a liking for the clothes of a lad, and they serve her well."

Declan and John looked to my breeches, and Declan said, "Serve her well, they might, and wear them well, she does!"

I blushed at his words. Seeing my rising to this, he continued with his friendly teasing.

"The wearing of the breeches even warms her face."

"Ah, that's the truth of it." Said Maura joining in the teasing. My face becoming even hotter.

W alking to the abbey I lagged ahint, watching Maura flanked by these two tall, strong men. They made her look so small. She loved these two. One with the love of a mother for her own son, the other as a mother would, a foundling. She linked her arms through theirs, walking proudly. I would liked to have walked so with my own sons. A wave of sorrow rippled through me, as I stepped with care among the toppled stones, and the brambles.

Declan took up the tinderbox. With little effort, he urged forth a flame. He took the lead, followed by Maura and me, with John ahint us. Though we were in no danger, it was a comfort having these two men as our companions. They made easy work of the heavy door that had taken Maura and me much might to ease open on the night we hurried here with our harps.

"We'll get the harps down first before we climb," said John, already halfway up the ladder. "I'll pass them down. Declan you grab them."

These men were tall enough for one to be up on the above floor and one to stand where we now stood, and the gap between to be bridged by our harps. First Maura's came. Declan stood it with care by the wall near the door. Then mine. It took only moments and with such ease, nothing like the effort it took for Maura and me to make the climb with them. Yet, on that night, with none of us knowing what would be the outcome of the lad and the yeoman's wife, there was much work to be done. There was no time then for the gentle passing of harps such as now. John climbed down with Maura's stool in one hand, the other steadying himself on the rungs.

"We'll be a while," Declan said to Maura. "Do you want to wait or go back? I'll take care of your harp if you have a mind to go."

Maura was already taking the cover off her harp. "No. You lot go. I'll keep my own company."

John having lit another lamp was, like me, eager to start up the ladders. "I'll go first" he said, already halfway up the first.

Following him, I climbed. My mind less on the rungs than on the one that followed me. A man who had shown no more interest in me than a friend or a teasing brother might, yet one who occupied far too much of my thinking. Now, here we were. Me, climbing ahead of him wearing breeches. Wearing clothing that showed much of the shape of a woman, the roundness of the backside, the curve of the hips, the features of a woman that lay in hiding beneath a skirt; my features. Now on show to a man, that unbidden, and unknowingly, had entered a place within my soul.

Up, and up we went. Ladder after ladder. I tried without success to shift my mind from Declan to the climb. John making headway, like a boy eager, now two ladders ahead of us, and us climbing in dim light. My foot slipped. I was in no danger, the ladders were short. But, with the quickness of a man used to defence, Declan held me.

"You're alright Orla. I've got you. On you go."

I hoped he didn't feel the quickening of my pulse or the thrill running in my body. The dimness, I knew, guaranteed the blood in my face went unseen. Hearing the noise of my slip, John hurried back to the floor above. Holding the lamp to see us better.

"Alright?" I looked past the lamp to him.

"Yes, I lost my footing." He waited only long enough for Declan and me to reach him, before he was off up the ladder.

"He knows well the reward that's waiting him," said Declan. Me, on the other hand, did not.

As we climbed out on the floor where John stood, there were no more ladders, only a domed roof. In the wall there were four windows. Each window faced a different direction. I went to one. As my eyes looked out, I gasped. I could see for such a distance. Green rolling land, crisscrossed with stone walls, and houses. Further beyond, trees and mountains. I thought up here, my view to be like that of the Golden Eagle. I went from window to window, each holding the same magic. The last window I went to looked out to the sea. The grey sky meeting the ink blue water, the gulls whirling; I could not move away. I felt the body standing ahint me. Not touching me, yet warm, and there, thrilling me!

"So beautiful, is it not?"

I did not breathe. Frozen, I did not want to turn and show my surprise, for the voice was not of the one I was thinking it to be. It was not Declan's, but John the Englishman's.

Still not turning, I nodded my agreeance. Looking out this window across the sea was as though you could see across the water, to where the world itself disappeared.

"I know why it is that Declan has a love for the sea," said John. "When you take to it, if all bodes well there is much to be seen. Countries, some like ours. Others, different. A newness. A thrill. Even the ocean itself, offers the excitement of danger and challenge. And the beauty of it!"

Declan slapped John's shoulder. "You know me well, brother."

Turning away from the window, I ran my hand over the stones in the wall. The workmanship, and care taken to shape and lay the stones was clear to the eye. Like the tunnels and the chambers, I wondered of those, whose hands had crafted such a thing. Truly, as I thought the first time I had seen this building, it was a feat of wonder. This tower was unlike any place I'd ever seen. And, I was now inside it! And, all the while we'd been climbing, Maura had been playing her harp. The music had floated up through the tower, yet, we could not listen well as we climbed. Now though, here at the top, looking across this land of ours, wedded to its music of the harp; it truly was a heavenly thing.

When we'd had our fill of the tower's top room, the climb down began. Looking out the windows, seeing such beauty had shifted my mind far from myself, making the climb more easy. I hadn't noticed the stopping of the music, yet, when we reached the ground level, Maura was waiting, her harp already packed. The men offered to carry the harps, giving me an opening for the teasing of John.

"So, you think us womenfolk too weak to carry our harps then? Am I after reminding you of how they came to be here?"

He laughed a little, squinted thoughtfully replying in a voice tinged with owlishness, "I think there is little you and Maura cannot do, if you set your mind to it." Then more lightly, "But, today Declan and I have a mind to carry a couple of harps about, and as yours are the only ones to hand, then they are the ones we will carry. Us, as men having the born right to do as we please, and you women having the born right to obey. Isn't that so Declan?"

I felt my body stiffen and straighten in readiness to argue. On seeing this, John and Declan both began to laugh.

"Orla, you really need to thicken that lovely skin of yours," said John.

Maura glared motherly at the two of them, "And you John Earnshaw, need to behave yourself. You're not too big for the getting of a clip around the ear-hole. Neither of you!"

We all laughed at Maura's words. Most at the thinking or seeing in the mind's eye this determined little woman giving these two great men a clout. Though, we all knew her more than able of doing so. Maura and me did not bid much fussing at the men's offer to take our harps to the chamber, and we parted from them where the tunnels met, us going back to the abbey, and them going on to the chamber.

Odd it was to hear John given his full name. I only thought on him as John the Englishman. Earnshaw... John Earnshaw. The name fitted him well. I'd come to think highly of Declan and John the Englishman. Both had treated me kindly, and with regard. Neither treated me as less than them. This meant much to me. Declan, the more fiery of the two, perhaps that being the Irish in him, John quiet and patient. Both bold, solid and generally good humoured. Fine men!

M aura and me wasted no time in making a plan for readying me to play at Declan's. Maura thinking now, as I was going to play six pieces, the lament could be one of them, though she said it best to play it early. My playing would move through the noble strains from Geantrai to Suantrai, then on to Goltrai, back to Geantrai, again to Suantrai, ending on the Geantrai. Much work lay ahead. Even with the lament as one the pieces, I still had two tunes that were only half-ready, and one that to me was yet a stranger; not heard, not met.

Maura went to the writing desk that sat quietly in the corner of the room. She took out paper, a quill and a small glass jar lidded with a tightly fitted cork. Removing the plug, she dipped the quill and made marks on the paper. She told me she was making a list of the pieces I would play, with the date and the place of playing. Keeping a record of this nature would be useful, Maura told me. Useful to those may be, who could read the marks. I could not.

I being eager to sit at my harp, rose early the next morning. I gave my blessing for the day, had a fire burning in the hearth, the chickens set free to peck and scratch, and the pot of porridge that had soaked while we slept belching its readiness by the time Maura joined me. Keenness fired my mood. I ate quickly. Washed my bowl, and waited. Maura was not to be hurried though she knew of my desire to make a start.

"Steady is the way Orla."

I heard her words, but had no mind to heed them. I had my own plan. I'd spoken with John, telling him I'd not come to see Raven for two weeks, needing to give my time to the harp. He gave his word he'd care for her, and knowing I'd be missing her, reminded me of how quick the time passes. I had no mind for the wasting of time. I had much to do. If I was denied spending time with Raven, then I'd surely spend it well on the learning!

I felt full of life as we made our way to the abbey, having not played my harp for a time. Maura told to me, absence often made the yearning for a thing that one was parted from, or denied to grow all the stronger. I'd no need for these wise words, this I already knew well! My children. My home. My parents. My husband. Now Raven and my harp. Some gone forever from me in this lifetime. Some, though out of sight, the promise of meeting again, of togetherness, real and likely. I'm not a one for dwelling on loss, it's not my way. Always looking ahead to what's coming, that's me! Carrying the memories of what has been as treasured gems, yet, not as weighty burdens. My loved ones wouldn't want that for me. I have no wanting of that! Even after all the pain and loss I've had, I still see goodness and beauty. And before me, it now stands; my harp!

S afely delivered by Declan and John, the covers taken off and stools placed by, our harps stood ready for our hands. Maura and me both made a little sigh on seeing them. A harp is more than a musical instrument. That is the nature of it. Once known, a harp of good fit is bonded to the harper. Though only having the harp in my life a short time, already I knew this to be so. For Maura, the union was long. I know her to look upon her harp and the music she played, with a deep love, as one might love kin, a love that she, with patience, was sharing with me.

Without much thinking or holding back, I placed my arm around her, and gave Maura a small embrace. No words. None needed. And in that moment, I made a silent vow to include Maura in my praying each night before sleep comes to me. She, surely worthy of such a favour.

We tuned, then I began the playing of one of my pieces. Maura stopped me. Me being eager, had not done the visioning, breathing, or calling to the Old Ones. This I must do every time, until it becomes as natural, and part of my harp playing, as the tilting back of the harp to the shoulder, she told me.

"It will take time. How much, none can say. For some, it's a short time, for others, perhaps many months. But, if you attend to this each time your harp comes to your shoulder, it will be something you no longer need to think on. It will be there. You'll be steady and your mind ready for the playing. Now, Orla begin again."

That my wanting to play saw me to forget this part, though I'd gone over it many times, told to me I was not a one for learning it in a short time. Though I learned the tunes with some ease, this, it was clear, I'd not learned well enough yet. It did not come to me in the way Maura spoke of it. Maura told me, betimes, one has to take a step back in order to make the placing of the footfall more sure.

We did not begin work on a new tune that day. Maura needed to think on which piece that would be. This was of no concern to me. I trusted her to choose wisely and instruct me with care. Besides, having the time away from the harp, I'd have gladly played one note over many times, if need be. I did not though. I spent my time visioning, playing through my known tunes, and working on the two that were not yet smooth; still faltering. I found much pleasure at the harp.

Though, most pleasing to me was, I'd taken charge of myself. I'd chosen to play six pieces. Hard work it would be, but I had chosen it. Another had not told me of what I would do. I was not having to obey another's word. It was me, Orla the harper, decreed it so!

# CHAPTER TWENTY-EIGHT

# EVERY SKERRICK OF SOUND

M aura set a piece and I began the work. She played through the whole tune. I listened. Then Maura played only the first phrase. I tried singing it back to her. When I could sing it, getting the phrase mostly as it was played, I took it to my harp. I visioned, breathed, and called in the Old Ones, then I played. Over and over, I did this and sound by sound it came. Like the other tunes, clumsy and stilted in the beginning, growing smoother over time.

Now, I had my six tunes, and a new bother. In learning a number of new tunes at the one time, they betimes became muddled, and I would find myself beginning one tune, and in my playing, it became another. Maura told to me, this was the way of it, when some of the tunes shared a run of strings, and one was attempting to learn with haste. To remedy this, Maura advised me to work only on one tune in the morning and another in the afternoon. She thought this helpful, as not only would I get the tunes solidly under my fingers, but it would, as well, give some time between the playing of each pair of tunes. This she told me would make my mind work hard, that being good for the remembering.

Maura was right. Working my tunes in pairs, one in the morning, one in the afternoon, and though we'd been humming and singing the tunes in the evening, returning to the playing of the first pair of tunes, each having one of the new tunes, was hard work! The new tunes being more easily lost. Some had holes in them, and Maura was no help. She said the more I used my own head, the stronger the tune would be and the better it would stay with me. I do not know if it was my earnest calling to the Old Ones for the help and guidance, but sound by sound the music came.

Once, I got the whole of each tune, it was there, for that day anyways! It was like they were hiding from me and I had to seek them out. After a time, when I changed my thinking, no longer trying to battle the tune but thought more on it as a game of hide and seek, I found the tunes more easily. It became a mischief. Peeking into the corners of my mind to find a few notes hiding here, a few there.

John was right, the two weeks away from Raven passed with great haste. Yet after spending many long hours at my harp, it saw me with my six tunes. I cannot say I played them nicely, but I had them. Now I could spend my time at the harp, doing what Maura called polishing and ornamenting them. My reward, a day with Raven!

Walking along the woodland path, my thinking jumped from the tunes, to Raven, to the being in the top of the tower, to the thrilling in my body when I felt the heat of another near me. A man I thought to be Declan, yet not. Even now, my face filled with colour. I had a yearning for the touch of another. At forty years, my body still desired the touch of a man. Not the warm embrace of a friend or kin, but a wild union, a thrilling knowing of another! My steps quickened into running, thinking to escape my own mind. Think of the tunes! Think of Raven! The whistle sounded.

I rode Raven that day like a wild thing. Galloping across the field, hooves thundering, me laughing like a woman mad of mind. Such pleasure! Raven knowing me, snorting and prancing, joining in the fun of it. The wind, the wild, the freeing! I was not Orla Connellan. Just for a short time, I was a wild thing! A spirit. A goddess. An untamed thing; I was alive!

I slipped off Raven at the door of the stables, lead her in and hooked the reins on the latch of the stall door. Having run up the stirrups, I was unbuckling the girth, when John appeared.

"Looks like you two have had a time of it then."

Bedraggled, my hair though most of it still in its plaits had loosened bits hanging round my face, and I was still breathing hard from the laughing and the galloping. Lifting the saddle showed the sweat beneath, telling of a hard ride.

"Were you running from something, or did you just want to gallop?" John asked good-naturedly, yet in a way that told me, he understood. The colour in my face rose a little, as one whose secret might almost be guessed, yet not quite.

"It was grand. And John, thank you."

"For what?"

"Taking care of Raven. I'll try and come to help every few days, if I can."

He called over his shoulder as he left. "Dry her off well before you brush her, and give her a good feed, it looks like she's earned it."

I lead Raven into her stall, returned my gear to the tack room, and got a bucket of water for her. While she drank, I went back to the tack room. There were many bins with all manner of horse things. In one of them were pieces of linen. I took some of these to dry Raven's coat, along with brushes and a pick. When I finished, I mixed her a feed, and gave her an extra biscuit of hay. Putting back the brushes, I headed homeward.

Nearing the gate leading out from the big house, I heard running footsteps ahint me. Turning, there was May. She told me some of the women would be making candles over the next few days, and to be sure to tell Maura. I gave my word.

Maura, was most excited on hearing the news.

"I'll go in the morning. You'll have to stay ahint to work on your music. I'll stay overnight. You'll be alright, won't you?" She asked, yet it was more out of good manners than concern.

With Maura's face wearing the eagerness, it was plain the making of the candles was something she took great pleasure in, and me, the one this woman had given a great many things, was not about to deny her this. The truth be told, the thinking of having some time to myself, I welcomed.

"I'll be grand. You go!"

With Maura gone to Declan's, I went to the chamber. Going alone, was now something I'd come to enjoy. I worked hard again all that day, breaking off only now and again. I did this more to practice the visioning part of my playing, than having a want to stop. I knew myself fortunate to be able to play for long stretches without my mind wandering or my body aching, as it had when I first began the learning. When I'd done enough for the day I went back to the cottage. How odd it was without Maura. Even on the days when she didn't come with me to the chamber, she was always in the cottage by evening. I was used to that being the way of it.

I did nothing much different without Maura there, yet I felt different. I liked being alone, and nowadays it was a rare thing; only in the chamber playing my harp, or riding Raven. I tended the chickens, prepared my supper, and ate it sitting by the fire, a thing never done! Maura and me always being sat at the table to eat. I washed my bowl and made a pot of tea. While it was brewing, I decided, not being ready to retire, to pour the tea into my flask, and return to the chamber. I made safe the fire in the hearth, took down my brat, and with my crane bag slung over my shoulder, pulled the cottage door closed ahint me.

Knowing well my way, I walked without light to the abbey. Reaching in, taking up the tinderbox, I lit the lamp and went to my harp. I'd only been down in the chamber at night when Maura and I ran with our harps to the tower, yet, it was the same. In the tunnels, there was no day or night only darkness, and the smooth, well-shaped stones keeping their secrets from the outside world. In here, I was one of their secrets, one of their mysteries.

I ran my hands over my harp to check it was in good voice. With the chamber not troubled by the weather of the outside, and the regular playing, my harp was rarely in need of much tuning. Still, never did I neglect the sweeping of my hands over it to check. As I made ready to play it came to me, that when I played the world round me, no longer was. I played myself into a mist of music! Just me, my harp, and the sound drifting from this place to another. A place, I knew not where. Coming late to the harp, and in the beginning, being unsure if I'd be ever able to play, I now knew this to be a right and true place for me. A right and true calling for me. Though still an apprentice, I was becoming Orla, the harper.

Having the order of the pieces I'd play at Declan's big house, I began. There was a shift in me as I played. Visioning, breathing, calling the Old Ones. Before raising my hands to the strings, I searched deep within for the nature of the tune. What was it that the one who made this tune wanted to tell the ear of those listening? This was something Maura had spoken of many times, and here alone in the night I heard what she was telling to me.

As I sat, I looked to Maura's harp. It sat on one side of the chamber, with me on the other. I thought on her harp as the one who listened; the one I played for. I played my first tune. One full of joy and brightness, then the second, the soothing one, then the lament. The lament I knew well enough to betimes close my eyes. The sadness in this tune flowed through me as did my own blood.

As the last strain drifted away, a whispered voice said, "That is truly the music of the gods."

This, the voice of a man, was not the voice of the unseen one I'd heard before. Declan stood leaning against the wall where the tunnel met the chamber. He did not move, or speak, neither did I... until every skerrick of sound was gone.

"**M**aura asked John to come and check on you, but as he had a mare foaling, I've come in his stead."

Walking back to the cottage together in the night, Declan spoke to me for the first time of my playing.

"I was taken to another world, carried away on the strains. The sorrow and the beauty touched me in a way I've never known before. I've heard Maura play many times, yet never have I been so moved."

I didn't know what to make of this, or what to say. To have this man, the one I was greatly drawn to, the one I had strong feelings for, feelings known only to me and Raven, to have him speaking in such an unguarded, and plain manner, made me to feel humble, disquieted and honoured, all at once.

"It is the way of the harp."

"No. It is the way you play the harp. You truly are the chosen one Orla. I've heard more than Maura play before, yet, your playing has a quality I've never before heard. You don't play the fancy way, but you have not a need to. There's a nature to your playing that can touch a man deep within. That is a gift. That is your gift."

In that moment, what I truly wanted was for him to kiss me, to join with me. I wanted him to touch me... deep within! I walked beside him in silence. As we neared the cottage his black nickered softly to him. Untying his horse, Declan waited while I unlocked the door. As I stepped through the doorway he swung into his saddle, saying in his smooth easy manner, that he'd report back to Maura all was well with me. I gave a small smiling nod.

I closed the door. Leaning against it my heart pounded as fast as the fading sound of cantering hooves on earth. All was not well with me! Long deep breaths charged with wanting filled my body. My breast rising and falling with longing for Declan's touch. I held my hands to my head. For a long time I stood waiting for the pounding to quieten, for the thrilling of my body to quieten, waiting for the calm to come upon me. The strength of my yearning for Declan's touch troubled me greatly.

The knowing, if he'd made any sign of wanting me, as I did him, I would have yielded. I would've given myself freely to him, there on that night in Maura's cottage, with no thinking or regard for what may have come of such a tryst. Again, Declan O'Malley had saved me from my own brazen foolishness. Anger replaced yearning as I moved to stoke the fire. Sitting there, I swore an oath to myself. Never would I be the one to seek the affections of Declan. If it was to be so, he would have to declare it.

M y neck ached and I was cold as I creaked awake still sitting in the chair by the fire that had gone out long ago. The cockerel was crowing as was his duty to call in the new day. Unfurling my legs, stiff with being tucked up on the chair, I slowly eased myself into the day, stretching and making my blessing. The mood of the night before trying to sneak its way into the morning. I sent it away with a coldness shown to the uninvited.

I ate a little bread and drank some water for my morning meal. I'd not readied porridge, or kept the fire burning, as was the way when Maura was home. I fed the chickens, and gathered wood, placing it in the hearth for when Maura came back. I picked up my crane bag. It had the flask of tea from yesterday. Taking out the plug, I smelled it. It would do me for the day. Taking a fresh supply of char cloth, and collecting some dry grass along the way, I went to the abbey.

I lit the lamp, and put the char cloth into the tinderbox, determined as I walked the tunnel to put all my efforts into my harp playing. I tuned, then went through my ritual. Visioning, breathing, silently stating my intention, and calling in the Old Ones. I then played through all six of my pieces, though if Maura was here this would not be the way, but she was not here. She would not always be with me, and on this day this was what I was called to do. Before beginning each tune, I stood, walked around, then went through my ritual before playing.

I'd be lying if I said I didn't look in hope, for the handsome leaning figure but he was not there, and soon the music took me over. For the rest of the day, I worked on one of the Goltrai tunes, the one that would be played last in my list at the big house. I could hear in my mind, the way I wanted this tune to sound, yet my fingers chose not to obey, finding it hard in the making of some of the shapes. I looked for where these troubles were and made up games for my hands to play. When it was a game and not work, they lost their defiance.

When it was nearly time to be leaving the chamber, I played once more through all six tunes in the order I'd be playing them. The last tune was now better; the game playing had settled the piece. When I got back to the cottage Maura was not yet there. I lit the fire and made ready the porridge for the following day. I was readying a modest evening meal of egg and barley gruel when I heard a horse.

With a rising hope, I tidied my hair with my hands and checked my clothes. A gentle knock sounded. One that did not match the rapping inside of me. Shaking myself, I stood tall and moved to open the door. It was not Declan, but one of his men come to tell me that Maura would stay one more night at the big house. I thanked him, and asked him to tell

Maura I was in good health and looked forward to her return.

When first the knock sounded, I'd hoped it was Declan. Relieved I was that it was not. Though, I'd made a vow to myself, I was unsure if I could keep it. Unsure if I could trust myself to be alone in his company. It was good to have the passing of some time to firm up my oath. Maura had many times spoken of the value of intention. I would use intention to keep my thinking about, and feelings for Declan hidden from all.

I kept a close watch on the gruel, stirring it often, not wanting it to burn and make the whole pot bitter. Like the night before I ate by the fire, but didn't go this time to my harp, not wanting to tempt fate. Instead I set myself to some needlework and humming through the tunes. I struggled to settle. Though I'd sworn my oath, I'd an ear for listening in the hope another would come to knock at the door. No one came. I readied the fire for overnighting and took to my bed.

Sleep came quickly, as I'd not rested well the night before. I dreamed of my children, my beautiful young folk. I dreamed of playing my harp, and I dreamed of Raven. Of galloping on her with my hair flying free, and riding to the grove, the peaceful, holy grove. I walked the avenue of stones, and like Maura and Declan, I spoke with the Old Ones. In my dream I knew how to speak with them. I heard the voice of the Old One, the man I'd heard before, the unseen one.

*You cannot keep your secrets from all. We the Old Ones, hear and see everything. We are here to help you and guide you through this life. We will never abandon you but you must learn to trust us. Open your heart to us. Trust yourself. Open your heart to yourself.*

I t was raining hard the next morning. Protected by my heavy woollen brat, I hurried to the tunnel. I worked at my harp as I had the day before going through my ritual, looking for the parts where my fingers found strife, and making up more games for them to play. I made my day a short one, wanting to get back to the cottage and make it ready for Maura's return. I had a nice cooking fire laid down, and a warming stew bubbling by the time she arrived. She told me all about the making of candles, and brought back a fresh supply of both candles and char cloth she and the women of the big house had made. It was plain Maura enjoyed the work, and had a great fondness for the women of Declan's household.

I told her of the work I'd done at my harp, and as I was speaking, a memory of my dream came. I spoke of this to Maura, leaving out the parts I did not want to share. I told her of the Old One who spoke to me, and what he'd said about the Old Ones being here to help and guide me, and about trusting them and myself. Maura told me I should take this as a sign that I was coming to know them. She urged me to be forever watchful for the signs that may come in many shapes, even in a game one plays to make stronger the way a hand is placed on the harp strings!

# CHAPTER TWENTY-NINE

# THE GREEN DRESS

The next weeks were passed by practicing for the sharing of my music at the big house, and an occasional ride on Raven. Though, the riding didn't happen often enough for me. John the Englishman was eager to accompany me the few times the weather was kind, and Maura deemed I needed to step away from my harp. I had much to share with Raven. Things I wanted, and needed to say aloud. Secrets I needed to hear spoken in my own voice in a bid to let them go. Setting them free into the clear, crisp air, I was thinking, the only way to stopping their constant invasion of my mind. This was not to be, not now.

The day arrived and so to did Declan with my harp in the back of the cart. As before, my harp wore its cover, and was placed with care resting on a bed of thick straw. This was the first time I'd seen him since his night visit to the cottage. He was his usual warm confident self, and me, on the outside anyways, was my usual self. Inside, my heart thumped, and my body thrilled again at seeing him, having him near. Yet, I'd made a vow and I would keep it!

We did not rush on that day. Maura telling of the need to stay quiet and keep my thinking on the music and my intention. This she told to Declan, he nodded his understanding, spending the time waiting for us to ready, by stroking the neck of, and talking quietly to his fine black. In my forty years, though I'd never met in truth many menfolk, never had I been so thrilled by one as I was by Declan O'Malley. A man that looked on me as a friend, nothing more. How I wanted it to be more!

Travelling in the back of the cart allowed me to watch those who sat afore me. The ease of being in each other's company, ever-present. The love shared, ever-present. As we bumped along the now familiar path, a calmness fell over me. I'd felt this before, the feeling that all's right in the world. Where it came from, and why it came at all, I cannot say. I could give it no name, this feeling, yet welcomed it and the comfort it brought. Was this one of the signs Maura spoke of?

In the morning I'd been filled with unease when thinking on playing for those at the big house, now this had left me. Now, I thought only of sharing my music with those, some of who'd grown to be friends, and others who perhaps, might be in need of my music. Now, as we made our way, my grand-mother's words came. *Playing of the harp, is a privilege!*

N earing the gates, there was no whistle. There never was when it was Declan coming to his own home. Declan, Maura and the gateman exchanged a few words as we passed. I nodded to the man, and he to me. Halting in front of the house, one of Declan's men came to the head of his black in readiness to take him to the stables. I jumped down, not wanting to feel my hand in Declan's.

Not showing any sign of taking notice of me getting myself down from the cart, with great care, Declan lifted down my harp, and carried it inside. Maura and me followed. Maura took our small bags upstairs telling me to go with Declan to get a feel for the room. The ballroom was beautiful... and big! A fleeting flash of fear peeped out from ahint my harp, but was quickly disappeared by Declan's taking off of the harp cover.

"It's not an easy thing to do, to take this cover off. We don't want you getting all het up struggling with this thing, before you have to play tonight."

I breathed out my joy on hearing this. Doing battle with the wretched beast before the eyes of any was not my want. More pleasing to me was Declan's knowing of the oilskin's defiance. Wresting apart bag and harp was a tussle that was not mine alone! Once my harp was standing in its chosen place, it was left to get used to the air of the room. Declan pulled the door closed as we left, he to his work, and I upstairs to Maura.

Entering the room I saw a dress laid out on the bed. It was most beautiful. Dark green velvet with a posy of buttercups stitched by a fine hand. The same buttercups danced around the hemline of the dress and edged the sleeves. Alongside it lay a matching sash.

"This is for you to wear tonight. Its colour will bring out your green eyes and show off your dark hair well."

"I cannot wear this Maura! This is the dress of a noblewoman, not a crofter's daughter."

"Ah, you're right, this is the dress of a noble-woman. Once you were a crofter's daughter, now you are not. You Orla, are a noble woman. Not by birth, but by the being of a fine woman harper. This is a dress befitting your station now."

I had no words. Running my hand over the finely stitched flowers on the bodice, feeling the silken velvet, knowing through my hand how this garment would feel on my body. I took it up and held it to myself. Even without slipping it over my head, I knew it would fit me perfectly.

"Clodagh had it made for you. Your grandmother knows well exactly what suits you. Now, why don't you go down and tune your harp. That way, you can come back, put on your dress and spend some time in it, so when you play, you will be at ease."

I thought on the dress, and my grandmother as I stepped down the stairs. Clodagh Moran had done well by me in so many ways. She'd given my children a life I never have could. She'd saved mine, when I could so easily have died with my parents and husband. She'd given me a fine horse, a harp, and now the most beautiful garment any woman could have.

I quietly opened the ballroom door and slipped inside, closing it ahint me, my need to be alone, great in that moment. My heart swelled in the same instant with thanks, love and pain. My hand clenched my tuning key with a force that matched the pain in my heart. A pain of longing for those I loved, those I'd lost, and those that would never love me. Blinking back the seeping wet in my eyes, I ran my free hand across the strings. I began the tuning of my harp and the readying of myself.

"I've drawn a bath for you. It will wash away the grime of the day and ready you for your dress and the evening."

Maura was such a wise woman. Though I didn't always agree with her ways I knew her to ever have the best in mind for me. And a bath I would enjoy. I had more than the grime of the day to wash away.

My hair was still plaited and pinned up, as was my way these days, making the journey to Declan's as a lad. Having removed my clothes, I stepped into the warm comfort of the tub. The water was hot and deep. As I sat down it cloaked my shoulders. Maura handed me a linen wash cloth before leaving me.

Closing my eyes, I leaned back my head and with little care dipped the cloth and put it to my neck and face, then my arms. Maura and me knew, though unspoken, that the bathing was more for my comfort than for my need of washing. With still a decent amount of time before playing, the bathing brought to me a calming.

When I'd had my fill, I stood and dried myself with the linen. Picking up the dress I held it once more to my body. Now alone, I looked at myself in the mirror. Holding it to me I whirled about. I slipped it over my head and tied the sash around my waist. It fit like a glove. I let down my hair and was combing it through when Maura came back. A great gasp escaped her lips!

"Oh Orla, you are so pleasing to the eye. Your look matches well your playing... quietly beautiful! Clodagh has indeed chosen well. As I've said before, do not wear your loveliness with coy. Orla, the gods have blessed you well. Do them the honour of wearing your beauty with your head held high."

I remembered well Maura saying this to me before. I did not blush this time. Us both standing before the mirror, I could not disagree with her. The dress set off my comeliness, and made me to feel as one that I did not know. When I spoke this aloud to Maura, she showed no surprise.

"Some will live their whole lives as one person, some will change many times. Some will be born as one, then become another. Few can know what life has in store for us. One thing I am sure of, is that you Orla Connellan, the beautiful woman harper, on this very day, will touch the hearts and souls of those of all who hear your playing."

G oing in for the evening meal dressed as a noblewoman was an odd thing. I entered the room and all the talking stopped. All eyes were on me. And there among them, were my kin. As I rushed to my sons and daughter I could see the pride in their eyes. Mary, Seamus, Uncle Jarlath, and my grandmother, Clodagh. They were all there.

It was Mary who spoke first. "Orla, you look so beautiful... and well." Always, the mother was Mary.

Seeing and embracing my children, and them me, swelled me with love. They were handsome young folk. Kathleen, like myself wore a dress, though of a more simple look. I'd never seen her in the clothes of a woman, she'd hidden well her true womanly beauty! My uncle gave me his usual warm wink of blessing. When all the embracing and surprise quietened, and the room began to hum once more with chatter, my grandmother came to me.

"I knew that to be the right dress for you Orla. I hope it is to your liking. It is one of fine needlework, yet it is more. It is, though not as needed as strings, or a harp key, it is the work dress of a harper! The Old Ones and those who love you, wish you many occasion to wear it."

T he meal over, as we walked to the ballroom, Kathleen linked her arm through mine.

"Oh Mammy, how grand this is. You, the bravest woman with your harp, leading the front for the souls of the people of Ireland. Oh, how I wish that someday, in some way, a chance such as yours is mine. I would gladly give my life for that."

I knew by the way it was said, that grand for Kathleen, was not about the splendour of the thing, but about the calling that had begun my new life. For my daughter, mine was a cause, a purpose. She lusted after such a purpose. We, most of us lust after a purpose! Kathleen saw the calling of me to the harp as a sacred thing, an exciting thing, a thing of great change!

I understood her want to know for herself, her reason for being. I knew this question lived within me; in most. Never had I shied away from the asking or the searching. I could be defiant and strong, when my wanting to know was great, or I believed a thing to be right and just. Though in me, this was tempered with a willingness to admit error if I found myself so. Of this quality in Kathleen, I was less sure.

G oing to my harp, I ran my hand across the strings listening for any that may have lost their tuning, then I sat and began my ritual. Closing my eyes for a few moments, I visioned, breathed, called in the Old Ones, and thought on the intention of the tune I was about to play. So practiced was my ritual, that it now took only one long deep breath to make the change from Orla Connellan to Orla the harper. I told first of what I knew of the tune, and raising my hands to the strings, the sweet sound of the noble strain Goltrai filled the room.

The music rose and fell over all like a magic veil of sound. I played through my tunes, telling of them what I could, visioning, breathing, calling in. I was not Orla Connellan wearing the green dress of a noblewoman. I was not making music for people. I played as a harper with the hands of a spirit-raiser! The sound, an unseen mist that wended its way in answer to the hearts and souls of those who without voice, called for it.

On ending my last tune, lowering my hands, I came back from a faraway place. Once more I saw the faces of those sitting before me, yet, no one spoke. All sat as if under a powerful spell. I knew this spell. It was the spell of my making! I stood, and with my words freed them from it.

"Thank you for accepting my gift. It has been given with a true heart in the hope that each will have heard the voice of the music speaking its message to you."

Like a soft gentle wind, the hum of voices and the moving began. Some moving towards me, some talking to others. Little by little the wind grew back into the gale of chatter and laughter that had earlier sounded around the large table where we'd shared a meal.

As was often the way, Paedar was first by my side. "Mammy, I have no words to tell of the way your music made me to feel." He threw his arms around me.

This was the way of the evening. People sharing their joy of the night. Like a circle, I gave, they received. They gave, I received. It'd be easy to be swelled by the high regard and kind words given, yet all the while Maura's learnings were with me. *You are merely the messenger!* Her teachings never were disregarded by me. I knew them to be given with honesty and good reason.

Maura did not come to me when my playing had ended, neither did my grandmother. The two stood together speaking quietly with an occasional glance my way. I did not need them at my side. I did not need to hear their words. Their eyes told me they were content with their choice of me.

I welcomed the distance from me they stood. I cannot say I enjoyed the attention given me, though I knew it to be akin to the life of a harper. Maura had spoken of this to me. It was something for me to get used to, she said. When all the fuss died down, I spent time with my children, and kin. What joy to see them! I stayed with them until my energy waned. I was tired from the playing and after a long night, looked to be alone. In turn, I kissed each of them goodnight.

Though, neither had come to me, Declan and John had for a long time spoken with Maura and my grandmother. I could not hear what they spoke of, yet their faces told me it gave cause for concern. I went to them, thanking Declan for the evening, kissing my grandmother and Maura, I went to my bed. I did not ask of what they spoke. If I was bound in it, I would in time come to know. I slept that night as one who had gone to their grave.

A t the bottom of the stairs next morning, I could hear the voices of my kin coming from the dining room. I made my way to the kitchen, taking down a bowl, I served some porridge.

Turning to go with it into the dining room, May said to me in her cocky way, "Issn it grand to play at th' harp an' to have th' eye o' th' two most handsome men in th' house. I seen th' way them both looks at you."

"And what two would you be talking of then, May?"

"Declan an' John, o' course."

"I'll not be thinking that's the way of it at all."

This set May going. Like a thresher the words left her mouth, telling me Declan and John could not take their eyes from me the whole night. Never, had she seen them eye a woman as they did me. My face took on colour as she went on with her teasing. Saying when I walked into the dining room their jaws were, "nigh on th' floor 'em was. You ask inny one. They'll tell 'e."

Touching my arm as I left the kitchen, I could hear her affectionate giggling trailing me as I stood waiting in the entrance hall for the blood to leave my cheeks. Not knowing who was in the dining room, I had no want to go in with my face all a flush!

"A h, Orla. Come sit with your kin before they take their leave," said Maura.

Declan was not there. I was glad, for had he been, my colour would've surely risen again. It was most pleasing to have time alone with my kin, taking a meal together as we'd done on the farm. Hearing all the news about what each had been doing, what was growing in the garden, new foals born, which horses had been sold. It seemed such a long time back since I'd been part of life on the farm. A small part of me envied my kin their simple life, yet, I knew there was no going back for me, not now. There was no surprise in my grandmother's words, as always seeming to know my thinking.

"Orla, your harp playing is coming well along. You have clearly put in the work, and it shows. My faith in you is well placed. We all have faith in you. Maura and I have talked with Declan and John about how best to begin the spreading of your work. We've made a plan. Yet, this is not the time to speak of such things. They will tell you of it. For now, let us enjoy the time we have as kin."

Looking at each of the faces of my kin, I could see the concern in Jarlath's, Mary's and Paedar's. Seamus and Connor gave nothing away. A skill that'd serve well one with a wanting for the selling, gambling, or the life of a trickster. Kathleen beamed with eagerness, seeing my life as a harper a great holy crusade. Then there was my grandmother. Clodagh Moran and Maura both wore the face of acceptance. Each, proud of me, but knowing what had to be done. Each knowing as did I, beautiful and magical as the harp is, taking on the life of a harper in these times could cost mine. Yet, I had agreed, and was not a one for going back on my word.

The meal was had. The chatter lifted, turning away from the thorny uncertainty of that what might befall me, to the readying for my kin's journey back to the farm. It was best for us to part. Knowing they were safe on the farm, I could give my mind and my heart to the work, and they, not being privy to my deeds, would be spared unnecessary concern. Goodbyes exchanged, the leaving done with, I made my way to the stables.

Maura and I would stay on one more night to talk of the plan made for my harp and me. So far, I knew nothing of this, and now my only wanting was to take my beautiful black mare out and ride in peace, just Raven and me. No rules, no plans, no judging! We called to each other, Raven and me as I walked through the stables, stopping at the tack room to get my saddle and bridle. Riding towards the galloping field, all was left ahint! The harping, the kinfolk, the big house, the wanting; now just me, horse and nature. Last night was already like a dream, a thing that might happen while one sleeps. I didn't go to the galloping field, Raven's head being turned by a hand not mine down the path to the grove... to the place of the Old Ones!

# CHAPTER THIRTY

# THE PLAN

Though only having gone to the grove a scattering of times, I well knew the way. I'd taken note as instructed by John the Englishman, of each path, where they joined, unusual trees, and when the sun shone, its place in the sky. On this day, there was no sun, the air crisp, with heavy clouds threatening to unburden themselves without care. I walked Raven for most of the journey. I had no mind to do any more. The playing of my harp, and the following nature of relief, thrill, and the much speaking with others, had left me in need of quietness. Raven's walking hoof falls and gentle motion matched in every way, my spirit, so too did the place I was heading.

On reaching the grove, I tied Raven on a long rein, and walked down the avenue of stones. Entering the stone circle, I stopped. What was I to do here? I didn't know the ritual for the calling of the Old Ones. I began to walk the circle as I had seen Maura and Declan do. I'd heard their murmuring, yet, knew not what words they spoke. As I walked, the rain began. Softly at first, then all at once so thick that looking through likened it to fog. I pulled the hood of my brat over my head, glad now, I'd worn it. I did not seek shelter. I kept walking. The sound of the rain making me bold to give voice. I called to the Old Ones. I called with a voice so loud I thought it not to be mine!

"Come to me those who have gone before. Be with me now in this place. I beg of you. Show yourselves to me. Give me a sign. Come so that I can honour you."

This I said over and over, walking all the time, not knowing what might visit me; perhaps the voice of the unseen one, or the great stag. Nothing came. Nothing did I see. The heavy rain fell upon me with my every step. Round and round in one direction, then turning to the other. Nothing! Just footsteps, sheeting rain, and my tears of desperation and disappointment. I dropped to my knees, sobbing. I felt a strong hand on my shoulder. I turned, yet saw no one. Hastily, I stood. I was alone, save for Raven. Even the rain retreated.

Miserable, I mounted Raven, yet with every step my spirit lifted. I'd felt a hand! The trees, moss and bracken grew brighter. The bird calls louder and sweeter than ever before. Oddly too, the path I rode showed no sign of rain. I felt my brat. It was wet. Raven's coat though drying from the ride, was the coat of a horse caught by the rain. Yet, nowhere were the tell-tale droplets of water on the leaves, or puddles along the path, the signs telling of a rain so heavy as we had known! I looked to the sky. The heavy clouds still hung in readiness with their menacing darkness. Even more odd, was that no question swirled in my mind, only acceptance. The knowing that something, a holy thing, had taken place in the grove, and Raven and I were part of it.

"**W**hat have you two been up to? You look as though you've been for a swim."

I told John the Englishman of the heavy rain that had blessed us. Holding the reins as I dismounted, he said, "You must have been in need of a soaking. The rain has not yet come to us here. But then isn't that the way of Ireland."

I knew he was fooling, and loved Ireland, taking it to be his home, but, that he was English had not gone far enough from me. His words brought about a rise in me causing me to speak more harshly than I'd meant.

"Well it may not have fallen here, but it surely did in the place that Raven and I have been. Any man with half-good eyesight can plainly see, and if you don't like it, go back to your own land!"

"My eyes see well enough. And my ears hear that for all your good looks and fine harping, your tongue has lost none of its edge." He teased, the hurt sounding.

I took the reins from him, and turned quickly towards Raven's stall, feeling the colour coming to my face. His words bringing to mind what May had said in the morning. I lifted the saddle from Raven and placed it on the stall door while I took off her bridle. As I hung them in the tack room, John stood in the doorway.

"Last night was a rare one, Orla. Your playing was as from another world, and Declan and I agreed as we watched and listened, we neither had seen a woman more beautiful than yourself." Then in his usual teasing way, he said, "Now, all you have to learn is to keep a mannerly tongue in your head."

He ducked and scampered out of sight as I threw a brush at him!

Brushing Raven, I thought on his words. I laughed softly, knowing how I must look. Bedraggled, smelling of wet wool and wet horse. Hair straggling about my face. Grubby hands, and likely a grubby face. Very few would know me as the harper woman who wore that green dress, yet, here I am. I am she.

Finishing off in the stables, I went up to the big house. There in the entrance hall as I hung my brat, I met Declan. His face showed his surprise at my state. My half-smile masked my awkwardness. I hurried passed and up the stairs.

"I've spoken with Maura, and we'll meet in my rooms after the evening meal." He called after me with amusement in his voice.

"Whissht woman! What have you been up to? You look as one who's been hunting in the wilds. Come, undress. I'll get some hot water."

As Maura left the room, I caught sight of myself in the mirror. It made me to laugh aloud. I looked not perhaps as one who had been hunting in the wilds but as one who was herself, a wild thing! I was grubby. I was bedraggled, yet I liked the woman I saw, the one who looked back at me. The one wearing the breeches of a man. The one who had ridden a fine black mare alone to the grove. The one who had walked the circle of stones in the pouring rain. The one who had felt the strong hand on her shoulder. I tilted up my chin and stood tall. I liked the woman of forty years, I was growing into!

A round the dining table that night there was much talk of my look, my dress and my harp playing. Sitting there clad in my clean, womanly garb of skirt and shawl, the clothes of an ordinary woman, there was a distance between myself and the harper woman. Yet, I knew them to be the same; two parts of me. I laughed with all when John told of the wild woman he had encountered in the stables, and Declan's telling of sighting the same, just outside of the dining room in the entrance hall.

"She flew passed me and up the stairs like a ban-shee."

These folk were such a tonic to be in the company of. Never, was I made to feel as though I didn't belong.

When the meal was done, John and Declan took their leave. Maura and I stayed on for a while. Then with a tilt of her head, Maura gave me the sign it was time for us to leave as well. As we walked the stairs Maura told me the talk around the table, was to be treasured. They are the times, she said, that a harper could call on to keep connected to the land and our people. They are the words that could give comfort to the harper when she was alone, or afraid, or far away.

"Always remember the love for you in that room on this night, Orla."

M aura knocked gently on Declan's door. John sat at a round table in front of a large window. Declan gestured with his hand for us to take a seat. As we sat, it was Maura who spoke.

"Orla. Do you recall clearly what Clodagh, your grandmother, asked of you?"

Well, I remembered. "Yes. She spoke to me of the the bringing together, and the healing needed by many of our land. How music had a power, especially the music of the harp. That it could cross unseen bridges, help people to mend. And, that me as a harper, was the one best to take on this duty."

"And you agreed."

"Yes." I had no want to talk of my resistance or my plea for another to be the one.

"Good. Now it is time for the casting of a wider net. You have played for your kin and for this household, yet that is only the beginning. You must share your music with more. We, Clodagh, Declan, John and I, have a plan, and if you agree, we can set it in place."

"And if I don't agree?"

"All will have been in vain. The plan stops here."

"Then I will agree."

The men sat in silence, yet the concern on their faces said much. I knew the life of a harper in these times was a life of danger, though until now, I'd known none of it save the scramble through the tunnels of Cill Ala, and the hiding of my harp in the tower. But in truth, it was nothing more than a bit of a caper. I knew well, my life could not remain mild and untroubled as it had in the past few months. The vision of the wild woman who stared back at me from the mirror. *I have courage enough, and a willingness to learn and to do what I must. I am well chosen.*

"There will be much danger, Orla." Said Declan.

"Do you think I don't know this? Do you think me some foolish, simple girl?" As the words spat from my mouth, I felt the strong hand grip my shoulder. I turned to it.

"What is it?" Maura asked.

I could not say for I did not know. "Never a mind. Tell me of this plan."

It was told to me. I was to play at a big house, another Irish house. Declan would ride with me. I would need at least another six tunes, and much thought would need to be given to the travelling. Maura told to us in times gone these big houses would have had their own harps. This would have made it all the more easy. It was now not so.

This was a plan that could not be hurried. Time would be needed to learn the tunes, make good the travel, and firm up an invitation to play. Though, the owner of this house, unknown to me, would require little bidding for this as he looked kindly upon our cause. All sitting who knew, agreed. It was settled! The music would be left to Maura and me, and the travel to Declan and John.

When all was spoke of, Declan poured us each a glass of his fine mead. "Sláinte," he said.

"Sláinte," we all said, knowing as we touched our glasses together, that our deeds could find us risking more than our health!

Not much happened over the next few months. I learned more tunes and rode Raven when I could. It rained much as is the way, and every so often Maura and I would spend a day or two at the big house. They be grand days, safe and exciting! In the evening after supper, the four of us, Maura, Declan, John and me would go to Declan's rooms, drink mead and talk of the plan.

The tunes were settled. It was now for me to practice them and get them solid under my hands. These, with Maura's eye upon me, I worked on with a will. Never forgetting the visioning, breathing and calling to the Old Ones. No longer did I have to think on this. It was just there now. It'd become part of my playing, just as the lifting of my hands to the strings. Some of the tunes came quickly with little effort, others not. In some tunes, it was a small bit that wouldn't come, or would come one day, yet the next went into hiding, needing me to call it back once more. This, in some tunes happened many times.

With Maura's words of comfort, I grew to know this as part of being a harper.

"Some will sit with you, others not. Always hold on to your intention, the reason for your playing. This will help you make friends with the tunes that are not so keen. After a time, if you're true, they'll take to you."

The choosing and learning of the music was more plain than the way of carrying the harp. Declan and John decided it would be best travelled on a pack horse. A horse that was not overly tall, so I could load the harp alone, if needs be. The thing they talked of carrying the harp, sounded like a wean's cradle fitted to a wooden pack frame. One that fitted like a packsaddle, but with wooden mounts so the harp could lie along the back of the horse.

The oilskin bag protecting the harp from the weather would need to have more straps fitted. These would tie the bag to the frame. Maura and I sat while the menfolk spoke of the problems and ways for them to be beat; speaking their thoughts aloud. Being caught up in the words, one could without effort forget the seriousness of the task.

"The horse needs to be fast and nimble. We'll have to train it to gallop with the harp on its back. It's likely there will be times when an escape will need to be made. Whoever leads the pack horse will have to be prepared to let it, and the harp go. Orla's life must be protected. There is little to be gained, if the harper is killed or worse, captured! Harps are hard to come by, and I know my English countrymen will, without hesitation destroy it. This loss might be difficult to bear, but not so difficult to bear as the loss of our harper's fingers, or her life! Let us not lose sight of this. Much danger may be found in our plan and we must prepare for it," said John.

I knew the time for leaving was coming soon when on one of the days I went to the big house I saw John in the galloping field with a horse going round him on a long rein. It had a thing on its back like what he and Declan had talked of. A thing what did look like a cradle for a wean. Round and round went the horse. Though I couldn't hear him, I knew John'd be clucking his tongue to get the horse to move, or telling him to whoa! He had the horse walking, trotting, and cantering. Though it didn't yet have a harp in it, the horse didn't seem to be minding the wearing of the thing on its back. When he saw me, John eased up the horse and walked it over to the wall where I was standing.

"This is the horse that's going to carry your harp Orla. What do you think of him?"

"He's grand, no mistake. What do you call him?"

"Henry. It's my little joke. After one of the kings of England. He's strong like Henry, but that is where the likeness ends. This little horse is fast and reliable. He's good natured and will do what you need. He's a half-brother to my bay."

The horse was a bay like John's, but smaller. Not small as a pony though. Plain with the black legs and mane and tail, and a kind brown soft eye. I rubbed Henry's nose and looked at the cradle on his back.

"Do you think he'll run alright with a harp in there?"

"He's pretty steady. We'll bring your harp up soon and see. You and Maura might have to come and stay for a few nights. I'll speak with Declan."

We walked along the wall to the gate, John and Henry on one side and me on the other. John told me he'd been working the horse for the past few weeks, getting him used to the putting on and off of the cradle and running on the long rein. He was ready now to have a go at carrying the harp and riding out with a few other horses. John had a way with the horses. He told me once he liked them better than people. He said that with horses you could understand the things they did, but not with people. At the gate, he handed me the lead rope.

"Get to know him Orla. I've got him in the stall next to Raven. When you come to stay, I'll get you to fit him out with the packsaddle. Henry needs to carry your harp, but you need to be able to load it."

A few days later Maura and I made our way along the woodland path; bags in hand. We'd stay two or three days at Declan's. Maura chattered as we walked and cursed the showers of rain that fell upon us. Though she liked living in her cottage, she always looked forward to spending a few days at the big house. When she was there, the other women without saying, made her the head woman, and she liked it well; they being good friends, Maura and those women, particularly May. I'd come to like them well, too. They always made me to feel welcome.

After putting our bags in Maura's room, I went to the stables. Raven was there, but not Henry. I took myself off to the field. As I expected, John was there with Henry. He had him walking on the long rein, this time, he had my harp on his back. Henry didn't seem to be minding at all, though he was only walking. Climbing over the wall, I made my way across to them. As I got closer, I could see that there be extra straps on the oilskin now, and these were lashed to the cradle. It looked alright up there, sturdy and all.

"Have you tried him at the trot?"

"Not yet. This is his first time with your harp. I'll get him used to the weight of it before I ask more of him. Slowly, is the way. He is a sound ride, but this is all new to him. I don't want rush and spook him. We need him to be firm in his task. Come Orla, walk with us. You lead him. The more time you spend with him the better."

He handed me the lead rope, and we walked along one of the long walls of the field. Henry walked easily beside me, John on the other side of me, away from the horse.

"Are you afraid Orla?"

"Of Henry?"

"No, of riding out and playing your harp for strangers in a strange place?"

"A bit. I'm not afeared of the riding, and only a little of the playing, but I am uneasy about who or what might meet us on the way. I'd be lying if I said I wasn't."

"You'll have Declan with you on your first ride. You could not be in better company. Declan is a good man, bold and fierce if he needs to be. He will protect you if danger comes to meet you. And I know he'll carry a pistol."

"A pistol! Why would he be needing a pistol?"

"Hopefully, it will not be needed Orla, but there is much danger in these times for an Irish harper. Never forget that. You need to keep your eyes and ears open, always."

John's face spoke more to me than his words. It wore the worry plainly.

"Take no risks and keep that savage tongue of yours quiet. Do what Declan tells you. Do not argue, or defy him Orla. Promise me!."

I wanted to lift the air, yet knew this was not a time for it. "I swear on my poor dead mother's grave, I'll do what Declan tells me."

When we got to the stables, John told me what to do to take the harp and cradle from Henry's back. I was glad of my strength. It was not easy to get the harp down. The untying of straps and buckles was easy, but I could've done with being taller, or Henry a bit smaller. Clearing the cradle was the problem. John stood by offering no help, as was his way. I worked out that once it was undone, I could tip the harp over and lift it off. It was heavy being well above my head, but I could do it. It would get easier the more times I did it. Glad I was that Henry stood still with all my huffing and puffing. Glad too was I that my cursing was silently spoken in my head and fell on no other's ears. The taking off of the cradle and pack saddle was easy, just the same as taking off a riding saddle.

"Good." Said John when I was done. "After we've taken our midday meal you can saddle him up again with the harp, and we'll take him into the field again and try him at the trot; see how well the harp sits."

Like the unsaddling, the saddle went on with ease, getting the harp up, not so. And once more John offered no help. I well knew how he worked. If I could do it for myself, then that is the way it would be. If I could not, he would help, and I would be made to feel as a helpless unfortunate. This I would not be. Not in John's eyes, not in any other's eye.

I thought on how I'd taken the harp down. I did over my moves. I lifted it over my head on its side, got it up into the cradle then pushed it up till it lay on its back. I buckled the straps.

"There! It be a brute of a thing, but I've it done!" I said proudly. John only nodded, yet I saw the smiling glint in his eye.

I lead Henry to the field, then John took him. Click- ing his tongue, John set Henry off at a walk. Clicking a few more times, Henry began to trot. The harp sat well, rising and falling in time to each step. Standing where I was facing back towards the stable, I saw Declan watching from the stone fence. John clicked his tongue again urging Henry into a canter. Still the harp sat well, rocking to and fro as it should. John looked to me, then raised his arm to Declan. Declan in return, did the same.

# CHAPTER THIRTY-ONE

# THE BEGINNING

The day came. Maura and I had spent the night before at the big house. She'd rolled up my green dress and packed it with care in my travel bag along with my comb and a few bits and pieces. My body throbbed with the thrill and the fear of it. We went downstairs. I left my bag by the large front door while we went to the kitchen to take our morning meal. I didn't feel like eating but Maura said I must, as the journey would be a long one. After eating, with little talking, I took up my bag, and Maura and me walked to the stables. We hardly spoke. There was nothing left to say.

John and Declan were waiting. All the horses were saddled, my harp was loaded. I looked to John.

"We had to do something with our time while we waited for one who tarried so." He smiled as he spoke, yet we all knew that danger might seek Declan and me out as we journeyed. The hope was that our ride would be marred by nothing more than our fine Irish weather.

We lead our horses out into the yard. Maura kissed my brow. She offered no parting words of wisdom, no final instructions for my harping, only her goodbye.

"Slán Orla."

"Slán, Maura," I returned as I mounted Raven.

"You have a fine day for riding!" said John in his teasing way, looking to the dark clouds above heavy with assurance of rain.

"We should be back in four days. Before the fall of night if all goes well. If we have not returned by midday on the fifth day, then send some to find us. Do not come yourself John. We've many a good man on a horse. I want you here! I need you here!" Declan's words were firm yet warm, such was the bond between the two. They embraced.

Declan then kissed Maura's brow, mounted his fine black, taking the lead rope from John's hand, nodding to me, turned with Henry in tow. I followed. There were no hurrahs, no tears of farewell, just a quiet walking of horses and riders out past the galloping field and down the path leading the way of the grove.

A peace flooded me, that wonderful feeling I'd come to know here in Mayo. All was well in my world. I sat atop my beautiful well-loved mare, walking behind a man, I'd though secretly, come to love, him leading a horse carrying the harp that I loved.

Knowing my kin and Maura to be well, if it were not for the possibility of meeting with others who had less regard for our Irishness, this was for me, close to heaven without being dead!

W e walked steadily for a time, how long I cannot say, for though the heavy clouds had not yet shared their wet load with us, they'd kept the sun well hidden from our gaze. I could not say if it was midday or tell to you the way we were going, only knowing that our journey began southward, the way of the grove. Though we'd started that way we'd taken a path new to me, one not coming to or passing the grove. Glad I was that Declan knew fully where we were. Never did he dull his eyes, his mind or his ears. Constantly watchful, turning his head this way or that, looking, listening, missing nothing that made movement or sound.

The woodland was thick with trees, the path not much used, with only a trace of it showing among the bracken. While I knew not where we were, with Declan, I ever believed myself safe, such was his unspoken oath. We were still in the saddle when the heavens opened. We rested and took shelter. Leaving the path we wove our way among the trees to a place where the arms of some large oaks held their limbs together as holding hands. The ground beneath, though always damp was shielded, so 'neath branch, cloak and brat, comfort was had.

We tied the horses but did not unpack them. Declan took an oilskin sheet from one of his saddle bags and spread it on the ground. I took one of the parcels of food that May had made for our journey, and we sat together drinking the tea from my flask and eating a boiled egg each and a little of the bread.

"We cannot stay too long. There's a place we need to reach to shelter for the night. We've still a way to go. Maybe two more hours. We'll be welcome there. They're good people. A woodcutter and his family. We'll be able to dry off if needs be. It's a good safe stop with a lean-to for the horses. John and I are well known to them."

We stayed a while longer, natheless, the rain did not slow. As we remounted, Declan thanked the gods for the lack of wind. With the rain falling straight down, our thick woollen hoods kept it from running down our backs or stinging our faces, and the well-made oilskin that I had battled with more than once, saved well my harp from any threat of wetting.

After a time the rain stopped and the wind picked up, now helping to dry us. Following Declan, we turned away from the path and rode among the trees. First, I smelled the smoke, then ahead the shape of a cottage. A horse whinnied out, and a man came from behind a small shed. A big thickset man.

"Patrick," called Declan.

"Welcome Declan. Ah, it's grand to see you. Come." He strode towards us, covering much ground with each step.

"This is Orla. She is a harper."

"You too are welcome in our house, Orla! Come, let's get you inside."

I went with Patrick to the cottage. Scampering to keep up with his long strides. Declan saw to the horses and my harp. Inside sat a woman by the hearth. She turned to me with eyes so dull at first I thought her to be blind.

"This is Emer, my wife. Emer this is Declan's friend, Orla." Then he left us to help Declan.

There we were, two women unknown to each other.

"Hello Emer. Thank you for letting us stay."

She stood. "I'll make us some food. You must be hungry. Warm yourself by the fire."

She spoke with a voice as dull as her eyes, and moved like a person alive, yet there was no life in her moving. Everything about her was dull. Though she did not drag her feet when she walked there was no spring in her. She was beautiful, quite a few years younger than me, but lifeless as a doll might be. No smiling, no frowning, nothing. Just there like a shadow.

"I'll help."

"No."

There was something about the way she said no, that made me to sit again by the fire. I felt awkward and looked into the embers. I wanted to do something but it felt wrong to move. I could hear Emer moving pots and plates, but never turned my head to her, feeling her not wanting my eyes to be upon her. She came after a time, to the hearth and hung a pot over the fire. Bending she put more wood in the embers and stirred the fire with the poker. Never saying a word, never looking at me. How I wished for the men to come. She sat back in the chair, staring at the fire.

"Have you lived here long Emer?"

"Five or six years."

"I'd never find my way here if it wasn't for Declan. It's well hidden away."

"Yes."

Oh, why don't the men come!

"I'm thinking there'd be much work to do here for a woodcutter."

"Yes."

There was something troubling about this woman. She made all the motions of a good woman, preparing the food, stirring the pot, the cottage was clean and tidy, but yet, there was something not right here. Emer made no effort to talk. She was not unkind, she was not cold towards me, she was nothing! Empty like. She was there, yet not, like a ghost. Finally, after what seemed a long time, the men's footsteps sounded, and the door opened. Declan stood my harp and went to Emer embracing her.

Stepping back, smiling, looking round with a fondness in his voice, he said, "And where's the lad, where's Fionn?"

"He sleeps alone in the cold earth," Emer said, with her beautiful eyes as dead as her son.

Shock and sorrow slapped hard Declan's face. "I don't understand. What happened?"

"The pox took him 'bout six months back. We made a grave for him. Come, I'll show you his place, where we laid him down." The two men left.

Oh, poor dear Emer. Now, I understood. Now, it was so plain. Her heart was broken. I've lost loved ones, but never a child of my own. I couldn't bear thinking on it, and here, this woman, this poor woman, was living every day with her little boy laying in the ground. His smile, his voice, his laughing, his crying, his childish joy, gone forever! I had no words. I quietly unpacked my harp thinking on what Maura had told to me.

*As a healer, there will be many tears. At times these will be your own, at times they will be the tears of others. You must not be afraid or discomforted by the weeping. In time you will learn that sorrowing aids the healing of the heart and spirit; this is your work.*

I lightly touched the strings to hear their tuning, and without a sound, took out my stool. Silently giving thanks to Declan for the making and packing of the stool, and to the harp cover that on this day yielded without battle.

Having now a dozen or more tunes, after going through my ritual, I began with the soothing, the Suantrai. Of this strain, I had a few tunes, and knew already I'd begin and end my playing on this day with this noble strain. I was well into the second tune when the men came back. Their eyes red, their bodies heavy with the sorrow upon them. I didn't stop. They sat. Having three Goltrai tunes, the strain of sorrow, I knew now was the time for a lament.

The men cried. Emer sat like a stone not shedding a single tear. When this lament was coming to an end, I played another. Such was the need there in the cottage; I could feel it! It had to be the tune Maura taught to me after telling me of her losing her love, Liam. It had to be the *Lament for the Seafarer*, no other tune would do. This I knew to be true, I cannot say how, but I had a knowing.

In the light of the fire, I saw it. A glistening on Emer's cheek. The deeper I went into the tune, the more Emer's tears came. Slowly at first. Dripping one after the other. Then a small sob crept from her mouth. Then another. Patrick went to her. She began screaming, slapping at him, sobbing all the while. Then the wailing began and Emer stopped the fighting and let herself fall into Patrick's chest. He folded his big strong arms around, himself crying, and held her; rocking her.

Declan sat with his head in his hands. I kept playing. That lament, then another. It had to be that way. As I went again to the noble strain of the soothing Emer quietened. She stayed, like a small child herself, in Patrick's safe arms. I kept playing until Emer moved. She kissed Patrick's wet face, then stood. With all eyes on her she came to me. Though we knew each other not, leaning down she kissed my cheek.

⚜

The meal we shared was a quiet one, with none of us eating much. I helped Emer clear away the dishes while the men checked on the horses.

"Thank you, Orla for making me feel again. Since Fionn's passing I have been numb to life. Like my little love I have been dead inside. I could not bring myself to cry for the fear I might never stop. I've been cold to Patrick. I know his pain is as mine, but all I have shown him is cruelty, and all he has shown to me is love and kindness.

Thank you for breaking the awful spell that Fionn's death cast over me. Without your music I may never have broken free of it. Please do not think me rude, but I am bone weary and have a great need for my bed. In the morning before you leave will you come with me to Fionn's grave and play for him?"

"I will Emer."

After she took to her bed, I went outside. I had a need to deal with my own sorrow. Declan and Patrick were nearly to the cottage when I met them.

"I want to check on Raven."

"I'll show you to her."

"No, Declan. Just tell me the way."

"She's in the lean-to ahint the shed, Orla. And thank you," said Patrick nodding the way.

"I'll be back in soon."

As my eyes fell upon Raven, a great bawling leapt from me, hurrying my steps. Reaching Raven, I buried my face into her mane, letting out all the pain for these people I had held inside me, that sorrow now demanding its freedom. When the river of sadness had flowed from me drying up my tears, I returned to the cottage.

T he next morning, I went with Emer as promised to Fionn's grave. A small grave. A beautiful grave, marked by a cross with letters on it.

"What does it say?"

"His name," said Emer.

I stood my harp, and took my stool from Emer's hand, touching it as I did. She smiled weakly at me. I sat and began. Thinking on the little lively boy, it had to be a tune from the noble strain of Geantrai, it could be no other; not for him, not for his mother!

A s Declan and me continued on our way to the big house where in the evening I'd wear my green dress and play in a place of grandness, I felt a strong hand on my shoulder. I didn't look round this time. I knew why it was there. It was reaffirming the power of the music. I could feel it in the touch, and knew it in my heart!

"Orla, I know it's early days for you as a harper, but I'm glad to have had you with me on hearing of Fionn's passing. You have the touch and your playing spoke to the heart of each of us. There was true healing in your music! I know the Old Ones were with you, but you have the way of knowing. You knew the right music to play for Emer, for the opening of her heart, for her sorrow, for all our sorrow. Fionn cannot be brought back and the pain of his absence will never be forgotten, but there can be healing. Now there can be healing! You, Orla the harper did that with your music, you opened Emer's heart ."

Though I knew not what joys and dangers lay ahead, as Declan's words fell upon my ears, I knew my journey as a harper was begun!

S ign up to my newsletter
at glendaunderhill.com.au

www.ingramcontent.com/pod-product-compliance
Lightning Source LLC
Chambersburg PA
CBHW030508120726
47904CB00005B/1387